M000210593

Also By Cathryn Grant

NOVELS
The Demise of the Soccer Moms
Buried by Debt
The Suburban Abyss
The Hallelujah Horror Show
Getting Ahead
Faceless
An Affair With God

THE ALEXANDRA MALLORY PSYCHOLOGICAL
SUSPENSE SERIES
The Woman In the Mirror
The Woman In the Water
The Woman In the Painting

THE HAUNTED SHIP TRILOGY
Alone On the Beach
Slipping Away From the Beach
Haunting the Beach

NOVELLAS
Madison Keith Ghost Story Series
Chances Are

Cathryn Grant

THE WOMAN
IN THE WINDOW

An Alexandra Mallory Novel

D2C Perspectives

This book is a work of fiction. References to real people, events, establishments, organizations, or locales are intended only to provide a sense of authenticity, and are used fictitiously. All other characters, and incidents and dialogue, are drawn from the author's imagination and are not to be construed as real.

Copyright © 2017 by Cathryn Grant

All rights reserved. No part of this book may be used or reproduced in any manner whatsoever without written permission except in the case of brief quotations embodied in critical articles and reviews. For information, contact D2Cperspectives@gmail.com

Visit Cathryn online at CathrynGrant.com

Cover design by Lydia Mullins Copyright © 2017

ISBN: 978-1-943142-34-7

1

San Francisco, California

When you leave — a job, a relationship, this planet — the water closes over the spot where you stood and breathed, ate and slept, danced and talked, as if you'd never been there at all.

After Tess shot and killed the man who was responsible for security in my apartment building, it was as if he'd never existed, never threatened us. His body disappeared. I never even saw a detective asking questions. A replacement head of security appeared within a week.

The new guy dressed in similar clothes to his predecessor — jeans, leather jacket — but instead of a ball cap, he wore a fedora. He spent a lot of time in the lobby and the second-floor lounge, strolling around, trying to appear casual but looking self-important. He was aggressive about keeping homeless people away from the front of the building or anywhere near its vicinity, and aggressive about discouraging people from loitering in the lobby. He was aggressive about making sure everyone knew who he was and that it was his job to make sure the building maintained its nicely-buffed reputation as a highly desirable place to live. There seemed to be more concern over the reputation for security than actual security. In my experience, threats arose within the building, they didn't infiltrate from the outside.

Every so often, the ripples of those who have

disappeared rise back to the surface. The man she'd murdered began to weigh on Tess. When she'd pulled the gun out of her purse, aimed, and fired directly at his head, her demeanor was cold and sure. She walked away from his bleeding body with equal ease, tucking the gun back into her purse as calmly as if she was returning her wallet to its place after purchasing a latte.

It wasn't that she regretted shooting that guy. He'd gestured as if he meant to slash her throat, so it was a fairly justifiable response on her part. It wasn't that she was haunted by guilt in any form. And she wasn't afraid of being found out. But she isn't a killer. She doesn't have the dispassionate view of the world that I have, and she now found him intruding into her thoughts at unwanted times.

As I settled into the small wooden chair across from her in the coffee shop for our usual Monday morning meeting, Tess didn't follow her usual pattern of immediately launching into an overview of the week's tasks. She peeled the plastic lid off her latte. "I've decided to take some extended time off." She took a sip of the creamy beige liquid. A smear of foam coated her upper lip. She licked it off. "There's too much. Steve. The painting...shooting that man...and, other things — pressure is a good way to describe it, I suppose." She turned and studied the people lined up to place coffee orders.

"How much time?" I said.

Without turning back to look at me, she took another sip of coffee. "Four weeks, maybe a little more."

"Nice."

She turned. "I've never taken that much time off. I've never even taken two weeks off." She laughed, the sound like something she'd manufactured, going on for a few seconds longer than it should have. "I hope I don't get bored."

"Where are you going?"

"Sydney."

"Australia?"

"It's the only Sydney I'm aware of."

"What made you pick Australia?"

"It's about as far away as I can get."

"What will you do?"

"Nothing planned yet. I might fly up to Queensland. Learn to dive. See the Great Barrier Reef before the human race wipes it off the face of the earth. Eat. Shop. Drink." She laughed. "See some kangaroos."

"Sounds like a good way to clear your head."

Four weeks outside of Tess's direct supervision might be just as interesting and head-clearing for me. Without her constant meetings and their endless demands for PowerPoint slides put together by me, my workload would shrink. Even though Steve Montgomery had proven himself as a misogynist, it didn't mean I couldn't still leverage him to possibly improve my earning potential. Removing Tess's interference would help me figure out the best way to handle him. I could figure out if that was what I even wanted.

"I never thought I was burned out," she said. "But as soon as I made the decision, I realized I'm counting the days until I'm out of here. Counting the *hours*."

I gave her an encouraging smile.

"Can I trust you to keep this to yourself until I'm gone?" she said.

"Do you really have to ask me that? After everything?"

"Just clarifying." She laughed. "The more I think about the trip, the less I care what happens around here. Some days,

I'll be sitting in a meeting and realize I've missed the last ten minutes of the discussion. When someone asks my opinion and I don't know what they were talking about, I don't even care if it looks like I don't have any value-add." She licked her lower lip and gazed at me as if I wasn't grasping the importance of what she was saying. "I really do not care."

"You'll feel differently after a break."

"We'll see." She tapped her phone to check the time. "But I have a favor to ask you. A huge favor. I trust you more than almost anyone, and…"

Her phone buzzed. She glanced at the screen.

"What favor?" I said.

She held up her index finger then swiped it across the phone. She stood and walked toward the door, leaving me with two cups of coffee, curious about what phone call she had to take outside of my hearing, and burning to know how demanding the favor would be. There's something about a favor described as *huge* that makes it sound threatening.

2

At dinner the night before, my own crimes were more on my mind than Tess's.

Isaiah and I had walked twelve blocks to Chez Monique. I'd been there once with Tess, but the experience was nearly obliterated by the memory of what happened after — the shock of Tess actually using her gun to silence the security guy who accused her of being a prostitute, before drawing his hand across his neck in a clear desire to slit her throat. Of course he only intended it metaphorically, but she'd viewed it differently.

Chez Monique was ultra-sleek with mauve-stained tables and divinely comfortable matching chairs. Unlike some restaurants with decor that focuses almost exclusively on the visual, Chez Monique's design and atmosphere invited diners to linger over their food and wine, to draw out the evening slowly consuming coffee and chocolate dessert — there were more than twenty desserts on the menu, all with at least a touch of chocolate.

The ceiling was glass, and above it, an atrium filled with hanging plants gave a feeling of sitting on a forest floor. The walls were painted glossy chocolate brown and were split by strips of mirror about four inches wide, causing the room to glimmer but avoiding the uncomfortable experience of watching yourself eat.

The server brought each of us the customary glass of champagne with a raspberry nestled in the bottom.

The wine list had a nice blend of California and French wines. Isaiah ordered a Napa Valley Malbec to go with our A5 Wagyu, which was the reason I'd suggested Chez Monique. He craves steak as much as I do.

After we ordered and the wine was poured, we toasted the lazy pleasure of Sunday. He took a second sip of wine. "No surprise, but I'm looking for a new place," he said. "A guy at the school said a room might be opening up in a house he shares with four people, which would be cheaper than sharing an apartment."

He was right, it wasn't a surprise. After his cousin turned up dead in a hotel room, Isaiah knew his uncle would eventually stop paying the exorbitant rent on the apartment. Isaiah's sole function in the apartment had been providing a stabilizing influence for his cousin.

The thought of Isaiah blocks or even miles away didn't make me happy. It was nice living two floors away from each other. Living together, but not.

If my studio apartment wasn't the barest livable space possible, I might have thought about asking him to stay with me, at least for a while. But anything longer than a night or two would be unbearably claustrophobic. The only escape from the breath and heartbeat and body heat and sounds of the other person was the balcony. And in San Francisco, you often need a hat and scarf along with a winter coat to spend more than a few minutes at a time on the balcony, so it's not reliable as expanded living space.

"I guess you can't afford a studio in our building?"

He shook his head.

It was a question with an obvious answer, but I felt I had to say something that sounded helpful, even if it was absolutely unhelpful. Isaiah was one hundred percent devoted to culinary school, he didn't even have a part-time job. He lived off his savings, following a meticulous budget. That was another bonus for Chez Monique, and quite a few other San Francisco restaurants. Isaiah's classmates and instructors provided contacts that meant lots of very good discounts, and quite a few meals offered for free.

"Too bad he's forcing you out," I said.

"I can't expect him to pay my rent."

"I know, it's just too bad."

He gave me a curious look. "I know you weren't that thrilled with David."

"He pissed me off." I blurted it out, not pausing to consider whether it was the right thing to say, in the situation.

Despite the sharp tone, my comment must have hit a solid note after all, because he went on, almost as if he hadn't heard me. "He had his rough spots, but I'm still kind of in shock. And…" He took a long, slow breath… "we knew each other our whole lives."

I didn't say anything.

"He was flawed, but…I can't believe he's gone." He shook his head and picked up his wine glass, tipping it sideways, letting the wine swirl around, then putting it down without drinking.

"Deeply flawed," I said.

"Yes." He stabbed his fork into the delicate greens lying on one side of his oversized salad plate. "But still my cousin. And friend."

I poked my fork slowly and relentlessly into small beet cubes, stacking them up on the tines as if I was arming it for a food fight.

"I have no idea where his head was. Why would he hire a hooker when he was with Jen?"

I ate the beets, wondering how far his grieving curiosity was going to take his one-sided conversation.

"I didn't know he was into that kind of thing. He never hired a hooker in his life, that I knew of."

I wanted to laugh but managed to cover my smirk with the large wineglass, touching it gently to my lower lip then taking a tiny sip. Of course he'd never hired a hooker. He wasn't *with* Jen. He threatened her and used her call-girl services for free. He deserved to die and I was satisfied that I'd killed him so smoothly, without a single mistake to put me at risk of discovery. I just needed to do a better job keeping my thoughts to myself.

"The whole thing is weird. A woman that makes enough as a hooker to have clients at five-star hotels…why would she kill someone for the few bucks in his wallet?"

I drank my wine. I ate a bit more of my salad and took another sip of wine. Isaiah put down his fork, waiting for me to help him speculate on the answer to that question. I was on thin ice, but I couldn't sit there saying nothing forever. "Maybe he had more, and he was flashing it around."

"I doubt he carried even a hundred bucks. He used apps to pay for everything."

I nodded.

"And why kill him? Couldn't she just tie him up and take the cash?"

"Maybe it wasn't about the money."

"What else?"

"It sounded like it was a game and something went wrong. The police seem satisfied."

"Satisfied?"

I swallowed. I doubted they were satisfied at all. They just didn't have anything that allowed them to pursue it further.

"It bothers me that they can't figure out who she was. That no one saw her," he said.

The server arrived with an entourage of sub-servers, carrying our plates bearing tiny pieces of first-class, mouth-watering filet mignon. The aroma made me forget everything Isaiah was saying, although a tiny thought stuck in my brain like a slivered piece of a thorn buried under the skin that you can't see, but sends out a sharp pain whenever you put pressure on it.

We cut into our steaks and marveled over their perfection. We toasted our perfect meal.

"David wasn't naive," he said. "I just don't get how he could allow it to happen."

"Maybe she pissed him off and he didn't have a chance," I said.

He put down his fork and looked at me. His eyes narrowed slightly.

I wasn't sure if it was a natural shift in his expression, or something I should be concerned with. It was a mistake to suggest the killer was pissed off after saying the same thing about myself. Although most times when you assume someone can guess your train of thought, that they've picked up on your revealing choice of words, their mind is going somewhere else entirely. Perhaps it had never occurred to him that a woman would kill someone in a rage. Or perhaps he was brooding over why the police hadn't done more, or still trying to figure out why David hired a hooker. He might have been feeling guilty that he was thinking about the steak more than his cousin, or fifty other things that had nothing to do with suspecting I was a killer.

He took a sip of wine. We started talking about the cheesecake class he was taking. The conversation flowed to other things, and then the meal was finished and we were walking home, entering his apartment, and falling onto his bed.

3

Tess spent twenty minutes outside the coffee cafe talking on the phone. I drank the rest of my latte, read through my email, checked Twitter, and she still wasn't finished. I thought about following her outside, but what would I do? I'd have to hover and try to keep a respectable distance so I didn't appear to be listening to her conversation.

Watching her mouth move, soundlessly spilling out words, was driving me mad with curiosity. She was doing a lot of talking, very enthusiastic talking. Her black hair swung around her neck as she nodded and shook her head.

Another few minutes passed and my curiosity turned to boredom. If she had a huge favor to ask me, this wasn't a very good way to set it up — leaving me sitting at a tiny table with nothing to do, watching the surface of her latte change texture. I stood, picked up her half-finished drink and my empty cup. I dropped them in the trash and went outside.

The moment the door closed, Tess looked at me and stopped talking. Her body language told me to move along, so I turned and began walking toward the CoastalCreative building. Behind me, I heard her resume her conversation in a low voice that taunted me with its even tone, following me to the corner without revealing a single identifiable word.

Sitting in my cubicle, I found myself lacking motivation to start on any of my current projects. The favor and the secret conversation consumed my thoughts. I entered my password and unlocked the screen. I opened the dashboard for the launch meeting later that morning and spent a few minutes fiddling around with different views of project status without any real purpose.

I played with spreadsheets for over thirty minutes before I got a text message from Tess: *U have time to stop by?*

I pulled my water container out of my bag and took a long, slow swallow. I launched a web browser and looked at the weather forecast. After another minute or so, I tapped back: *Sure. Now?*

Tess Turner: *We need to finish our conversation.*

I stood and walked past the row of cubicles to the outer hallway. I felt like a puppy on a leash, yanked back at the whim of the owner, trotting where she told me to go. I stopped outside her office. The glass walls give the building an open feeling, allowing everyone to see the view of the city and the often menacing charcoal color of the San Francisco Bay.

She looked up and waved me inside. I sat across from her and settled one leg over the other, staring at the toe of my shoe for a moment before I turned my attention to her.

"So, the favor," she said.

"Yes?"

"Will you do me a favor?"

"What is it?"

"It would really help me."

"With what?"

"I bought a…" she laughed. "Don't think I'm crazy."

"Never."

"I bought a Cockatoo."

"Okay."

"There was this exotic bird show and he charmed me…

anyway, this was before I decided on the four weeks off."

"I don't have room for a Cockatoo in my apartment," I said. "You've seen it, there's barely room for me."

"I know. I was wondering…would you be able to stay at my place?"

I took a slight breath, hoping she didn't see the excitement that raced through me. A month in her gorgeous condo? You could hardly even call it a condo. The only thing condo about it was that there were multiple units in the eighteen-story building. Her place was larger than a lot of houses — twenty-seven hundred square feet of hardwood floor and panoramic windows.

"I know it's a lot to ask."

I smiled.

"He doesn't require much work. He's well-behaved."

"How can a bird be well-behaved?"

"He sits on his perch. He talks. He'll keep you company."

I'm perfectly fine keeping my own company. And I certainly didn't need a one-way conversation with a large bird.

"He even stayed in my bedroom last night, and I fell asleep while he was murmuring to himself."

"You definitely need this vacation," I said.

She laughed. "I'm not crazy."

"That's what all crazy people say."

Her smile faded to a look of uncertainty. "I would really appreciate it. I trust you."

"Sure. No problem."

"I promise. He's very well-behaved."

"The term bird brain wasn't invented out of nothing."

"That's not nice."

"Well your cockatoo and I aren't going to become best

mates. Is that why you bought it? Because of the Australian thing?"

She folded her arms and leaned back slightly. "No."

I wasn't sure I believed her, but I smiled and left it at that.

"My plants will need watering. I'll write down instructions for everything. It's actually easy, I don't mean to make it sound like more than it is. And you'll get to stretch out with more space. Enjoy some luxury."

I nodded.

"I really appreciate it. Really."

"No problem. It'll be a nice change of scenery."

"I'll be able to relax more, knowing everything is taken care of. Knowing he's well-cared for."

"Sure."

"One thing. I want to be clear about this — no guests. And especially not Steve Montgomery."

"Why the hell would I invite Steve Montgomery over to your condo?"

"I don't know. You have rather permeable boundaries. And despite my request to the contrary, he's going to keep trying to recruit you. I don't know what's going on between you two. And I get the feeling you're flirting around with what he has to offer."

She was right about the boundaries. I smiled. "I'm not flirting with him."

"I didn't mean it in the traditional sense, but you're doing something to keep him…off balance, convincing him he needs to hire you."

"Not really."

She studied me for a moment. I kept my face blank.

"So we're clear?"

"Absolutely."

"Once he hears I'm out for an extended time, he'll double down on trying to get you to move to his org."

"He doesn't know yet?"

She shook her head. She uncrossed her arms and clasped her hands on her lap. She leaned forward. "I mean it. He doesn't know where I live, and it needs to stay that way."

"Of course."

She smiled but she didn't look convinced. She didn't look as if she trusted me at all.

There was no scenario I could imagine where I'd want to invite Steve anywhere, much less to the place where I was sleeping and enjoying my free time. But she definitely had it right about my boundaries, and I suppose she wanted to cover even the most far-fetched possibility.

She was right. I would continue to string him along, to see what kind of salary he might offer me, to continue my mental debate about whether working for someone with a paternalistic, territorial view of women was worth a significant rise in my income. With Tess gone, anything might happen.

"Can you promise?"

"Tess — you murdered a man. You didn't worry whether I'd tell anyone about that."

"This is different."

"How?"

"I need to feel my personal life is my own."

"That's understandable."

It didn't really make sense, not compared with shooting someone, but she was quite agitated, and I didn't want to lose my chance at her glorious twenty-seven hundred square feet of paradise. Balcony space not included.

She stopped pressing after that. She didn't seem to notice I hadn't promised. I don't like making promises — it's impossible to foresee what might happen to change the situation.

4

The only other time I'd been to Tess's condo was at night. Stepping out of my Uber ride onto the street during daylight was an entirely different experience. The sky was cloudless blue, and the eclectic mixture of newly constructed condos and apartments alongside early twentieth century Edwardian and Spanish buildings were bathed in warm light, making the newer, taller buildings appear less sinister.

The bay windows, white molding, and columns framing the front stoop of the Edwardian-style building next door to Tess's looked fussy compared with the sharp edges and rectangles of Tess's high rise. A buff and pink paint combination made the stucco resemble human flesh fighting for its life beside industrial green.

Tess had given my name to the clerk managing the lobby desk. This time, instead of a visitor's card, I had my own laminated ID card with a bar code that would allow me to pass the desk easily as I came and went. Printed in a large red font was the expiration date — one day after Tess's planned return. They were very security-conscious. Or, she was.

I rode the elevator to her floor. There were only two units on each floor. Hers was number 13-2. I pressed the round button beside the doorframe. There was no sound to assure me a bell was letting her know I was there, but I doubted it had malfunctioned. The place was only four years old.

A moment later she opened the door. Her feet were bare

and she wore navy blue leggings and a white sweater. Her hair was pulled up into a short ponytail. The smudged, smoky eye shadow and heavy liner was the same as always, but the clothes and ponytail gave her a quieter, not *in-control-of-all-things-at-all-times* demeanor.

"Hi." She stepped back. "Do you want a glass of wine before I show you around?"

"Sure."

"Chardonnay?"

"Sounds perfect."

She went to the kitchen and I followed. I'd seen her kitchen and eating area as well as the formal dining room the last time, but like the exterior, seeing it in daylight made me realize how truly magnificent it was with its white cabinets and the de rigueur stainless steel appliances. A huge picture window behind the sink gave a view over her street and a glimpse of other buildings, new and old, stacked side by side on Russian Hill.

She took a bottle of Chardonnay out of the fridge, removed the cork, and filled two glasses.

A voice in the other room said — *Chardonnay please.*

Despite questioning her judgment in buying an expensive talking bird, I couldn't stop my laugh. The bird sounded like a human being. It obviously had grown to know Tess very well in its short time living there.

"Did you teach it to say that?"

She smiled. "He learns fast."

She touched her glass to mine and took a sip of wine. "The plants on the window sill should be watered every five days."

I nodded.

"I'll show you the rest." She walked through the dining room into the semi-circular sunroom that opened into the living room. The sunroom had closely spaced windows that started five or six inches from the floor and reached nearly to the ceiling. The only furniture was a love seat, a low table, and an armchair perpendicular to the love seat. The wall across from the windows was painted pale yellow and featured two black and white photographs — scenes from Yosemite.

Opening out from the living room with magnificent folding glass doors was a balcony running the entire length of the room. Past the living room was a hallway leading to her office, a small bedroom, and two master suites — both bathrooms featuring Jacuzzi tubs and spacious showers. The larger suite also had a balcony.

"You can sleep in this room." She gestured toward the more sterile, smaller suite. It held a queen-sized bed with a slatted curved teak head and footboard, a teak dresser with an oval mirror above it, and a dark blue armchair with a matching footstool in the corner. There was an open, empty walk-in closet.

She took me into the smaller bedroom. A bookcase with glass doors stood in one corner. In the other corner, the large white bird sat on a perch, putting it at eye-level with me.

The bird glared at me. Its white and yellow crown feathers were fanned out, the top ones pointing straight up. The thick beak curved to a sharp point, harder than any part of my body, harder and less penetrable than even my bones or teeth. The alert way in which it regarded me was somewhat charming, but that beak said it all. This was a wild animal and no matter how pristine white and sunny yellow its feathers, no matter how much it planned to converse with me, or rather at me, it was an untamed creature.

Hello.

I startled. The voice sounded so polite. But it was no different from a robot, programmed to sound gracious, doing nothing but mimicking human speech and inflection.

"Aren't you going to say hello?" Tess said.

I looked at her. "You're kidding, right?"

"Don't be difficult, Alex. Besides, his speech is reinforced when he hears you speaking."

"What's its name?"

"Not it. He."

"Okay."

"Damien."

"That's an odd name for a bird."

"Why?"

"Aren't they supposed to be Tweety or something?"

"Are you trying to irritate me?"

"Okay. I'll be nice. Hello, Damien. You better not peck me to death in my sleep."

"Alex!"

Hello, gorgeous, Damien said.

"He has a sense of humor," I said.

"He's very intelligent."

"I have no doubt."

"Anyway, his care instructions are in the notes I left on the dining room table. It outlines how often you need to provide food, change his water, and clean the floor mat. There's a list of foods he can eat. Don't deviate."

"Of course not."

"It doesn't seem as if you're taking this seriously."

"Of course I am."

"Are you ready to hold him?"

"No thanks."

"You should get to know him before you're alone with him."

"Tess. He's a remarkable creature, although I think he'd have more going for him in the wild, rather than sitting inside a condo repeating nonsense. I'd love to see one in its own..."

"You need to let him get used to you."

I walked up to the bird.

"Hold out your arm," Tess said.

The bird lowered his head, keeping his crown feathers spread to make clear he wasn't making a submissive move. He turned sideways, then twisted farther and looked up at me.

"Come on. I don't bite."

He laughed, sounding strangely like Tess when she really let loose.

I continued to stand there. After a few seconds, the bird reached out one deadly looking foot with dark, sharp nails. He placed it on my arm. He squeezed firmly, and then lifted his other foot off the perch, settling onto my arm.

"He's heavy."

"About two pounds," Tess said.

She moved up close beside me and rambled through a series of comforting phrases and cooing sounds. Then she began speaking as if he were a colleague. "This is Alexandra Mallory. She'll be staying here while I'm away. You can trust her, and she'll treat you well. I expect you to do the same. No shouting or screeching. And don't do anything to frighten her."

She held out her arm and allowed him to use it as a stepping stone back to his perch.

"I'll be fine," I said.

"I'm just telling him the rules."

I didn't respond.

She was losing her mind, it was a good thing she was taking four weeks to get out of the country.

This was indeed a huge favor. I was giving up the peace of mind that comes from sleeping alone in exchange for time in a luxury apartment. I hoped it was worth it. As we turned to leave the room, Damien seemed to be keeping an eye on me.

5

After a second glass of wine and another run through the instructions, Tess gave me a key and I left.

On the street, I stepped up close to the building and pulled my phone out of my bag. I ordered an Uber ride, checked email, and responded to a message from Isaiah. With my finger hovering over the keypad, I thought about typing a message that I had a temporary housing solution for him. He could buy himself four more weeks by staying in my apartment. It wouldn't get us into closer proximity now that I was an Uber drive away. In fact, I was also planning to move my car to Tess's building where it would be secured in one of the two additional slots she was allocated. Even though he wouldn't be close by in the evenings, he was still a few blocks from work and my gym.

Better to tell him over a martini so I could watch his jaw relax as relief passed over his face. The Uber would arrive in the next five minutes or so. I tapped a message asking him if he wanted to come over for a drink. When he messaged back that he did, I replied with a martini emoji.

I stepped out to the center of the sidewalk, turned, and looked back at my temporary home. The structure rose above me so that I had to stretch my neck to see the top edge. I lowered my head and looked at the building next door.

Part of the adobe was chipped away along the line where the sidewalk met up with the building. The steps leading to the heavy oak door were worn and tinged with gray from years of feet going in and out, but otherwise, it was in beautiful condition. I walked to the curb and turned to study it further. It was a building with stories to tell. I guessed it must have been built soon after the earthquake and fire in 1906. I wasn't sure how much of Russian Hill was destroyed in the earthquake, but since eighty percent of the city was leveled, there weren't many structures that still existed from the nineteenth century.

As I stood thinking about the past, the sheer curtains on one of the second story windows moved slightly. The window appeared to be closed, but it was hard to know for sure from where I stood. The curtains moved again. I put on my sunglasses to reduce the glare. The curtains moved steadily now, swaying from side to side.

A moment later, the curtains parted.

Fingers touched the window, pressing against the glass so the pads appeared flattened and bloodless. As I watched, the rest of the hand came into view. The fingers were slim and a little on the small side. The edges of the palm showed a narrow hand. A woman. The hand was small enough, it had to be a woman. Or a boy. It remained in the same position, continuing to press hard against the glass, looking as if it wanted to push its way through.

Was he waving at someone? Signaling something? She? I glanced over my shoulder. No one else was watching. Was it directed at me, or just a calming ritual, practiced to let the cool, solid, unmoving glass provide some sort of grounding?

I squinted. Along the edge on the pinky finger side was a smear of red. I closed my eyes for a moment. It couldn't possibly be blood.

For several minutes, maybe longer, the hand remained flat

against the window and I remained mesmerized by that palm and fingers and the yearning that seemed to seep through the glass. Considering it was full daylight, there was something eerie, almost chilling about it.

The hand moved slowly down the glass, as if it were a drop of rainwater trailing away, leaving behind a smear of blood.

A car honked behind me. I jumped. Normally, I'm hyper alert to my surroundings. I doubt I've startled like that more than two or three times in my entire life and now I'd done it twice in the space of an hour. My mind was consumed by the palm of what I'd decided was a woman's hand.

The Uber driver waved rapidly, as if she was in a big hurry. I stepped into the street and got into the car.

"You're supposed to be waiting for me," she said.

"I was."

"You weren't watching." She pulled into the street, eyeing me in the rearview mirror instead of looking for traffic. Fortunately, there was none.

"Classy area," she said. "You live here?"

"No."

"Visiting your guy?"

"No."

"Aren't you talkative."

"Just need some time to think," I said.

"Well excuse me. I was just being friendly."

"No worries."

She jutted out her jaw, pushing her lips together, making sure her head was turned so I could see her annoyed expression in the mirror.

The rest of the trip back to Howard Street was dead

silent except for my heart, thudding much too loudly. I felt blood pumping through my limbs, throbbing in my hands, and all I could see was that woman's blood smeared on the glass.

6

Jen thought having David Lasher out of her life would make her days infinitely better. Blissful, almost. And they were, for a week or two. But the desire to be rid of him had been replaced by something equally strong — she wanted a normal life, or at least sort of normal. A life that didn't involve a job she had to keep secret. A life where she might be able to find a real boyfriend, maybe even fall in love again. She wanted a life where a man like David Lasher didn't believe he could use her for sex, just because she took money for sex.

Meeting Alex, and then Tess, had changed everything.

They had actual jobs. Jobs they were proud of! They could talk to people at a party or in a bar, laughing and telling stories without trying to hide every single thing about themselves. Alex could walk in and out of the apartment building without worrying she was being watched, her habits broadcasting an abnormal pattern, her clothing scrutinized. Alex and Tess could worry about things like getting to the dry cleaners before it closed, or whether a man was hitting on them at the gym.

Jen's life felt like standing on the balcony railing, twelve floors above the street.

That first time Jen had taken money for sex, it hadn't seemed like such a *thing*. Nothing at all, really. The guy was a guest at a party, a friend of a friend...of a friend, more or less. He was a little over six feet tall and she could tell he worked out, but not in an obvious, bulging, strutting way, just in shape. He wore jeans and nice leather shoes. She always noticed shoes, even more on men than women. She wasn't sure why. She supposed it said something about the man. An instinctual part of her noticed whether the shoes were well-made, cared for. It wasn't as if she could describe a guy's character based on shoe type. It was just a feeling. And his shoes were nice.

He was clean-shaven, and his eyes were dark blue, with depth.

The way he asked hadn't been insulting, although she'd had three glasses of champagne, so maybe her radar was dulled. It wasn't as if he called her a slut or anything like that. He'd handed her a glass of white wine. When she took a sip, he said, "Hey, are you the one?"

"What?"

"My buddy said one of the women here is an escort." He laughed, but he sounded nervous, uncertain about how she might respond, which was charming. "If you're not, sorry. I just blurted that out. Too many glasses of wine already. But you're hot, so I assumed…" He smiled. "And you seem like you can read people, that you're astute, so it fit, and I thought I'd ask. He said pricey, but you're definitely worth it."

She took several sips of wine. What was the right response? Most women would have been horrified, some might have slapped him, but at that moment in her life, she had no idea who she was any more, so why not? Something about those blue eyes, his very straight, fine, light brown hair made him look kind, if that wasn't too much of a leap. He was polite and he seemed more like he specifically wanted her, not just sex. He seemed to like her.

She was getting desperate for money. She'd been out of

work for three months, ripping through her savings like someone had dropped a match in a pool of gasoline.

"Don't be pissed. Sorry if I got it wrong," he said.

She smiled. "You're very astute yourself."

"Okay, cool. Good." He laughed. "That's a relief. Four hundred is what he said, but if there's a tip, that's cool too. I…"

She took two sips of wine. Then two more, quickly. This guy was charming and good looking and she was drawn to him. And she was going to get four hundred dollars, maybe more, out of making love? It had been so long. She ached for a man and she hadn't even realized it.

"Should we go somewhere?" she said.

They'd gone to a hotel in Palo Alto, a few miles from the party. She told him her name was Heather. She didn't feel cheap and no one gave them strange looks. In fact, it felt kind of classy. It was a nice hotel and he'd paid. Without being asked, he produced a condom from his pocket, and afterwards, he'd let her stay in the room as long as she wanted. He'd asked for her number and offered to tell his friends.

So easy. She hadn't felt like a whore at all.

Now, she felt cheap and used and tired every single day. Fifteen times a day she asked herself whether it was too late to go back to being a normal person. Every time she walked into a hotel room, she wondered how she'd acquired this kind of life. It was like living in a nightmare, unreal sometimes.

When she was in high school, when she lived with Jake, she'd thought her life was headed in the right direction. She'd never in her most frightening, bizarre dreams or worries imagined she'd end up a prostitute. How did that even happen? It was unreal. She pressed the heels of her hands on the bathroom counter and leaned close to the mirror. Her face didn't look like it belonged to a hooker. Even when she wore make-up, she thought she looked just like other women her age, not…

She turned away as tears rushed into her eyes and the image grew blurry.

Other people had career counselors and recruiters and re-training courses. What was there for her? She tried not to think about it too often. But the days ran into one another, and she was starting to think she was on a long, slow slide to decay. She'd be too old, no man would want her, and then what?

7

Jen walked up Howard Street toward her apartment building. Her stomach was pleasantly full with Pho. It was her staple since moving to San Francisco — easy to find and endlessly comforting. The broth felt good in her stomach even when she had no appetite, and she always managed to eat the vegetables and beef once her belly was reminded that food really was a good thing.

Pho was inexpensive. She had plenty of money, she did well, and she could afford the outrageous rent on her studio apartment and manage to save a little at the same time. Still, she liked to watch what she spent. If there was ever any hope of re-starting her life, it would require money. Every dollar counted.

Often, she had the Uber driver drop her off and pick her up at the Pho place. Somehow it felt safer, more anonymous. Walking home from there at twelve-thirty at night seemed more natural than arriving at the apartment entrance.

The handful of call girls, escorts — whatever — that she knew preferred cheaper apartments, places where the management wasn't so vigilant about making sure hookers didn't darken their doors. Jen had a different strategy. She laughed to herself when she thought in those terms — strategy! All those years listening to her ex talk about business strategy had sunk into her subconscious. An apartment building like the over-priced one where she lived, close to the financial district, the bay, and the iconic Ferry Building, had zero tolerance for illegal activity, especially prostitution. Because of that reputation, the cops didn't watch it as closely. If she managed to blend in with her successful neighbors, she had better protection than at a less classy place. And she never brought men to her apartment. Never. It was the first rule. Well, condoms too. So maybe it was the second rule. Or rule 1A.

As she approached the entrance, she saw a huddled form pressed up against the side of the building, partially hidden by a rack that held four turquoise bicycles. The bikes were designated for anyone to take on a short ride, leaving the bike at a similar rack elsewhere — the ultimate in city transportation, shared and inexpensive. When traffic was gridlocked, cycling was faster.

The figure was motionless, wrapped in a dark brown sleeping bag, a brown wool cap pulled low so no face was visible. A grubby hand clutched the edge of the sleeping bag. A woman's hand, it turned out — thin, with small fingers and chipped blue nail polish.

A visceral pain shot from Jen's throat to her pelvis. This could be her. Every time she saw someone sleeping on the sidewalk, especially a woman, especially a woman with normal hands, not swollen and discolored from years on the street, she felt it could be her. Someday, it would be her.

Until she became a call girl, she never would have imagined ending up homeless, hungry and filthy, all alone. But that was before she knew how fast life changed. How suddenly everything good could turn to shit. In a single day, your almost-fiancé was with another woman and you were fired from your job with no references for the next job. You were forced out of your home, abandoned and alone.

Without any warning, you were drifting in another dimension, and then you were deciding that a man offering to pay you a decent amount of money for sex was a godsend.

She knelt beside the woman. Behind her was a backpack, stuffed so the stitching pulled at the seams, and beside that a black plastic garbage bag, equally full.

Jen reached into her own bag and pulled out a snack bar. She moved closer and tucked it inside the top edge of the sleeping bag. The woman didn't move. The odor of unwashed skin rushed into Jen's nostrils and spread through her body as if she'd eaten something spoiled. She jerked away and landed on her ass.

The doors to the apartment building opened and a man in an overcoat stepped outside. He looked familiar — someone's boyfriend. He tossed a piece of paper at the sleeping woman.

"What are you doing?" Jen said.

He laughed. "Giving the bitch a lottery ticket. She could use it, don't you think?" He walked to the curb and consulted his phone.

Jen picked up the ticket. It was from last week's drawing. "Hey!"

The man ignored her.

Jen pushed herself to a standing position. Feet and ankles tingling from having the blood flow compressed while she knelt, she stumbled to where the man stood and held the ticket out to him. "This is expired."

He studied his phone.

"I'm talking to you."

"Get lost or I'll call security."

"I live here."

He looked at her, clearly not accepting her word. "Fuck off."

"You can't treat her like a piece of trash."

"She shouldn't assume she has the right to turn a nice building into a slum."

"She has nowhere to sleep."

"I'm not discussing the root cause of homelessness with you — but she would have a place to sleep if she wasn't addicted to drugs, alcohol, and sheer laziness."

Jen shoved the lottery ticket into his hand.

He let it fall to the ground.

"What's wrong with you?"

"I told you to fuck off." He moved away and tapped at his phone.

She bent and picked up the ticket. She moved toward him and tried to slip it into the pocket of his overcoat. "Take it."

He shoved his elbow at her forearm and the ticket fell on the ground again.

"Don't push me!"

"Then back the fuck off."

A white Prius pulled up to the curb. He stepped into the street, yanked open the back door, lowered himself into the car, and slammed the door. The Prius hesitated for a moment, then pulled away.

She picked up the ticket and put it in her pocket. He was not getting away with this. The unabashed cruelty of the human race amazed her sometimes. It was easy to forget, easy to insulate yourself from it. She was lucky, she knew that. Her clients treated her with respect in many cases, and certainly decency. She'd never been beaten or verbally abused. She'd never been assaulted or degraded, although she was aware every single day that was a distinct possibility.

Sure, there were rude clerks in stores and restaurants, selfish people who took your parking spot or cut into lines, unfriendly neighbors. The list could go on indefinitely, but downright cruelty was easy to push outside your range of vision. It took place in other countries or other parts of the city. It took place on dark streets, or behind locked doors, not in front of a luxury apartment building on a clean, mostly safe city street in beautiful San Francisco.

But it was there, pulsing beneath everything. She turned and went to the door. She glanced at the woman. The snack bar had slipped out of the sleeping bag. The woman must have turned and readjusted her arms to make them more comfortable, an impossible effort on the cold concrete beneath her thin sleeping bag.

Jen walked back to the woman and tucked the bar inside the sleeping bag, more securely this time.

Inside the building, the guard sitting at the lobby desk eyed her as if he'd never seen her before. She flashed her ID card and went to the elevators. Hopefully, the woman would find a new place to sleep, a safe place.

8

Portland, Oregon

Lots of kids run away from home. Adults love to laugh at the charming nature of this running away.

As if.

Little Jessica was absolutely adorable, they chirp. *She used her pink Tinker Bell suitcase. She packed her teddy, her plastic crown with its red gemstones, and what was left of her Halloween candy. She put on her jacket and announced she was running away! I bit back my smile and offered to pack a sandwich. She asked for peanut butter with honey. She walked down the street and I could actually see her footsteps starting to drag. When she reached the corner, she turned and looked to see if I was following her.*

So cute! You should have seen her. I couldn't stop laughing.

Nice. Maybe they should have stopped laughing at her first show of spirit and tried to figure out why a small child thought she was better off without her parents. It's all brushed off as meaningless drama, but maybe it's not so meaningless. Maybe it's something that settles that woman on a therapist's couch or in rehab thirty years later.

Usually kids run away when they're fairly small. Maybe I was a late bloomer, or maybe I just bided my time. I didn't run away from home until I was ten, and by that age, I knew to take a lot more than a crown and candy.

I stashed two pairs of jeans and several shirts along with changes of underwear and socks in the corner of my closet, ready to shove into my backpack before I left for school. My father's small carryon suitcase was also in the closet. The entire suitcase was consumed by a sleeping bag, a small canvas tarp, and a downy pillow, easy to smash into a tiny form, with a few air pockets left for paperback books. Before I made my move, I spent two months collecting coins I found around the house and on the floor of the car.

On top of the pile of clothes in my closet was a plastic bag filled with granola bars. The day before I left, a plastic bag of apples joined it. I also grabbed a package of fish crackers. I had a refillable water bottle, two boxes of apple juice with straws stuck to the side, and a flashlight.

For a ten-year-old, I was well-prepared and resourceful. But I didn't have a clear view of the long-term picture. All I knew was that I didn't belong in the Mallory family, cowering in fear of a vengeful god with very specific rules.

I had a vague plan, dreamlike in its flimsiness, to find another family that would take me in. This is where my resourcefulness broke down. I hadn't identified this more flexible, less self-righteous family, and I wasn't really sure where I would stay once my plastic bags of coins and granola bars ran out.

My escape was well-planned. I hid the suitcase under the back porch. My backpack looked puffier than usual when my mother drove us to school, but with five kids and five backpacks and five brown bag lunches, she didn't have the time to notice slight variations. Besides, she was too focused on assessing our appearance — making sure teeth were cleaned, hair combed in an appropriate way, and clothes met my father's standards. In most cases, my brothers consumed her energy with their failed attempts at keeping their hair under control and their hope that she wouldn't notice the grubby condition of their pants.

After stopping at the junior high for the two eldest, she took the rest of us to the elementary school. It was a chaotic atmosphere, parents pulling in and out of the parking lot, double parking, backing up without warning, so she usually dropped us a block away.

As she continued on to the grocery store, her usual habit on Thursdays, I began the eight-block walk back home. It was a sunny day, the air somewhat warm for early May. Why we couldn't walk those eight blocks to school to begin with, I never completely understood. She seemed to feel more certain the handoff to school personnel was cleaner, safer by car. But if that was the case, why drop us a block away? We were without adult supervision for the short walk, and once we reached school property, it wasn't as if anyone paid particular attention to us until we were in our classrooms and roll was taken. There was easily half an hour or so during which no adult knew exactly where any of us were.

At home, I dragged the suitcase from beneath the porch and set out walking. The temperature was growing warmer by the time I arrived at the park four blocks from our house. There were quite a few moms with infants and preschoolers clustered around the small climbing structure and slide, far too busy to pay attention to me.

I went to the public restroom that was housed in the same building as a landscaping supply shed. I'd seen a piece of plywood outside the shed. I dragged it into the restroom and placed it over the toilet in the last stall. I stacked my suitcase and backpack on the plywood and took my coins with me.

The first act with my new-found freedom was to find a swing. I spent the rest of the morning, soaring up until I felt my toes might touch the trees.

Unlike all the cute kids who run away as a tactic to grab parental attention, I wanted out of that house. Unlike kids who were terrified the minute the sun went down, I stayed away for two nights.

9

San Francisco

It was one of those gorgeous fall days in San Francisco, clear enough to see the far side of the bay and out to the Pacific Ocean past the brilliant Golden Gate Bridge. Everything smelled clean and the air was warm, making it feel like summer, while summer in San Francisco often feels like winter — thick fog blowing in from the ocean, wind, and bitter cold.

Russian Hill was teasing me with the possibility of running up and down hills, some of which looked as if they were forty-five-degree angles, but in reality were less than twenty. The sidewalks were narrower than in other parts of the city where they were designed for flocks of tourists. Like a lot of suburban neighborhoods, there wasn't much pedestrian traffic.

I hadn't brought much to Tess's condo, just two small suitcases and a garment bag. It only took me thirty minutes to settle in. I planned to return to my apartment on a regular basis so it didn't seem worth half a day of schlepping from my place down to the parking garage, then Tess's parking garage up to the eighteenth floor. A few days before she was due back, I could take the same trickle approach back home, dropping things off before I went to work or the gym.

I opened the refrigerator and surveyed the welcoming food she'd provided. There were two bottles of Chardonnay, not to mention the wine displayed on a rack in her dining room. Also in the fridge were several containers of deli food, a paper sleeve of sliced turkey, three kinds of imported cheese, a small pot of homemade barley soup, and a package of Italian sausage. On the counter was a loaf of fresh sourdough bread, and in the freezer — Grey Goose Vodka. If I felt like it, I didn't have to leave her apartment for the next week.

Even though it was only three in the afternoon, I mixed a martini and put some soft cheese and slices of pear on a small plate. I went into her living room and sat on the sofa, looking out toward the bay. I sipped the martini, ate cheese, and let the silence swallow my mind. And the space. Such vast, relatively empty space, enhanced by fifteen-foot ceilings. Her thoughtful decorating style presented blank walls as art, with a single table or chair well-placed in front of it. Spread out before me was a view of early twentieth century buildings, trees thick with yellow and pale orange leaves, and beyond that, the shimmering bay, dotted with white sails.

When the olives in my martini were gone, I washed the glass and put away the cheese. Running was out of the question, but a walk with a pleasant martini buzz was appealing. I put on jeans, boots, a black tank top, and a short black sweater. I put my hair in a ponytail in case I walked farther than planned and got too hot. Although, I had no route mapped out, so walking farther wasn't really a valid concept.

In the lobby, the desk guard greeted me by name. Definitely not the anonymity I was used to in my building of several hundred residents. There were thirty-six condos in Tess's building, and I guess when you pay close to two million for your half of a floor in a high rise, they make sure to know who you are, as well as anyone staying in your place longer than a few days.

I waved and went out the front door. I turned and started walking, gazing at the blend of modern and old around me. It felt good to be outside, moving my legs, without battling the aimless weaving behavior of people on the crowded sidewalks near CoastalCreative or around my apartment building. It didn't feel like I was walking in the heart of one of America's largest cities. It was almost like suburbia, especially on streets where all the buildings were older and they weren't battling with slick high rises.

I walked for five or six blocks, then turned. When I'd walked in a large rectangle and was nearing the building next to Tess's, I slowed, waiting to see if the woman who'd touched the window would make another appearance. I leaned against the balustrade running up the steps. I reached into my purse and pulled out a cigarette and lit it quickly. I imagined people emerging from nearby buildings to chastise me for my filthy habit, for tarnishing their sedate, genteel streets, for loitering.

It was a Saturday afternoon, surely some of the buildings were occupied.

I turned so the sun was on my face and neck. I closed my eyes and inhaled. I opened them and released the smoke slowly. I took a few more drags, thinking of nothing.

10

The sun was soft on my skin as it slipped close to the buildings across the street. When my cigarette was gone, I put it out and lit another. I closed my eyes again and enjoyed the smoke and the last of the sunshine and the lingering hum of vodka in my veins.

"No smoking on the sidewalk."

I opened my eyes.

A few feet away stood a woman about my height. She was slender, dressed in wool camel colored slacks, flat brown leather shoes, and a brown leather jacket over a white shirt. Her silken white hair was coiled on top of her head. She was easily eighty years old, but she stood erect, her shoulders back, and her arms crossed, no sign of a tremor or weakness in her hands or arms.

"Put it out."

"It's a public street."

"Loitering is crude. This isn't The Castro."

I took one more drag, dropped my cigarette and stepped on it.

"Are you going to pick that up?"

"Absolutely."

She glared at me. "I've never seen you before. Do you live around here?"

I nodded toward Tess's building. "I'm staying at a friend's place."

"Who?"

"I doubt you know her."

"Try me." She pulled her large dark glasses down along the bridge of her nose and eyed me over the top edge.

I moved away from the steps. I tucked my fingers into the front pockets of my jeans and glanced at the building to my right, lifting my gaze to the second floor. The curtains hung motionless and no hand appeared.

"Well?"

"I'm sure you don't know her."

"Why are you staying there?"

"She's out of town for a while."

"Do you live in San Francisco?"

I nodded.

"Why does she need you at her place?"

"She has a bird. I'm looking after it." Telling her about Tess seemed like a violation of some kind. Maybe Tess didn't want a woman next door knowing about her life — her comings and goings, and Damien.

"Smoking is bad for you." As if to suggest she'd been holding my smoke in her lungs the entire time she'd been talking to me, she let out a deep, phlegmy cough. "I should know. I did it for thirty years."

"Why'd you stop?"

"It'll kill you. Quit now, while it's easier."

"Maybe in a few years."

She laughed. "You're like I was. You think you're invincible."

Despite her sharp tone, I found her entertaining. For someone so old, she seemed a little invincible herself. "It's relaxing."

She nodded, her head slightly to the side, as if she'd

heard the excuse before. "Where do you live?"

"Near the financial district."

"It's nicer over here."

"Of course it is. The cheapest apartment is over a million bucks."

"That's not what I paid."

"I'm sure not. When did you buy it?"

"Nineteen-fifty-four." She smiled.

"What floor do you live on?"

"Third."

"And the whole floor is yours?"

"Yes."

I moved toward the curb. "I should get going."

"Why?"

I looked up at the second floor. The curtains still hadn't moved.

"Things to do."

"Like what?"

I gave her a thin smile. "That's my business."

"You're very much like me. You remind me of me when I was your age. Feisty. But you have class. That's nice. It's rare."

"Lots of women are feisty, and classy." I smiled.

"You're like the daughter I never had." She removed her glasses and wiped at the corner of her eye. She put her glasses back.

"Well I'm sorry you didn't get what you wanted." I could have said the same — she was like a mother I'd never had — sharp and independent.

"What's your name?"

"Alexandra."

"That's beautiful. And your last name?"

"I think Alexandra is good enough for now."

She held out her right hand, weighted down by a ridiculously large ruby on her ring finger. "Lorraine Clayton. I'm not afraid to tell you my full name."

"I'm not afraid." I shook her hand. The ruby pressed against my finger, scraping it slightly as she removed her hand from my grasp.

"Yes, it's real."

"I didn't doubt that it was."

The sun slipped behind the buildings across the street. It was suddenly cold.

"I'm sure I'll see you around," I said. I glanced at the second story window again.

"Why do you keep looking up there?" she said. "Are you casing my apartment?"

"Absolutely not. I saw something a bit strange the other day, and can't stop thinking about it."

"What was that?"

"A woman put her hand through the opening between the curtains and pressed it against the window."

"Why is that strange?"

"You don't think it is?"

She didn't respond.

"It seemed odd, not pulling the curtain to the side and looking out, if she wanted to look out. Do you know her? The woman who lives on the second floor?"

"She's not someone I socialize with."

"Is she new?"

"No."

"How long has she lived there?"

"I don't recall, exactly."

"Is she young? Old?"

She shrugged her shoulders with a slight, gentle movement.

"How strange to not know someone living in your building."

"Does your friend socialize with everyone in her building?"

"Probably not, but there are five or six times the number of apartments."

"Not everyone associates with their neighbors. Most don't."

I studied the building. It was gracious and spoke of a time when people didn't sequester themselves in front of entertainment systems or computers, ordering takeout or eating in restaurants, only going out before dawn and returning home in the dark.

But that hand on the glass hadn't looked right. A woman yearning for something she couldn't have? A woman trying to find a connection to something outside of her apartment? An older woman lost for decades in her own imagined world who drifted around among antiques and memories all day? It was a rather dramatic thought, a secret world of San Francisco, of any large city, where people are isolated, living out eccentric lives, dying alone in apartments crowded with furniture and books and ornaments from the past.

That would never be me. Money saves you from that sort of existence, a sad, unnoticed progression to death. "Nice meeting you." I lifted my hand in a farewell greeting and started toward Tess's building.

"What's the rush?" Lorraine said.

"No rush."

"You're leaving in the middle of our conversation."

"No, I'm not. I said it was nice meeting you. Maybe I'll see you again sometime."

"Absolutely."

I looked over my shoulder. She gave me a tiny smile and I knew she'd deliberately repeated the word I used too often, but is so well-suited to so many situations.

11

It was after midnight when Jen stepped out of the Uber driver's car in front of her building. She'd been too tired to consider getting dropped off at the Pho place and walking. She closed the car door but it didn't latch. She opened it and slammed it shut. As she turned toward the lobby entrance, she saw the security guard just inside, watching her.

Too bad. He didn't know where she'd been. She was being paranoid and she had to shake it off. It would give her a nervous appearance if she started thinking he was looking at her more closely than he should, wondering why she went out nearly every night of the week, and arrived home later than most on weeknights, sometimes not until two in the morning. It was none of his business. Lots of women had active social lives. There was nothing about her that looked any different from her neighbors. Her hair was combed and her makeup under-played. She wore knee-high boots and a wool coat. She carried a large canvas bag that was a little different than the usual laptop or leather bag, but it didn't look out of place.

She straightened her shoulders.

He continued staring at her, arms folded, legs spread in a wide stance. He acted as if he thought he was a real cop. He didn't wear a uniform because they didn't want to give the impression of force, or someone interfering in the ambiance of the building. They wanted more of a private detective kind of persona. A man who quietly took care of things.

Before she'd gone three steps, the left door opened and

the security guy came out. He looked at her as if he thought about holding the door for her, but then let go and it eased itself closed.

He walked along the front of the building.

Jen stopped.

The homeless woman was there again.

The security guy bent over and yanked down the top edge of the sleeping bag. "Get up."

The woman groaned and struggled to pull the bag back over her face.

He held it tightly. He poked his toe at her lower legs.

Jen walked over to where he stood. "She's not hurting anyone."

"She can't stay here."

"What does it matter?"

"Building policy."

"You can't even see her."

"She needs to leave. Go on inside. I'll take care of this."

Jen touched his back. "Please."

"What's it to you?"

"She has nowhere to go."

"Well she can't stay here."

"Why not?"

"It's not up for discussion."

"I just don't see…"

"I said you need to leave." He shoved his toe at the sleeping bag again and tried to pull the top edge lower.

The woman groaned.

He put his hand on the woman's shoulder. "Wake up. You need to get out of here."

"Leave me alone." The woman's voice had a growling quality.

He knelt on the pavement and felt around the edge of the bag. When he found the zipper tab, he unzipped the bag in one swift motion. He folded the bag back, exposing her like he was opening a flap of skin for an autopsy.

Jen had no idea why that image came to mind, but it seemed the same — a violation of something that should be kept hidden. "Please don't," she said.

The woman thrashed and whipped her knees up to the security guard's elbow, knocking him hard.

He stumbled back. "Don't start with me, or I'll call the police." He moved around to her feet, grabbed the fabric and yanked, pulling the bag off most of her body. He put his hand on her shoulder and rolled her onto the sidewalk. "Get up."

"Go away."

"You can't stay here." He began rolling up the sleeping bag. He pulled the elastic strap around the lumpy coil he'd formed, picked up her backpack and the plastic bag and carried everything to the curb. "I don't want to see you here again."

The woman heaved herself into a standing position. She pointed at him with her index and third finger formed into a V-shape. "A pox on you!" She stumbled to the curb and picked up her backpack. She slipped her arms through the straps and hoisted it onto her back. She picked up her other things and turned in the direction of The Embarcadero.

"That was cruel," Jen said.

"It's gotta be done. We can't have a homeless camp here."

"It's not a camp. She's one person."

"They breed. Like flies." He shoved his hands in his pockets and walked away from the building.

Jen went into the lobby. Looking over her shoulder through the floor to ceiling windows, she couldn't see either one of them. The woman would surely be back. It was a safe place. The streets that tolerated homeless people, where no one asked them to move along, were swimming with deranged men and alcoholics and people crazed by meth and crack. There were shelters that might help her, but they usually overflowed their capacity.

Jen walked to the elevator and pushed the button. It was all too much sometimes.

12

Although I found Damien unnerving, I had an inexplicable desire to introduce him to Isaiah.

Tess had said no guests. Did the security people who rotated through at the lobby entrance know that? If they didn't know her rule, would they report unauthorized visitors to her anyway? I had to assume they would. Would she be angry enough to punish me in some way? It wasn't as if I was planning a party, or that Isaiah had some sort of skin disease with the potential for infecting her condo.

I stood at her six-burner gas stove, sautéing prawns, Italian sausage, and shiitake mushrooms in garlic flavored olive oil. A small pot of steamed rice sat on one of the back burners. Another minute and a half and my dinner would be ready.

I tried to imagine what sort of punishment she'd mete out once she discovered I'd broken her rule. Mostly, she'd been thinking of Steve. She'd thrown in a general restriction as a bit of a CYA, a last-minute thought. Maybe she'd forgotten, or just wanted to make sure I wasn't inviting an array of guests who might scuff her floors or stain her lovely sofas and chairs.

The aroma of garlic filled my nostrils. I inhaled deeply, exhaled slowly, and turned off the gas.

I scooped a serving spoon of white rice onto one of Tess's small white plates with a red dot at the center, like the drip off the tip of a paintbrush. I covered it with a few prawns, slices of sausage, and shiitakes. I carried the plate to the bar, re-filled my wineglass with buttery Chardonnay, and sat on the equally buttery white leather cushion of the stool.

There was no way to sneak Isaiah into the condo. Like my building, the lobby desk was occupied twenty-four-seven. The garage in her building also had a security guard. The ID cards were scanned but they were there to make sure each entrant had one, or a guest pass.

I sipped my wine and stabbed a mushroom. I let my mind wander, trying to think how I might get around security.

Damien let out a human-sounding laugh, then shouted — *Watch out!*

A chill ran down my arms. Had the bird read my thoughts? I laughed at my ridiculous thought.

The bird laughed in response. *Dirty bird!*

At least I didn't need to remember to clean up the mat beneath his perch. He reminded me. Clearly. Loudly. Daily.

I slid off the stool and plugged my phone into the speaker at the end of the counter. I scrolled through my music, looking for something that would soothe him rather than entice him to screech in an effort to make himself heard above it. I chose Liszt, slowly increasing the volume. He was quiet and I finished my dinner in peace.

The moment the kitchen light went out, Damien began murmuring to himself. The darkness in the kitchen when Tess was finished with dinner must have signaled something to him. It wasn't food. Her strict instructions outlined one meal at breakfast and one the minute I got home from work. The *minute*, no pausing for a drink or to change clothes. Damien was hungry!

In fact, after I agreed to bird sit, she'd informed me that

if I had evening plans, I needed to come back to the condo first to feed Damien. Why had she taken on a pet that severely restricted her social life? I wondered what she'd do when she was back in the swing of things and traveling overseas every two or three months. Did that mean staying at her place might become a regular gig? I wasn't sure how I felt about that. There was something subservient about it — as if she viewed me as her assistant rather than an employee with independent value.

I went into the bird's room. A floor lamp kept his space illuminated twelve hours a day. The light was on a timer so at least I didn't have to think about that.

Hello.

"Hi, Damien." There was an involuntary change in the pitch of my voice, as if I thought I needed to be friendly and warm and enthusiastic to it…to him.

Chardonnay time.

"Been there, done that."

He cackled and I grinned in spite of myself.

He turned his head, his crown feathers fully extended, as usual. He didn't trust me any more than I trusted him.

"So, what's up? Is there something I'm supposed to do before your light goes out?"

Chardonnay time.

I took a cautious step closer. "I bet you know all of Tess's secrets."

He opened his beak, exposing the thick tongue, like something prehistoric. It moved as if it had a life of its own.

I was supposed to talk to him, but it felt ridiculous. He was a bird. "What am I supposed to talk to you about?"

Sydney.

"How did Tess teach you that in such a short time?"

Time. Chardonnay time. He laughed. Was it my imagination that his laugh now echoed Tess's?

I couldn't escape the sense that Damien was more than just a bird craving food and flight, that he wanted to communicate. Of course, the poor thing would never know outdoor flight again. And from that perspective, I thought Tess was a little cruel. At the same time, the bird seemed quite satisfied with his circumstances.

Isaiah had to meet him. Tess couldn't expect me to stay at her place for an entire month and never invite anyone over. She couldn't require that I put my life on hold while she drank her way up and down the east coast of Australia, or whatever she was doing. She was in a power struggle with Steve and it showed how much she'd let him get under her skin that she told me not to invite him over. I would never do that. But Isaiah had nothing to do with her.

As they say, it's better to beg forgiveness than ask permission. What could she do to me?

13

Like a homing pigeon, Steve showed up at my cubicle the first Monday of Tess's extended absence.

He leaned his arms on the top edge of my cube wall and grinned. "The cat's away."

"That's trite."

"But true."

"I still have plenty to keep me busy."

A fine pale stubble glistened along his jaw. It was unusual for a sales SVP to come to work without shaving. Especially on a Monday.

"Too busy for a drink after work?" He winked. "I know I botched the last one." His expression changed to one of genuine sorrow, like a regular guy wanting to make amends. He didn't look like he was trying to flaunt his authority over me and there was nothing flirty about it. "Are you mad?" he said.

"I don't get mad easily."

"Or you hold it inside? I can see that in you. A smile to the world while the rage burns in your gut."

I smiled.

"Proving my point."

The condescending words flowed out of him so easily — like his earlier suggestion that I would be thrilled to become his protégé, or informing me in no uncertain terms that the glass ceiling no longer existed. The list went on…but maybe he wasn't the misogynist he appeared to be, maybe that was all an act meant to provoke a response.

"Keep guessing," I said. "Because you have no idea what I'm thinking."

"Is that a challenge?"

"No. It's an impossible task."

"Liquor is a truth serum."

"Is it?"

He nodded, the flirty look back in his eyes, twisting across his lips. "So. How about it?"

"I have some things to do after work, but seven would work."

"What things?"

"Not really any of your business."

"Fair enough. I guess seven would work. Although that's dinner time, so…"

"A drink. That's all."

He straightened. "Yes ma'am."

I sighed. "You're not always as clever as you think you are."

He looked confused. "I can pick you up. Where…"

"I'll meet you there. Wherever there is."

"O'Brien's. On Gough."

"Sounds good. Seven."

"See you then." He walked away.

If his offer of a position in sales was still on the table, I sort of wanted to string it along. Unless I managed to find something crazy different, and not necessarily legal, it was my only current option for a significant increase in salary. But he was just so…I didn't want to use the word *slimy*. A better word was…

Slimy.

It was difficult for me to get my head around the idea that a man born well after the feminist movement of the 1970s — living in a post-feminist era, if you will — could be so clueless. Or maybe he wasn't. Maybe I was right in my earlier thought and it was all an act. A power play. After all, I'd never seen him around men. Maybe he played similar games, used similar controlling and sometimes demeaning language with men. Who knows. But he was just so crass. Who says those things?

CoastalCreative is a good-sized company, with an up-to-date Human Resources department, delivering mandatory harassment training. And the training wasn't just a little video or a web page — it was a two-hour course with animated interactive exercises, structured so you weren't able to skip through it to the final pass/fail quiz.

Of course, watching videos and playing interactive games where you had to spot tiny images of wall calendars with bikini-clad females, or desktop religious art in your quest to identify all the offensive things hidden in an office illustration, as if it were an adult *Where's Waldo* game, didn't mean you actually learned it. Disrespect for other human beings is difficult, probably impossible to cut out of a person's mindset in adulthood. Training didn't mean you felt compelled in any way to apply it to your life.

The things he said could be, often should be reported to HR, but how many women do that? It's a brave woman who stands up to even outrageous harassment and quid pro quo pressure for sex from a superior. To complain about a man telling you there's no glass ceiling, trying to describe how offensive that is, somehow manages to make the complainer look small. Oversensitive. Misogyny and bigotry are so engrained in culture, people don't even recognize it.

Women are too sensitive. You need to get a sense of humor. Come on, guys, we have work to do! Products to market and sell! High-pressure reviews to get through! We already work so many hours, bleeding into weekends, up late at night when a major event is on the horizon. Is an offhand remark about a glass ceiling really hampering your ability to do your job? Really?

You took it the wrong way. It's not what he meant...

A drink at night was going to be significantly different from our last get-together when we walked along sun-washed sidewalks to a bar near the office and tossed down a quick drink.

Tess would tell me to run fast, to refuse the drink, to build my career with the support of her mentoring. She would tell me the promise of easy, fast money wasn't worth it, that it wasn't as easy and fast as he made it sound. She'd tell me to watch out for him. Maybe. But curiosity trumps wisdom with me. The adrenaline starts pumping and I'm desperate to know what might happen, how things will play out, what someone will say and what I'll say in return. I have to know. It's a game. A very exciting game, better than any sport.

That adrenaline was already flowing at increased speed into my veins. I was planning what I'd wear, how quickly I could shovel food at Damien, and thinking about the entertaining possibilities ahead. I didn't want to get too dressed up, to look as if I'd put in effort.

A change of my shirt, with a jacket over it so he wouldn't quite remember if I'd been wearing the same thing when he issued the invitation. A bit more eye makeup for the dark lounge. Brushing my hair. Standard stuff, but it was tricky to look good without looking like I'd had a complete do-over between leaving work and arriving at the bar.

I put in a request for an Uber to pick me up at Tess's at six-forty. I worked until four-thirty, only half paying attention to what I was doing.

Getting a Senior Vice President to want what I had, more than I wanted what he was offering, was like getting set to run a marathon.

14

Damien was fed and busy slurping fresh water. His insistence that it was *Chardonnay time*, had followed me out the door. I wondered what the other person living on Tess's floor would think if that door opened as Tess's was closing and that strange, human-but-not, voice echoed into the shared space around the elevator.

I was a few minutes late arriving at the bar. O'Brien's was Irish, obviously. It seemed like an odd choice. Steve didn't strike me as an easy-going Irish guy, although I suppose his light hair and eye color suggested he might have some Irish blood. Not that you need to be Irish to enjoy an Irish bar, but I would have expected him to choose a more upscale place, a place that suggested wealth and the upper crust — executives and attorneys and real estate moguls only — step inside and pay double what you'd pay elsewhere for a top-shelf shot.

Even on a Monday night, people were crowded around the entryway to the bar, pushing forward, craning their necks as they looked for small tables or a seat at the bar. It was the longest bar I'd ever seen — it ran along the right side of the room and wrapped around to the back wall. Every seat was taken.

Steve waved at me from where he stood beside a small table in one of several rooms that opened into the main bar. I walked toward him. He smiled and skittered around the side of the table, pulling out the chair for me before taking his own seat.

In the center of the table was a silver dish on a wire frame with a flame beneath it. Sautéed mushrooms and calamari simmered gently. Beside it was a tiny basket of crackers so thin they looked as if they would turn to dust if you picked one up. There were two bottles of mineral water and two glasses of ice with a slice of lime tucked among the small cubes.

"Vodka martini?" he said.

"Yes."

He half raised his hand to signal a server, glanced around, and stood. "It's faster to go to the bar. Enjoy the appetizer."

I stabbed a toothpick into a mushroom and put it in my mouth. I wasn't sure how they went with the crackers, it wasn't as if you could set a mushroom or even a slice of calamari on top. Maybe they were just a change of pace between garlic-doused flowering fungus and fish. I took a cracker. It was sturdier than it looked. And very tasty. Sesame.

The plate of mushrooms and calamari was half empty and my mineral water was gone by the time Steve returned. He placed the martini glass in front of me. Vodka slithered over the top and ran down the outside, trickling along the stem, and spreading a small pool around the base.

"Sorry, that took longer than expected. I should have ordered here after all, at least we could have talked. Instead I left a beautiful woman sitting alone."

He plunked down in his chair and took a sip of his scotch. "Sorry again." He raised it toward me. "To opportunity. Cheers." He took another sip.

"Cheers." I picked up my wet glass and drank.

He handed me a cocktail napkin. I wiped my fingers and the side of the glass.

"Sorry about that." He grinned. "Three apologies in less than a minute. I usually don't say I'm sorry."

"I don't imagine you do."

He ate some calamari and went into a long story about his golf game the previous day. He described, shot by shot, his progress off the tee, up the fairway, into the sand, out of the sand, and onto the green, ending with a flourish of his glass as he explained his remarkable putt. Golfers, maybe all sports lovers, seem to think everyone is as fascinated by every second of the game as they are. He acted as if he'd completed brain surgery and was recounting the miraculous outcome.

"I'm boring you, aren't I," he said.

"No more than a football fan."

"You don't like sports?"

"I like running. And weight lifting."

He nodded. "I can tell."

I smiled.

"Golf is a good game. You should take it up. It would help your career. Lots of partnerships and alliances get formed on the golf course."

"So I've heard."

"Just a piece of advice."

I sipped my drink, flicking my tongue at the single olive. I'd have to pace myself. If I'd gone to the bar myself, there would be three olives waiting for me as I sipped my way to the bottom of the glass.

"Here's another bit of advice," he said.

I stabbed the last mushroom and popped it into my mouth.

"Do you want more?"

"Advice?"

He laughed. "No, mushrooms and calamari? Something else? Dinner?"

"I don't have a lot of time."

"Why?"

"Because I don't."

"A date?"

"We agreed on one drink."

"Okay. Okay. Fair enough. Then I'd better get to the point."

I sipped from my nearly empty glass, longing for the olive, but wanting to save it until I was ready to leave.

"I know I haven't been consistent with this, but I really think you'd be happy with a position in my organization. And I apologize for dropping the ball on that."

"You haven't given me an offer."

"Since we've gone around in circles on it, I wanted to get a sense of where your head is now, before I put time into something formal."

I smiled. There was no *we* going in circles, only him.

"So are you interested?"

"How can I be interested if I haven't seen an offer?"

"This isn't how it works."

"How what works?"

"Don't play games."

"I'm not."

"If you think you can play Tess and me against each other, you're wrong."

"I'm not playing any games or any people."

"I get the sense that you are."

"I just want to understand what you're offering. And I

want to discuss it with Tess."

"Why would you do that? You land a job...*then* you tell your boss you're moving on, you don't discuss it. That's the last person to discuss your career with."

The pimento poking out of the olive eyed me from the bottom of the glass. I folded my hands on my lap and leaned forward slightly, pressing them against my thighs. "I thought your manager was supposed to help with career development."

"You're kidding, right?"

"That's what it says in the annual performance review forms — put down your goals, where you want to grow, what interests you're..."

"That's all bullshit. You're smart enough to know that. Now I know you're playing me."

"Think what you want."

"You can be a bit of a bitch, did you know that?"

"I thought you appreciated my bluntness?"

"It's a fine line."

I leaned back and waited.

"I'm not giving you an offer until I understand whether you're serious. I don't want you discussing it with Tess, or taking it to another company, for that matter."

I sipped my drink.

"Tess is done at CC. Do you realize that? Why do you think she ran off to the other side of the world?"

"That wasn't my impression."

"These things happen at levels above you. It's not visible to average employees."

"She didn't seem..." I stopped. I wasn't sure he was telling the truth and I was on the verge of saying too much about Tess. I shouldn't discuss her with him at all. He had an insatiable desire to turn every conversation back to her. Even though he was telling me how it was in his view, I still had the sense he wanted to extract whatever information he could from me.

"What were you going to say?"

"That's rather harsh," I said.

"It's a harsh world."

"What did she do?"

He shrugged. "It's more what she didn't do."

"I thought she was well-respected."

"She's not aggressive enough. And she's a little emotional, if you want to know the truth."

"Emotional?"

"Changes her mind without warning. Moody."

I stared at him.

"You've seen that side of her, haven't you?" He swallowed the rest of his drink. "Are you sure I can't persuade you to have dinner?"

I ate my olive and nudged the glass away from me. I pulled out my phone and put in a request for an Uber. The app informed me a ride would be there in seven to eight minutes. I stood and pulled out my wallet.

"No, no. My treat. I invited you."

"Thank you."

"I don't feel like this conversation is over," he said.

"It probably isn't. But my ride will be here in less than five minutes."

No harm in adding a bit of a buffer, I didn't want to drag it on any longer. How could I consider working for someone whose presence I couldn't wait to escape?

Maybe I didn't really want to work for him. I just liked playing him, and he knew it, which didn't make it much of a game.

15

Portland

About two miles from the park where I'd spent the morning of my escape on a swing, there's an awesome park that's heavily wooded. It features all kinds of large shrubs creating the kind of secret hideouts kids crave. Usually, kids explore these places while mom and dad are seated on a picnic blanket within shouting distance. I'd done plenty of that, but now I was on my own.

The open grassy area spreads out and dips down about four feet into a sort of valley that's undisturbed by tables or benches or climbing structures. People play Frisbee there and eat picnic lunches. Beyond that, as it rises back up to street level, there's a brick retaining wall. Above that is more grass and the trees are more dense. The grass gives way to dirt and dead leaves as it slopes up again to the hillside filled with the shrubs that offer private enclosures. It was the perfect place for me to sleep for a few nights while I figured out where I was going to find this mythical family who would take me into their home.

Already the school would have called my mother to confirm my absence from class. I wondered if she'd called the police immediately, or my father. I imagined him advising her not to *panic*, not to *over-react*, not to get *hysterical*. I imagined her doing all of those things. I imagined him suggesting this was family business and shouldn't involve the police. I certainly hadn't been abducted. Despite our personality clash, he knew me well. Better than she did.

Two miles wasn't a huge distance, but for a ten-year-old wearing a backpack and dragging a suitcase, it wasn't only a long walk, it was two miles of potential exposure. I decided to wait until close to the time school let out. That way, it would be assumed it was an early release day and I wouldn't look quite so out of place. Pulling a small suitcase wasn't entirely odd, some kids used them to bring their books to school. I figured chutzpah was half the trick to success, maybe more. I didn't know the word chutzpah at the time, but it fits perfectly when I think back on it. I understood a lot of things before I knew the words that defined them.

I sat on a bench and ate the lunch my mother had packed for school, took a few sips of water, and returned to the bathroom to refill my bottle from the sink faucet. The towel dispenser was empty so I wiped my hands on my pants.

My small wristwatch said it was two o'clock. I thrust my arms through the straps of my backpack and extended the handle of the suitcase. I walked out of the bathroom and turned left. On the sidewalk, I moved quickly but not in a way that looked as if I was running from something. I realized it was perfectly reasonable that I might be headed to soccer practice, with my uniform in the suitcase. The thought made my shoulders feel looser, and my pace became more of a stroll.

Half an hour later, I reached the park where I planned to sleep.

No one was picnicking on a weekday afternoon. I followed the blacktop path past a play area with two slides coming out of a cube. Circles were cut in the sides of the cube so kids could peek out. There were three swings, and several plastic farm animals on large springs that bounced when you sat on them. The path curved down the slope to the valley area, looped around a grove of trees, and met itself again. I collapsed the suitcase handle and picked it up.

Crossing the large expanse of grass to the retaining wall was a struggle with the over-stuffed suitcase banging against my shin, but I had to walk fast. I needed to get to my sleeping spot soon. Assuming my mother had called my father first, they were surely not still arguing about panic levels. By now, she would have prevailed and a patrol car would be driving through the neighborhood with last year's school photo.

I lugged the suitcase up the incline and through the first wooded area and found the grouping of shrubs I was looking for. There was a flat area with two leafy bushes that grew their tendrils around each other. At the bottom, between the two bushes, was an opening. I crawled through and I was inside a ring of plants near a small maple tree that reached over to provide a covering. Plenty to shield me from the sun but not rain, which in Portland, should have been a bigger concern than it was. The sky was clear and we hadn't had rain for three or four days, but that didn't mean clouds wouldn't move in before bedtime.

I spread the tarp on the ground and unrolled my sleeping bag. I opened a snack bar and ate it as slowly as I could, trusting that chewing each bite for an extended amount of time would make me feel more full. For dinner, I planned to walk to the Speedy Mart where I could buy beef jerky and potato chips. I needed to go well before dark, so I didn't arouse curiosity in the clerk. Lots of clerks aren't curious at all, they just want you to complete your transaction without any hassle, but you never know.

The books I'd stuffed in the empty crevices in my suitcase were part of the *Fear Street* series. They were my favorites because I felt my own life disappear when I read them. I made it through a few chapters before my aching shoulders demanded attention. I stretched out on my back, staring up through the leafy canopy, and fell asleep.

When I woke, the sky was slate colored and it was cold. I sat up, shoved my book back into the suitcase, and put on my jacket. I arranged everything in a tidy pile, as if that would keep my possessions from being stolen. I tucked the bag of coins into my pocket.

I walked to the Speedy Mart a block away, bought my unsatisfactory dinner, and returned to my hideout. Already I was getting bored, but I was not admitting defeat.

16

Isaiah had a weird mixture of gratitude and guilt over the chance to stay in my studio apartment while I was camping out at Tess's place. The shared house possibility had fallen through, and if he didn't have my place, he'd be sleeping on a friend's couch while he looked for a new home. Finding an apartment in the city is complicated and time consuming — locating that trifecta of availability, location, and affordability. He was grateful for his good fortune regarding the timing of it all, but he felt guilty for some reason he couldn't seem to articulate.

As best I could figure it out, he didn't like being dependent on me.

I didn't see it that way at all, but at the same time, I knew I'd think the same if the situation was reversed. When I figured out what was probably bothering him, I was even more drawn to him.

Dependence makes my skin crawl. It means you aren't in control of your own destiny. Everything could fall apart without your consent if you're leaning on someone else for your home, your livelihood, or for your sense of being a valuable human being, for that matter. I don't like depending on CoastalCreative or Tess. It's a necessary and hopefully, temporary evil. I envy people who know how to invest, how to take advantage of stock market fluctuations to create money. Of course, you need something to start with, so maybe there's not a lot of creation involved.

I envy those who have the nest egg to invest in property, expanding their ownership relentlessly until their lives are buffered by passive income. Anything where money can recreate itself and you don't have to count on unreliable, uncertain, unpredictable human beings.

From the time I was ten years old, I craved independence. I wanted to follow the rules that made sense and ignore the absurd. I wanted to organize my life in a way that looked interesting to me. Instead, I had to depend on my parents to feed me. I had to adhere to their bizarre view of the world and their unbearable fear of wrath streaming out of the heavens and doing…I was never sure what.

After death, of course, there were the flames of hell, the eternal suffering that was also slightly vague. Did the suffering refer to more than fire searing your skin? Constant hunger? Thirst? Lack of sleep? Ear-shattering noises, screams maybe? If you look at some of the paintings by the masters, that's what they suggest, quite vividly. But it was never spelled out.

Once, my mother said the suffering was the heartbreak of eternal separation from your creator, but as far as I could see, they were already separated from their creator on planet earth.

Isaiah had insisted I enter my apartment with a key whenever I chose, but I knocked, nevertheless.

He opened the door and I stepped to the threshold. He brought his mouth to mine, kissing me for several minutes without touching me except for our joined lips and tongues and breath. It's quite erotic when he does that, and it makes me crave him even more. We moved away from each other and went inside.

The room smelled different. Nothing overtly male or Isaiah-specific — no foreign shampoo or odors of unfamiliar foods. Just…different. Not me.

"I want to kidnap you," I said.

"Any time. Do you want a martini?"

"Now."

"Okay." He went to the kitchen area and opened the freezer.

"Not a martini. I want to kidnap you now."

He laughed. "Okay. Sure. Where are we going?"

"If you knew, it wouldn't be a kidnapping."

He extended his arms, wrists pressed together. "Are you going to cuff me?"

"I wish. I guess I'm not prepared. Still, get your jacket."

He went to the closet and pulled out his black leather jacket, scuffed and worn from years of constant use. "Blindfold?"

"You're liking this too much. You should be nervous," I said.

He mimed biting his fingernails.

We went to the underground parking garage. He got in the passenger seat of my car and we left. He pestered me with questions all the way to Tess's place, continuing to wonder why he wasn't blindfolded. As we turned onto her street, he was suddenly quiet. "Are you taking me to Tess's?"

"Maybe."

"I don't think we should…uhm. You need to respect her place."

"I do respect it."

"I don't think we should do anything there."

"That's not why we're going."

"What is it?"

"I want to show you something."

"Can't you take a picture?"

"No."

"Now I'm curious."

"You should be." I pulled up to the curb in front of Lorraine's building.

"Nice place," he said.

"She's in that one." I pointed to the high rise.

We got out and walked to the lobby. We went inside and approached the desk.

I smiled, friendly and confident of easy access. "Hi."

The man sitting at the desk smiled without showing his teeth, the barest smile that could still be called a smile. Doing his job of friendly welcome without giving me any advantage or a welcoming feeling whatsoever. "Hello, Ms. Mallory."

"I need a guest pass for my computer repair guy."

The man looked at me, holding my gaze. He didn't even glance at Isaiah. "Ms. Turner only authorized access for you, Ms. Mallory."

"But he..."

"No exceptions."

Isaiah took a few steps back.

"She didn't want me having dinner guests, a party, that sort of thing. But this is..."

"No exceptions."

I smiled. "I don't think you understand."

"I understand perfectly. No guests. No exceptions."

"He's not a guest. He's..."

"Yes, computer repair. You'll have to take your computer to a shop."

"But the internet…"

"Is there a problem with the internet?" The man picked up the handset on his phone. "I'll have someone check it immediately."

"No. It's fine."

He smiled with smug satisfaction that *of course* the internet was working.

I considered texting Tess and telling her she needed to make an exception, but trying to explain that in a text message might not go well. I was doing her a huge favor, dealing with that bird. All I wanted to do was introduce him to Isaiah.

I smiled. "Okay, then." I turned and we walked out the door.

"What did you want to show me?" Isaiah said.

"I'll figure out another way. I don't want to spoil the surprise."

"He seemed pretty firm."

"I know. I just wanted to find out what Tess told them. I have another idea."

We returned to my car and drove to Chinatown. We had a fantastic feast while I tried to figure out how I would get the bird into my car and drive him to my apartment and get him inside without risking his safety. Isaiah had to see him. More important than seeing him, he had to listen to him speak.

17

Jen climbed slowly out of the battered Honda. Why did the shittiest cars always pick you up after two in the morning? She knew the answer to that, of course. But still, it was the last thing she needed. A rip down the center of the backseat, foam spilling out like semen, the stench of cigarettes and some kind of nearly spoiled food filling the car. Didn't Uber have principles their drivers were required to follow? Possibly. But not after two a.m. At that time of night, you were grateful if a car showed up on time. You were supposed to give a good rating just for the fact they were even available.

It had been embarrassing, climbing into a car like that in front of such a snazzy hotel. She might as well have announced to the doorman what she was, what she'd been doing inside despite the management's vigilant efforts to keep the place upscale and free of scum like her.

The night hadn't been one of her best. Her client...she laughed. She knew it was dumb to call men her clients, but in a self-delusional way, it made her feel better. What else to call them? Johns? Tricks? Those words made her feel ashamed.

He'd been referred by an attorney, but she knew the minute he offered to buy her a Cosmo at the bar where they met, that there was something unkind about him. And that was being kind herself. She wouldn't call him cruel, but he was rough and he saw her as a piece of meat that he reluctantly required to keep his body functioning properly.

Mostly, he thought she was dumb — he told her that

right away. Not that good looking — he told her that repeatedly, as if it justified everything that came after.

He'd had her three times, always from behind.

After, she felt raw and pinched.

He smacked her face. She didn't know why anyone had to do that. There was nothing erotic about it. Just cruelty. Keeping her in her place, letting her know how unimportant she was. In some cases, she might have walked out immediately, but since he was a friend of a good client, she felt it would be a mistake with repercussions.

Hopefully, he wouldn't message her again. And hopefully, she could move on and the experience would fade to a dull, barely remembered pain. The torn strap on her bra, the rawness that screamed with every step, the ache in her cheekbone. Worst of all, the way she felt about herself. Disgusted and ashamed and most of all, stupid. She'd had it good so far. No abuse, no bruising or broken bones or cuts, nothing that she hadn't experienced in her normal sex life prior to turning into a pro, if that's what she was. Maybe her luck was running out.

She tugged at her skirt and shifted the strap of her bag higher on her shoulder. Cold air slipped inside her nostrils, releasing a slide of mucous. She turned away from the building and pulled a tissue out of her bag. She wiped her nose and stuffed the tissue back inside. She looked up.

The homeless woman was in her usual spot, undeterred by the diligent security guy. Jen smiled. She took a step forward and saw the woman wasn't alone. A man stood with his back to Jen. So, he was here after all. She moved closer to the front doors.

A splatting sound echoed softly in the deserted street, like rain falling on carpet.

She took another step forward.

The man remained motionless, his head bent slightly. Was it the security guy, or someone else getting ready to shove his foot into her kneecap, or worse? The man wriggled his shoulders and turned slightly.

Jen walked up closer. "What are you doing?"

His head jerked toward her, but the rest of his body remained facing the sleeping woman.

The sound of water dripping on pavement, followed by a faint hissing, filled her ears with a roaring that threatened to drown out the other.

She charged at him, shoving her shoulder into the center of his back.

"Hey! Fuck off," he said.

"What the hell is wrong with you? What are you..." She was crying. She slammed her fist into his back. He hardly seemed to feel it through the thick wool coat.

He whirled around and grabbed her wrist.

His pants were open and she saw his wet penis wobbling in response to the sudden movement.

"You pig. You...pig is too good for you."

"Get off me."

He shoved her and she stumbled backwards. Her bag slid off her shoulder and fell on the pavement. She left it there and charged forward again.

He pushed her away and reached down to yank his zipper into place.

"That's disgusting. That's..."

"Fuck off," he said.

"It's you! What's *wrong* with you?"

It was the same man who'd thrown his useless lottery ticket at the woman's sleeping body. The human race was disgusting. Had it always been this way? Were there just more people now, so it seemed more depraved because it was spreading out of dark crevices, more visible by the sheer number? A lot of people would tell her she was one to talk, but it wasn't fair. She treated people with kindness. This was the worst thing she'd ever seen. She wanted to cry.

She walked to the door and flung it open. She half-ran to the desk. "Where's security?

"Right here."

The security guy appeared as if out of nowhere. "Is there a problem?"

"That guy," she waved her arm toward the door. "He peed on that woman. He's pissing on the sidewalk, and he…" She began crying. A sob came out of her chest that she hadn't known was there.

"What guy?"

"He…he doesn't live here. But he visits a lot."

"So what happened?" The security guy strode toward the door.

Jen hurried after him.

Outside, the man was getting into a cab.

"Stop!" She raced to the street. Her bag sat in the center of the sidewalk where she'd left it a few minutes earlier.

The cab door closed.

She lunged toward it, pounding her fist on the back window. "Get out!"

The security guy grabbed her arm. "You don't need to get hysterical."

"He peed on her!!"

The security guy said nothing and the cab pulled away.

Jen glared at him. "You need to watch for him next time. You need to…"

"What's your name?"

"What does that have to do with anything?"

"I need it for my report."

"On what?"

"On the disturbance."

"I'm not the disturbance. He is."

"I'll get rid of her, again. And see if we can get a regular police patrol to keep her out of here."

She was breathing hard, making it difficult to speak. "She's not the problem. That…that…piece of crap is."

"Calm down."

Jen grabbed her bag and slung it over her shoulder. "You have it all wrong."

"What's your name?"

"I don't have to tell you anything." She felt tears spilling out of her eyes. The security guy was blurry now, but the tears didn't obscure the stubborn expression on his face.

How could he turn this on her? She wasn't sure which was worse — a man who pissed on a human being or a man who didn't care and was more interested in causing problems for Jen. He couldn't know her name and she couldn't risk becoming someone he paid attention to. It was probably too late for that now. Her stomach heaved as she hurried to the elevator, sickened by the realization that she couldn't do anything to help that poor woman. Her hands shook, thinking how he'd begin to take note of her every time she left or entered the apartment building.

18

The next morning, Jen woke at seven, not that she'd slept much, so it was an exaggeration to call it *waking*. All through her dreams she'd seen the man peeing as if it were the most natural thing in the world to cover a woman's body with your filth. She smelled the pungent odor, felt the warm liquid on her own skin, making it feel as if her shower before bed hadn't done its job.

She took another shower, turning the hot water up until the temperature was almost unbearable. When she was dressed, she sent a text message to Isaiah.

Jen Miller: *Do you have time to grab a coffee before you go to class?*

She was standing at the kitchen counter, staring at the coffee pot, trying to decide if she should go ahead and make her own, since he wasn't answering. She lifted the carafe off the hot plate and her phone buzzed.

Isaiah Parker: *Sure. 7:45? Lounge or out?*

Jen Miller: *Lounge is fine. See you.*

She blasted the dryer at her hair for two minutes, then put on socks and Ugg boots with her jeans and turtleneck sweater. The rawness in her body from the night before made her ache for comfort clothes — softness and warmth, a thick protective exterior.

When Jen arrived, Isaiah was already in the lounge, standing at the serving station waiting for coffee. He waved and held up two fingers indicating he'd already bought her a cup. Such a nice guy. Every time she saw him, there was a prick of jealousy in the bottom of her throat. Alex got him and Jen was left drifting alone, even though she'd known him first. Of course, most guys didn't want a hooker for a girlfriend. No guy that she wanted.

The desire was growing more difficult to ignore, fueled by the previous evening. She had to do something, figure out something, do *anything*, to get out of the too-easy trap she'd fallen into. Taking money for sex. What could be easier? And what could be worse? She'd been lazy and stupid and now she was trapped.

She settled in an armchair and waited for Isaiah to join her.

He crossed the room and put the oversized white cups and saucers on the table. Jen's was creamy with milk, his was dark brown. Simple and straightforward, like him.

He picked up his cup and took a sip. "What's up?" he said.

"Something horrible happened last night."

He put his cup down hard. The clink of ceramic caused a man sitting a few feet away to look up, startled. He frowned and went back to his tablet. "Are you okay?" Isaiah said.

"It's not about me. I'm okay." She would keep that to herself. Forever. Telling anyone, especially a man, would make it more humiliating, once it was out in the light of others' pity and disgust and blame that she would allow those things to be done to her.

He picked up his cup again.

Jen did the same, but she didn't drink. "That homeless woman that sleeps near the entrance?"

"Yeah?"

"She, well the security guy keeps chasing her away."

"That's his job."

"I know. But there's this guy, he visits here a lot…last time I saw him, he threw a used lottery ticket at her."

"Not cool."

"It's worse."

"What?"

"I can hardly say it."

He waited, looking down into his cup as if he thought avoiding her gaze would make it easier for her to talk.

"He peed on her!" Her voice caught and all that came out was a squeak. She swallowed. "He was standing there, piss going all over her sleeping bag. Probably in her face."

"Are you kidding me?"

She shook her head.

"What a pig."

She took a deep breath to steady her voice. "I tried to talk to the security guy and he wanted my name. Like I was the one with a problem."

"I doubt that's what he meant."

"He just wants her out of here. He didn't care what that guy did."

Isaiah nodded.

"I don't know what to do."

"Do?"

"I can't just let it happen."

"It already did."

"You know what I mean. I want to do something. I want…"

"Like what?"

She sipped her coffee. "I don't know. I can't just let that

happen. I don't want to live in a world where that's okay."

"No one said it was okay."

"Security implied it. And what's to keep it from happening again?"

"If she stops sleeping there, I guess."

"So you think it's not a big deal?"

"Of course it's a big deal."

"Why don't you want to do something? Why aren't you angry?"

"I am angry, but I don't see what anyone can do. Unless he's caught in the act. I guess he could be cited for public urination, but that's about it."

"I have to do something. But I don't want…I can't have the security guy noticing me. You know what I mean?"

He nodded.

"I can't let that happen to her."

"What are you going to do?"

"I'm not sure. I guess, for now, I just wanted to tell someone. I wanted someone else to feel as upset as I do."

"You got it."

"Thanks. And thanks for the coffee."

"Any time," he said.

"If I think of something…"

"Sometimes, you need to know the world sucks, that people suck big time, and just keep going."

She didn't say anything. He was right, but also wrong. She couldn't just keep going.

19

I was standing on the street before heading to work, smoking and keeping my eye on the second story window of the charming Edwardian building next door. The sun was just coming up and it was cold, but I was wearing boots and wool pants and a thin sweater with a wool coat over that, a scarf wound twice around my neck. The only thing missing were mittens and a hat.

The sheer white curtains covered the window where I'd seen the woman. Heavy drapes hung behind the sheers, but they hadn't been closed the few times I'd looked at the window. Now, they were. The glass gleamed, not even a fingerprint of blood. The window was so clean, it must have been washed and wiped with a squeegee. All the windows on that floor were equally clean.

I inhaled and blew out a long thread of smoke. It remained in the still air, made more visible by the cold.

The cigarette was almost gone when the front door opened. I'd half hoped for another conversation with Lorraine, but a man emerged. He wore a black fedora and a black overcoat. He looked like he belonged in the antiquated building and the building belonged to him. He wasn't quite as old as Lorraine, but definitely up there — well over seventy.

He walked slowly down the first few steps, his back straight, no smart phone in sight. It made me sentimental for a world I'd never known — one with hats and overcoats, one where people enjoyed their own thoughts instead of cluttering their heads with tweets and memes. A world that probably wasn't as glamorous as it appears in photographs and movies. A world where smoking a cigarette wasn't a crime against humanity.

He touched the brim of his hat. "May I help you?"

"No. Just having a quick smoke. I don't mean to loiter."

He smiled. "You've met Mrs. Clayton."

"Yes." I returned his smile. "I live next door. Or rather, I'm staying there, watching my friend's place."

He nodded. He took another step down and paused.

He stepped onto the pavement and moved closer. He leaned forward ever so slightly, in an uncertain bow. "May I have a cigarette?"

"Absolutely." I pulled out the pack and held it while he eased a cigarette out of its place. I touched the flame of my lighter to the tip.

"Thank you." He held out his hand. "Frank."

I took his hand. "Alexandra. Have you lived here long?"

"Over fifty years."

"Nearly as long as Lorraine," I said.

He nodded once.

"Do you like it?"

"Russian Hill is a beautiful area."

We smoked in silence for several minutes.

I tapped my cigarette and the ash fluttered to the ground. I turned to face him more directly. "Mind if I ask you a question?"

"Go ahead."

"Do you know anything about the woman on the second floor?"

"Why do you ask?"

"She…there's something not quite right."

He put the cigarette to his lips and took a long, deep drag, more than I would be able to manage. I expected him to cough, but he let it out slowly and easily.

"I saw blood," I said. "On her window. Her hand was bleeding, and she…"

He nodded as if it was the most natural thing in the world. "She's not right in the head."

"What's wrong with her?"

"You shouldn't stare at her."

"I wasn't."

"Don't even look up there. It only encourages her."

"Encourages her to do what?"

"I really shouldn't say. It's not something I wish to talk about with a lady."

He was so quaint, so polite, I felt an unusual, unfamiliar restraint, so I spoke gently. "What if I'm not a lady?"

He smiled. "Of course you are."

"So what's wrong with her?"

"She does things. She behaves in a way that's…disturbing. She's trying to get attention."

"Why?"

"She just wants people to notice her. She wants to shock. And appall."

"There must be a reason."

"I suppose everyone has a reason for their behavior," he said.

"How can you live in the same building for decades and never speak?"

"It's possible."

"How many people live in your building. It's only one

apartment per floor, isn't it? So the lobby and four units?"

"Yes."

"Then how…"

"We're private people. It's not a social club. She wants to be left alone, and so do I."

"Are you sure?"

"Sure about what?"

"That she wants to be left alone. Maybe she needs help."

"She lives in a beautiful apartment, which obviously requires money, so she has plenty. Why would she need help?"

I could think of a thousand reasons.

"You don't think it's a little unsettling that she's smearing blood on her window?"

"As I explained, she simply wants attention. Some women are like that. Most women. They all have different methods of getting it — some positive, some not."

Had it escaped his notice that he was talking to a woman? I thought of my earlier sense that he represented a lovely bygone era, but I was now jolted into the matter-of-fact misogyny of that undefined era. The 1920s? Forties? Fifties? The more he dismissed her as attention-seeking, the more concerned I was about why she was so fervently seeking it. If it was simple loneliness, why didn't she come outside?

For some reason, his view of her, Lorraine's opinion, seemed manufactured in their own minds. If nothing else, why weren't they curious? Was seeking attention enough to explain it all away so they lost interest? It wasn't enough for me. I wanted to know why. Maybe because I'm a woman and I do not believe women do shameful — whatever that is — disgusting things simply for the attention. "Does she ever look out? Or does she just put her hand on the window?"

He stared at me as if I'd asked him how often he had sex.

After several minutes of silence, he dropped his cigarette on the ground. He stepped on it and performed his little, uncertain half-bow. "Thank you for the cigarette, and the lovely company." He touched the brim of his hat, tugging it forward so I could no longer see his eyes. "Have a good day." He began walking.

"Bye," I said to his back. He didn't turn.

Was he tired of discussing her, or was there a reason he didn't answer my question? I couldn't be sure. His demeanor was so impassive it could have been hiding several different things. I looked up at the window.

The curtains moved slightly.

20

For nearly ten minutes after Frank walked away, I stared at that window. The curtains were motionless, but I knew she was there. She was watching me watch her. We had now entered into some sort of game. If I could have managed it, I would have gone without blinking. I wanted another cigarette but the slightest glance toward the tip as I flicked a lighter might mean missing the fluttering sigh of a curtain.

Lorraine and Frank both decreed she was best ignored. They came close to insisting I ignore her. Were the residents of the city really that cold, that isolated from people living and breathing inches from their own walls? Or in this case, below the floors they walked across all day long? It was true in my building. I'd only met a handful of neighbors. Most, I passed without greeting, some barely exchanged half-hearted smiles. But there were hundreds of occupants. As far as I could tell, Lorraine and Frank lived alone, meaning this charming structure from another era had, at most, six to ten residents. The ambiance of that earlier era gave the impression it would be friendlier, neighborly, characterized by formal greetings on a daily basis, teas and cocktail parties. I couldn't comprehend living that close to people for decades and never speaking to them.

I'm not a social butterfly. I'm not the type of person who chats it up with everyone I meet, who wants to invite every person in the neighborhood for a holiday open house. I don't want them creeping into my space and taking over like unwanted spiders spinning webs in the unreachable corners of the ceiling, taking far too much interest in my life. But I'm curious to know who they are. I'm interested in knowing their names, and a bit of their stories. These two apparently wanted to live as if the people nearby didn't even exist.

It was chilling. And unsettling. And slightly unbelievable.

The curtains hadn't moved. It was time for me to leave for work, but without Tess there, did it really matter all that much? My first meeting was at ten, it was only seven-fifty.

Finally, I reached into my bag, felt for my cigarettes, slid one out of the pack, and put it in my mouth, all the while keeping my gaze glued to the window. I located the lighter and held it to the tip, nearly going cross-eyed making sure I could see the window while connecting tobacco and flame.

I inhaled and dropped the lighter in my bag.

The curtains moved, as if the odor of smoke had drawn her to the window. I squinted, trying to determine whether the window was cracked open. It didn't appear to be, but possibly the ledge beneath it blocked the narrowest opening.

A few minutes passed, during which I only put the cigarette to my lips twice, mesmerized by the gossamer curtains more than the smoke trailing out of my mouth.

The street was silent. The songbirds who'd been vocal earlier had quieted down or left the area. The occupants of Tess's building were nowhere in sight. The lobby doors hadn't opened and no cars had emerged from the underground parking during the time I'd been standing there. I shivered as the cold pavement seeped through the soles of my shoes and threaded its way along the bones of my legs.

A hand appeared on the glass. The left hand. It was pressed hard, the skin sickly white as circulation was slowed by the impervious glass, leaving the skin bloodless. She relaxed the pressure and the fingers traced their way down the glass. Then, the hand was gone.

I inhaled smoke and released it.

The right hand appeared. The tip of the index finger was thick with what looked like blood, although I still refused to accept that's what it really was.

She touched the window on the left side near the frame. She began to move her finger, writing with smeared red liquid. The first letter was an elegantly scripted *I*. The liquid left a thick stroke, but as her finger continued its path, there wasn't enough left to form complete letters. She ran all of the letters into a single word, further preventing me from making out what she was writing.

The movements were large, sweeping from the bottom edge up to the wood that formed the top of the pane of glass. The intensity of her movement grew with each indecipherable letter. They blurred into a series of loops and curls, like waves of water trickling along a creek, rising over rocks and circling around fallen branches and outcroppings of earth along the bank.

I took short puffs and blew them out quickly, as if the rapid activity would free my brain to see what she was writing. Why would she write on the window, knowing I was standing there, yet not make any effort to actually communicate? Had she even considered I was reading it backwards? In addition to the evaporated red and endlessly connected letters, like an overdone hashtag that has to be deciphered slowly, I also had to think in reverse. Or was she writing in reverse? I didn't think so, starting with the upper-case *I* like that, but there was no way to know for sure.

The ash fell off my cigarette without my noticing it had grown thick. I took another drag, dropped the cigarette on the sidewalk and crushed it with my foot. I picked up the butt and flipped it into a nearby trashcan wrapped in wrought-iron bars to give it a stately appearance.

My head hurt from the effort of staring, straining to read, aching to comprehend. The woman wanted something but I had no idea whether it was just an effort to command my attention, to take moments of my life for herself, possessing me, or if she actually wanted me to read the words she'd written.

I turned back to the window. All that remained clear was the red upper-case *I*.

21

After work and a visit to the gym, in order to get my mind off the woman writing cryptic messages in blood, I decided to focus on taking Damien out for a visit to Isaiah.

Everything I understood about the world, and all my human intelligence, knew without a doubt that the bird was repeating phrases he'd heard from Tess and his previous owners. He was a fast learner. Cockatoos are smart — they can pick locks with determination and skill. They toss rings and knock over plastic blocks with as much enthusiasm and purpose as any human toddler. He'd learned to associate phrases with other things going on around him. It was possible he repeatedly heard a wine cork popping out of a bottle at the same time he heard the mantra — *Chardonnay time*. It was rote learning. The bird was not graced with a personality that allowed it to have a two-way, intelligent conversation with a human being.

There was no way that bird was talking to me.

But his posture and clarity of speech gave the impression he was, and I had to see a reaction from someone else to help ground my thoughts in reality. Maybe I'd spent too much time with him already, feeling him listening to me as I cooked and ate, stretched before my runs, and dressed for work. I felt him listening while I slept. I'd never seen him close his eyes. Did he sleep?

Damien.

Hadn't there been a movie with a child named Damien?

A child with demonic tendencies, fathered by the devil? Why had an elegant bird been given that name?

He was a beautiful creature. Pure white feathers, the splash of pale yellow on his crown, making him look warm and playful and friendly. But it was a bird. A wild bird. He wasn't a carnivore, but a hungry wild animal will eat what it needs to in order to survive. Nothing is above eating whatever it can find when the point of desperation is reached. The Donner party comes to mind.

Tess hadn't specifically pointed it out, but a cage sat in the closet of Damien's room. I had no idea how to get a large bird into a cage. Thinking I might lure him with a treat, I opened the door and put a piece of mango on the floor of the cage. I went to the kitchen and poured a glass of Petite Syrah. I sat in the sunroom, looking out at the city lights as they came on in random patterns, lighting the dusk. I sipped the wine and waited.

There wasn't a sound from the other room. It was a stand-off — human brain versus bird brain and I suspected Damien was going to win. I picked up my phone and Googled *how to get a bird into a cage*.

The suggestions offered nothing useful. Either lure it with food, or grab it, holding its wings near the tops, and ease it through the opening. Simple advice for a parakeet or canary. For a bird that's over twenty inches tall, with feet like pinchers in a carnival game. Food was the only viable option.

I put down my wine as softly as possible, trying to avoid the click of glass on wood. I tiptoed into the hallway and up close to the door of his room. I peered around the corner. The bird sat on the rung of the opening to the cage, leaning in, eating the mango, his enormous tail and half his body still outside of the cage.

This one was proving the intelligence of cockatoos on a regular basis.

I tiptoed up behind him.

He turned slightly, chewing mango while eyeing me.

I moved closer.

He continued masticating.

I took one more step and closed both hands around his body. I tried to ease him farther into the cage. He wrapped his feet around the bar and squawked.

I pushed harder, making sure to maintain a gentle grip at the same time, afraid of crushing his heart.

Back off.

"Come on. I want to take you for a little ride. Get inside. It'll be fun, you'll see."

I glanced behind me, as if my instinct feared someone was listening to my ridiculous conversation.

Back off.

"I'll give you more mango."

He squawked. *Mango. Delicious mango.*

"Just get inside."

Mango.

"Yes. I said you can have more, but…"

Mango! Mango!

"Get inside the cage."

Then, suddenly, he unclasped his feet from around the bar and leaned into the cage. I settled him on the bottom and closed the door.

Mango.

I went to the kitchen and cut a piece of mango into three chunks, wrapping plastic around the remainder and putting it back in the fridge. The bird had yielded to my wishes, but the only thing he accomplished was increasing the sensation that there was some sort of two-way communication. I'd bribed him and he responded.

Instead of opening the cage door, I slipped the pieces of mango through the bars and let them fall to the floor. He grabbed a piece and began working his beak around it, tipping his head in that annoyingly adorable way he had, while keeping his crown feathers standing straight up in a never-ending warning that he didn't trust me. I smiled at him and he worked his beak harder, mango oozing out the sides. He bobbed his head and moved his upper body, starting a little dance over the thrill of delicious mango. Delicious was a rather complex word, but he'd seemed to have it down very well. There was no mistaking what he'd said.

On a shelf in the closet was a large cloth with a slit in the center which allowed it to cover the cage while leaving the heavy-duty handle accessible at the top. Pieces of ribbon were sewn to the edges so it could be tied snugly around the cage. The cage and bird weighed close to ten pounds, which wasn't a problem, but the shape would force me to hold it out to the side. I might find muscles I'd neglected in my workouts.

I texted Isaiah that I was coming over with my surprise.

22

I put the cage on the passenger seat. Damien was so quiet, I pulled aside the cover to make sure he was okay. He glared at me. He didn't blink, although I hadn't really noticed how often he blinked. Without exposed eyelids, it seemed easier to miss the movement.

As I exited Tess's parking garage and turned onto the street, he began squawking. The sound pierced my ears and bored into my brain, making it hard to think about where I was going. I drove past a woman pushing a handcart containing two bags of groceries. Despite my rolled-up windows, she turned and looked, startled by the sounds.

"Shh. Stop it."

He shrieked louder.

"Now would be a good time for you to talk, instead of this. It's hard to concentrate on driving."

He let out a squawk that bored into my ear and tore at my nerves. I imagined I felt his deadly claws sinking into the flesh of my shoulders, his beak close enough to take a large bite out of my earlobe.

By the time I reached Howard Street, I head a headache.

I pulled onto the ramp leading to the underground garage, fed my card into the reader, and waited for the gate to open. It seemed to take forever, Damien continuing to shriek as if someone were trying to murder him. I'd assumed he might enjoy the ride, but possibly keeping the cage covered upset him. If he could have entertained himself with new sights, it would have shut him up. But I needed to be sure he stayed warm. I didn't want to explain a case of bird pneumonia, or worse.

Tess hadn't said a word about taking him out. She left contact information for his vet, but didn't mention a procedure if I actually had to take him for medical care. Maybe she'd expected me to get in touch if he got sick or I was worried about his condition. Maybe she only left the vet's name to make herself feel better, never imagining there would actually be a problem of some kind.

I rode the elevator to my floor and lugged the cage down the hall. This time, I unlocked my door instead of knocking. I wanted to make a dramatic entrance. Isaiah was sitting on the couch, working on his laptop. It always struck me as odd that someone studying at a culinary school would have homework that required a laptop instead of spoons and pans and wickedly sharpened knives, but he had quite a lot of it.

He closed the laptop and put it beside him.

"What is that?"

Damien shrieked.

"A bird?" Isaiah stood and walked toward me.

I untied the ribbons and swept the cloth away from the cage. "The reason Tess needed me to live at her place instead of just dropping in to water plants."

The bird bobbed his head. *Chardonnay time.*

Isaiah laughed. "What the hell?"

"I know."

I dropped the cloth and started toward Isaiah. He met me half way. He slipped his arm around my waist, pulling me closer, lower body first so our hips were pressed together. He put his other hand on the back of my head and his mouth on mine. As his tongue moved into my mouth, it seemed to probe to the center of my stomach. My muscles collapsed and my body became pliable in his arms.

The bird laughed.

Our lips twisted with the desire to laugh, but we continued kissing despite the mocking sound that filled the room.

Isaiah wove his fingers through my hair, then tightened his grip, making me feel as if he wanted to possess my mind.

Nice going. The bird laughed again. *Nice going.*

Isaiah laughed, his lips growing tight. He let go of my head and we moved away from each other. He walked to the cage and knelt beside it. "What's its name?"

"It's a he. Damien."

"That's the name of the kid in that old movie — Omen. Who would give a beautiful bird a name like that?"

"I don't know." I realized Tess hadn't mentioned whether she'd changed the bird's name or he'd come with it. I guessed it would be the latter…he seemed to respond to his name, so it must be familiar to him.

"What else does he say?"

"A lot of things." I walked over and sat on the floor beside Isaiah.

"Tess is okay with him leaving her condo?"

I shrugged.

"She didn't okay it?"

"She'll never know."

He looked at me. "Is that a good idea?"

"Why not? I wanted you to see him. To be honest, I wanted to know…"

"What if something happens to him? You're responsible."

"What could happen?"

"He could catch a virus, or some kind of infection. You could be in a car accident and he'd be hurt."

"Traffic crawled. I never went over thirty. In fact, I was riding the break most of the time. Any accident wouldn't be enough to hurt him."

"You don't know."

"He'll be fine."

"It's a huge risk."

"I like risks. I wanted you to hear him talk."

"How many things does he say?"

"I'm not sure yet. I haven't been around him enough. It's kind of eerie, he…"

Isaiah stood and went to the couch. "I was going to suggest you take him out of the cage, but if Tess doesn't know…and we might not be able to get him back in."

"Have you ever been around a bird like this?" I said.

"A large bird, or a cockatoo specifically?"

"Any large bird that talks."

"I've seen them in pet stores. Never known one personally."

I smiled. "How much do you know about their ability to speak?"

He shrugged. "They mimic what they hear. Sometimes it's articulate, other times just the inflection."

"It seems like the things he says apply to the situation."

"How is that?"

"He says *Chardonnay time* when I open wine."

"I'm sure it's the time of day, or the sound of the cork."

"That's what I thought. But…" I looked at Damien.

He glared back at me. *Delicious mango.* He bent and picked up one of the forgotten pieces of mango.

Isaiah laughed. "That's funny."

"But you see what I mean?"

"What are you trying to say?"

I kissed his jaw and leaned against him. "It's crazy."

"Yes?"

"It seems like he understands me. It seems like he talks to me as if he wants to…I know it's just mimicking, but I feel like there's another person staying in the condo with me."

Isaiah laughed again.

Damien laughed, his tone altered to sound like Isaiah's. His crown feathers were standing straight up, as usual. He obviously didn't trust either of us. He moved his wings, stretching them out to the sides, and let out a horrifying shriek, like a human being screaming in fear for her life.

Isaiah shuddered. "Okay, there's…maybe you should take him back home."

"I wanted Jen to see him too. But I mostly wanted to know, does it seem like he's communicating with us?"

"Of course, because it's so unusual to have an animal making human sounds. Your mind wants to put more meaning into it."

"I know he's not really talking to me, but still…"

He put his arm around me. "Of course not. It's not like you to be so fanciful."

"I know. He's getting on my nerves, I guess."

Ha!

"Think of it like a dog barking." He turned my face toward his and began kissing me.

Kissy face!

Isaiah pulled away. He smiled. "Maybe you should cover his cage."

I went to the bird and put the cloth over the cage. Damien let out a horrific shriek. *Bad girl! Bad girl!* He shrieked, then said it again. *Bad girl.*

23

Damien wouldn't stop shrieking. I removed the cloth again.

"He obviously doesn't like being covered," Isaiah said.

I studied the bird. He cocked his head, but his raised crown feathers gave a mixed message of hostility only slightly mitigated by a seemingly friendly come-on. It wasn't simply being trapped behind bars with a blank sheet blocking out the world that made him shriek. He hadn't made a sound when I covered the cage before leaving Tess's condo, and he was quiet when I'd placed his cage in the car. The racket started when I turned out of her building. It was the car ride itself that upset him. Covering him again now, told him he was headed back to the car.

His accusation unnerved me.

Was he chastising me for taking him away from home? It was a ludicrous thought. I'm not an imaginative person, believing I see human emotions in the eyes of animals, or entertaining fantasies of angels, or marveling over determined destinies between people with similar astrological signs. My logical brain knew the bird had mimicry skills. That was it. And yet, he continued to use the pieces of his vocabulary in shockingly accurate ways.

Not believing he was actually communicating with me made it more unsettling than if I did believe such a thing were possible. I knew he wasn't, but felt it nevertheless.

While Isaiah opened a bottle of wine, I sent a text message to Jen, telling her to come to my apartment if she wanted to see something freaky. She texted back immediately that she was on her way.

Jen arrived with a bag of homemade tortilla chips and a plastic container of guacamole that she'd picked up from a taqueria a few blocks away. She'd planned a comfort-food evening in front of the TV, but was eager to share it with Isaiah and me.

A bottle of Pinot Noir, very spicy guacamole, and fresh tortilla chips kept our conversation to a minimum for several minutes. Damien filled the empty spaces with chatter about *Chardonnay* and *mangos*, adding his laughter at appropriate times, shifting his imitation from Isaiah's voice, to Jen's, to mine. After a few unflattering chortles from the bird, all three of us began adjusting our laughter, softening our voices, smiling instead of laughing out loud, or swallowing an involuntary laugh with a quick sip of wine.

"I wish I had a bird like that," Jen said.

I dipped a chip into the guacamole. "You might want to spend more time around him before you say that." I bit the chip in half and let the avocado and jalapeño and chili warm my mouth.

"Why?"

"He can be extremely annoying," I said.

"Like when a child repeats everything you say?"

"Worse."

Jen scooped up guacamole and shoved the chip and soft green topping into her mouth. Her voice was garbled and thick. "Why?"

"There's no way to make him stop. And he talks when you aren't expecting it. Sometimes I feel like someone has snuck up on me, or broken into the condo."

"I'm sure you'll get used to him."

"I don't think I want to."

"He's cute. And funny."

"You haven't heard him shriek. And you didn't try wrestling him into the cage. Look at that beak."

"He looks so friendly. The feathers on his head look like a tropical flower."

"A flower that shoots poison," I said.

"How can you think such a sweet, pretty bird is dangerous?"

"I don't care if he talks or sits on the perch in his own bedroom, he's still not domesticated."

"They're popular pets," Isaiah said. "If they were dangerous, that wouldn't be the case."

"It belongs in the wild. Just my opinion." I swallowed the last of my wine.

We were quiet for several minutes. Even Damien remained silent.

"Did you hear what happened to me?" Jen said.

Isaiah went to the kitchen counter. He took a bottle of wine out of the cabinet and peeled off the foil.

Jen stuck a chip in the guacamole bowl and scooped some up. She took tiny bites and told me about a man pissing on the homeless woman that slept in front of our building.

I wrinkled my face, imagining the scene. "That's disgusting."

She nodded. "Security didn't even care. He wanted *my* name, and wasn't at all interested in finding out the name of the guy who did it."

"Do you know who he is?" I said.

"He doesn't live here. I think he's with a woman who

lives in the other tower. I'm pretty sure I saw her with him a few times. I know I've seen him leaving at night."

Isaiah poured wine into our glasses. I picked up mine. "Just one more glass for me. I need to get the demon bird home."

"Don't call him that." Jen pouted. She stood and went to the cage and began talking softly to the bird.

The bird hissed. He raised his voice and shouted — *Bad girl!*

She jumped back. "Oh. That's not very nice."

I took a sip of wine and waited.

"You're such a pretty boy," Jen said. "You should learn to say nice things."

Bad girl!

Jen glanced at me. "I feel like…"

I nodded. I wasn't the only one imagining a personalized comment from his well-trained throat.

She returned to the couch and picked up her glass. She took a long swallow of wine.

"Are you going to try to find out that guy's name?" I said.

She shrugged. "If I can do it without being obvious. But then what? I don't want security bothering me. I don't want to be on their radar, if you know what I mean. I don't understand what I have to do with it or why he wanted my name. Every time I think about it I want to punch someone."

I wished I could do something. But I'd already taken care of Jen when I killed David and I couldn't have her getting too curious about me. I finished my wine. "I should get going."

I covered the cage while Damien shouted about what a *bad girl* I was. He carried on all the way down in the elevator, then grew quiet as I put him in the passenger seat of my car.

The drive home was a skull-piercing repeat of the trip over.

He was a gorgeous creature, but I wondered whether his cranky attitude was because he agreed with me. The ride in the car reminded him he was trapped. He preferred a life in the wild, not stuck in a cage or consigned to a single pole, not even the branch of a tree, instead of being surrounded by hundreds of trees, delicious mangos, and others of his kind. Not to mention a female companion.

24

A text message arrived from Steve, asking me to join him for dinner so we could *continue our conversation* about my *career opportunities*. I rarely pass up a free dinner, especially a dinner like the type he was offering at La Grenouille — food that melts its way through your body, wine that doesn't even suggest there's alcohol laced throughout because it's so smooth and easy on the tongue. A room with good lighting, comfortable chairs, and a serving staff watching your every move to make sure your meal is the highlight of your week.

I took an extremely long shower in the palatial bathroom of my en suite, enjoying three streams of water coming at me from different angles. I shaved my legs and wiggled my toes on the heated tile floor while I spread lotion over every inch of my body, closing my eyes to imagine the day when I'd have a similar bathroom of my own. Making the transition back to my studio wasn't going to be easy. It takes only a moment to get used to luxurious surroundings, but so much longer to return to a more mundane world.

I chose a fitted black dress with a wide cutout below the collarbone, slightly revealing without being flamboyant, and a mirroring, larger cutout in the back. I finished it off with four-inch heels and gold earrings shaped like raindrops. My foundation was paler than usual, my eye makeup heavier and completely wrong for an interview, but everything about the situation was wrong, so I figured it was best to give it my all on every front.

Steve was seated at the table when I arrived. He wore a white shirt with a gray and blue striped tie and gray suit. A business envelope lay beside his assortment of forks. My full name — Laura Alexandra Mallory — was written in obscenely large script on the front. The letters were loopy and graceful, reminding me of the strokes used by the woman next door to Tess, as she wrote on her window.

He stood and waited while the maître d' pulled out my chair and placed the napkin across my legs.

"You look great," Steve said.

We weren't off to a good start, professionally speaking.

Steve ordered wine and pâté. It wasn't surprising that he didn't bother to ask what I'd like. I wasn't really annoyed, it was simply another tick in a box on the list of his privileged approach to the world. He assumed his choices would be superior, and assumed they'd be welcomed gladly and praised with enthusiasm. I wondered if he even realized he did it or ever considered that it might be off-putting.

He toasted CoastalCreative and we each took a sip of wine. It was indeed spectacular and I gushed over his choice. With utmost honesty.

When the appetizer arrived, he reached for a paper-thin toasted slice of sourdough bread, spread the putty-colored pâté in an elegant swoop across the bread and held it out to me. He kept it a few inches from my lips as if he expected me to eat it from his hand. The symbolism wasn't lost on me. Without touching his fingers, I pinched the sides of the toast between my thumb and index finger. He let go and I brought it over the tiny plate in front of me. I held it for several seconds before taking a small bite.

He smiled.

We polished off the pâté several minutes before the salad arrived. Mine was butter lettuce, soft as silk while still managing to be crisp. It tasted sweet all on its own, but was lightly drizzled with herbal vinaigrette and decorated with small pieces of goat cheese, pine nuts, plum tomatoes, and finely sliced strands of radish. Steve's was a traditional Caesar, including two large, plump anchovies, which he ate unadorned before starting on the lettuce and croutons. He ate rapidly, as if it was his first meal of the day.

He told me about a few of the CoastalCreative customers he'd taken to dinner at La Grenouille, and the deals he'd sealed at the very table where we were seated.

Leaving quite a bit of lettuce, but having devoured all the croutons, he pushed his plate to the edge of the table, dismissing it from his sight. He looked at me. "Why did you reject my gift?" He picked up his glass and held it for a moment before taking a long swallow of wine.

"What gift?"

"The appetizer. Didn't you know it's a tradition in Russia for a woman to take her first bite of a meal from the man's hand?"

"I've never heard of that."

"Have you been to Russia?"

"No. But I read a lot."

He smiled. "I didn't think so." He put down the wineglass. "It's not the same. Not at all. Life needs to be absorbed through the senses. You can't take in the world through black marks on a screen or a sheet of paper."

I put a tomato in my mouth and chewed it slowly.

"Even if you didn't know the custom, it was clear I was offering you a gift. You declined. I wonder what that means."

"First, you don't need to offer me any gifts. Second, the way you describe the tradition, it sounds like an intimate ritual between a man and a woman, not a business custom."

"Not necessarily."

A tickling sensation grew at the base of my skull, begging me to run my fingernail across it. Instead, I took a sip of water and lined up another tomato and a piece of cheese on my fork. I put them into my mouth and held them for a moment before chewing.

"You don't trust me."

I chewed slowly and swallowed. "Why do you say that?"

"The purpose of the ritual is to demonstrate trust."

"Between a couple."

"That's not important." He touched the envelope lying beside his two remaining forks. "Why don't you trust me?"

I pushed my plate to the side, it was empty except for a smear of vinaigrette and a tiny pebble of cheese. "I don't know you."

"I think you do."

I studied his face, trying to figure out if he realized what he was saying. Did he know that I had him profiled, so to speak? Unless my countering instinct was correct and his behavior was all a great big charade to keep the power securely in his hands. I was still on the fence about that. There's power in people not knowing who you really are, believing they have you figured out when they're actually clueless about your real thoughts.

Our entrees arrived and we began eating, the conversation drifting forward to something less fraught with hidden meanings and power plays.

He dragged the steak knife through his filet mignon as if

the meat were made of soft wax, a thin slice falling away without any effort on his part. He ate nearly half the filet without speaking. Then, he put down his fork and folded his arms across his ribs. "So do you want to work for me or not?"

"Still waiting for the offer."

He didn't glance at the envelope and neither did I.

"You're very flirty, you know that?"

"I don't think I am. I think I've been pretty clear."

"In a flirty way."

"I don't intend to come across like that."

"Then why the sexy dress?"

I'd thought he might have guessed why, but apparently not. Unless that too was an attempt to mislead me. If he was going to continue sending mixed messages, I had to fight back with the same. If he wanted to draw out this offer over weeks or months, it was okay with me. "You say a lot of politically incorrect things," I said.

He sipped his wine. The mashed potatoes and baby carrots and delicate green beans lay untouched on his plate. All he'd tasted was the beef, and even that was now looking neglected. I continued to plough through my steak and truffled macaroni and cheese, trying not to wolf it down, but everything was so good, so perfectly cooked.

He refilled our wine glasses, pouring slowly so that it took longer than necessary. He set the bottle on the table. "I say what I think."

"Even to customers?"

"For the most part."

"I doubt that."

He smiled.

"Some women might consider your comments offensive."

"But you're not like that."

I smiled. He continued to believe I was one of the boys. It was quite a thrill, actually, wearing four-inch heels and a shit-ton of makeup and having him think I was a good ole' boy. "You don't know that for sure. Don't you take harassment training?"

He laughed. "I haven't watched one of those bullshit courses in years."

"But it's required. I get warnings every day if I'm late taking the refresher." It seemed very egalitarian of the company — requiring women to take the same training as men. Ridiculous in ninety-nine percent of cases, but I suppose there's always one percent that make it necessary.

"Only the plebs take those."

"It's required."

"If you saw the list of non-compliant people, it would be pretty much the executive roster of CoastalCreative."

"And there aren't any consequences? Those are the people who are most at risk of a lawsuit." I couldn't believe he was bragging about it.

"We have lawyers for that." He picked up his knife and sliced through the meat. He put a large piece in his mouth and chewed, smiling around it.

We ordered dessert and didn't talk about harassment or career opportunities for the rest of the meal. By the time he paid the bill, I knew the dress was a mistake. He kept his gaze stroking my hair and skin, and never glanced at the envelope. It seemed as if he'd forgotten why we were there.

25

Watching Steve watch me during dinner, a slightly sick feeling had begun to take shape inside of me, knowing that I was putting up with, even encouraging his creepiness. What was he after? Surely there was no benefit to him in having another junior sales rep. It wasn't as if he believed I would single-handedly drive up his organization's sales numbers.

Outside the restaurant, he took my elbow as we turned toward the parking garage. I slipped it out of his hand and moved to the side, putting another foot of space between us. He laughed and slowed his pace, dropping back half a step to watch me walking on a slight incline in my higher-than-average heels. I slowed, forcing him to catch up, and adjusted my stride to mirror his.

We turned the corner. Tucked into the entrances to most of the buildings were people wrapped in sleeping bags and blankets. Bulging black trash bags were piled nearby as if they were constructing bunkers that might protect them from the enemies on the other side of the economic divide. It's a constantly spreading problem in San Francisco, despite efforts to provide shelters and support programs.

As we neared the middle of the block, a man lurched out of an alcove that had five or six steps leading up to a tiny entryway secured by a black iron gate. He faced us and stopped, wavering slightly. He held out his hand, suddenly very stable and in control. "A few bucks to help a guy out?"

Steve grabbed my elbow and veered around him.

"Hey, come on, man. I'm just an average guy. It's not for dope. Promise."

Steve walked faster.

The man followed, his booted feet heavy on the pavement. "I know you got it."

"Sorry, I don't."

For a savvy guy used to city life, I was surprised Steve didn't know that getting into a conversation with a panhandler wasn't a good idea. Either hand over a few bills or walk faster, pretending the human being doesn't exist, their voice is inaudible, their stench something organic that has nothing to do with the decay of human life.

Untied boots clunking as he broke into a lumbering jog, the man pushed past us. He ran a few yards ahead and stopped. He turned to face us, shoving his hand in his jacket pocket.

Steve tried to steer me toward the curb, but the man was surprisingly adept, leaping in front of us.

"You got it all, and you can't share ten bucks?"

"I thought it was a few bucks," Steve said. He sounded snappish and not at all in control, the alpha male receding in the face of a clear disadvantage, foolishly hoping he could end the encounter on his terms. But there was no end. The garage was still a block away. "I hate this shit," he mumbled.

I sighed. Every sound out of him was making it worse.

"You got the babe. I imagine you got the luxury car and the paycheck and the nice house. You wouldn't have the babe if you didn't have any of that shit. Just a twenty."

"I don't carry cash."

I ached to tell him to shut up, but it was too late. The best thing was to keep moving, despite the drag created by the pinch of his hand which had grown uncomfortably tight, no longer a grip of reassurance but one of mild panic.

The man looked at me. "Chicks always have cash. It's a rule. It's their safety valve."

The man was very astute. He didn't seem high or drunk or insane, although clearly there was something out of alignment or he wouldn't be here. Maybe he was new to the streets and still had a working knowledge of the civilized world that was slipping out of his peripheral vision ever so slowly.

He took a step closer. His breath had the odor of something that had been closed up for a long time, spoiled food and bacteria-laced saliva. He pulled his hand out of his pocket and with expert grace slid it past the sides of my unbuttoned coat and down the front of my dress. The moment his skin touched the skin of my breast, my body reacted. My left knee came up and slammed into his balls.

He bellowed and doubled over, but his hand remained lodged inside my dress, pinching and probing. Between the male hand on my elbow and this, I felt that I was being grappled by an octopus. I drove my heel into the top of his foot. He let go of me and stumbled back, shouting, half-crying.

Steve yanked me into the street and we walked quickly toward the corner. The man continued yelling after us, cursing every part of my body.

Inside the parking garage, Steve asked if I was okay.

"I'm fine."

"You handled that well." His tone wasn't begrudging, but resentment flickered across his eyes. The shame that he hadn't proven himself as a protector. The realization he'd been out-maneuvered by a homeless guy and a female.

"That didn't end as I'd planned, but we'll try again. Next week," he said. Assuming I'd agree. Grabbing back his control.

I realized the envelope that had rested beside his plate throughout the meal had disappeared without my noticing.

He held out his hand for my parking receipt. I gave it to him. He pulled out his wallet and gave both receipts and a hundred-dollar bill to the valet. Apparently, my dignity wasn't worth a hundred bucks to him.

26

Every morning before work, I smoked a cigarette by the Edwardian building. I waited for the woman's hand to emerge from behind the curtains, caressing her window in some new way. I waited for Lorraine and Frank — hoping to extract some thread of information about the faceless, formless woman, even though they insisted they were ignorant of her problems.

I didn't believe them.

A light drizzle started while I was getting dressed and I worried it would prevent me from following my ritual. A ritual that couldn't continue much longer because it was starting to interfere with my running. It seems as if my body can handle a certain amount of nicotine and tar without objecting, but once I cross a threshold — somewhere around five or six smokes a week — I feel it when I run. A vague tightness in my lungs, a faint rasp in my breathing.

Continuing the despicable habit indefinitely is not a good idea. I have this conversation with myself nearly every month, but smoking is so relaxing, so mind-altering in the way it forces you to stay in one place, the way it moves your thinking into a rhythmic pattern that follows your controlled inhalations and exhalations.

The cockatoo seemed to agree that the weather wasn't to his liking. He was muttering and making a loud clicking sound. I couldn't make out what he was saying, but it sounded like *dreary day*. Finally, I closed the bathroom door and put on my Rachmaninoff playlist to drown him out.

I put on dark brown leggings, a long turquoise sweater, and chocolate-colored riding boots. I've never ridden a horse in my life, although I could see myself doing it. Someday. It looks freeing and exciting — feeling a powerful, silent beast carrying me away from civilization, hair flying behind me, heart beating in time with his pounding hoofs. All a fantasy, but still, I would add it to my list of things required for the life I dreamed of.

Meanwhile, the soft leather riding boots looked very cool and were extremely comfortable.

I borrowed an all-weather coat from Tess's closet and put on a cloche style hat that belonged to me.

The street was deserted. I lit a cigarette and hoped one of the absurdly uncurious neighbors would come outside for a walk in the mist. After several minutes, Lorraine opened the front door. She moved her feet carefully down the steps, slick with moisture that had taken on an almost oily consistency.

"Good morning, Alexandra. How are you? I was hoping I'd see you again."

Immediately I felt myself pull back. I wanted to see her, but I wasn't thrilled that she had some reason for wanting the same. Mildly friendly was fine, but I didn't want to be a person on whom she began to depend. I admired her. I liked talking to her. I felt I could have a life like hers someday. Hers, only better, but I didn't want her to start clawing the protective coating of my life, working her way inside, demanding time and attention.

"Nice to see you." I turned slightly and exhaled my smoke.

"It's not a good day to be standing outside," she said.

"Sort of a habit."

"Indeed." She smiled.

"I met one of your neighbors," I said. "Frank."

She nodded. "He's a gentleman."

"It seems like all of you are friendly with each other except the woman on the second floor?"

She turned her head. Her white hair was combed to perfection, coiled into a French twist. She wore one of those clear plastic folding rain hats over it. I didn't know those things still existed. My mother loved them. She liked that they were so tiny she could tuck the plastic sleeve holding the folded hat into her coat pocket. She liked that it didn't flatten her hair like a regular hat did.

Lorraine wore a navy blue all-weather coat. Navy blue pants extended beneath the hem and her shoes were also the identical shade of navy blue.

I waited for her to turn back to me, but she continued looking across the street.

"Is something wrong?" I said.

She shook her head.

"I'm just curious. She's very disturbing and…"

She whirled back to face me. "Yes, she is."

"It's so strange. She worries me."

"I told you I don't want to discuss her."

"But she lives in your building."

"So?"

"Aren't you curious, if nothing else? Or concerned? She was writing on the window with something that looked like blood."

"I'm sure she was."

"That doesn't worry you?"

"It's not my business." She tugged the ties on her rain hat, drawing the plastic straps more tightly into her flesh, which made her chin protrude slightly. "Please don't ask me about her again. And don't encourage her antics."

"Who else lives in your building?"

"You're very nosey."

I laughed. "Like I said, just curious."

"Well then," she said.

"Where are you going so early?"

"I volunteer at a boutique. We sell handmade clothing and household items, quilts and knitted scarves, that sort of thing. The proceeds go to Children's Hospital."

I smiled. "How nice."

"You seem like a nice girl," she said.

"Thank you."

She moved closer. "Living alone is hard."

I didn't agree, but I smiled sympathetically. Besides, what did I know about living alone for decades? Maybe it did get more difficult after a while.

"Would you like to come over for tea? Saturday?" She took another step toward me. I felt her breath on my jaw, warm and somewhat moist. "I make the best cream puffs. And I have fifteen varieties of tea."

I wasn't a big tea fan, and cream puffs are okay once a year or so. I couldn't imagine eating a plate full of them, and I had no doubt there would be a plateful. On the other hand, I would get a chance to see inside the building.

Lorraine took my hand. "You don't want to?" Her eyes filled with tears.

"I'd like that."

"You took a long time to answer."

"I was trying to remember whether I have plans Saturday."

She moved away. "Oh. Of course. You probably have a very active social life."

"But it's fine. I can come over on Saturday."

"Three o'clock?" she said.

I nodded.

She gave me a big smile, showing her gums and the rather precarious situation of her teeth embedded in those gums.

I shivered.

"Are you cold?"

"I am. I should get to work."

"Of course, dear. Of course. You're so busy. Thank you for making time for me."

"I'm looking forward to it."

She lifted her hand and wiggled her fingers at me. She turned and began walking.

I looked up at the window. The woman was watching us. The moment she saw my head lift, she moved away and the curtain fell into place.

27

Portland

The sun didn't wake me my first morning away from home. When I opened my eyes, it was light, yes, but the thing that had brought me up from my dreams was a woman sitting near the foot of my sleeping bag pinching my toe. I yanked my foot away from her. She grabbed the other foot, with a firmer grip this time, making it impossible for me to get free.

She had long dark curly hair woven into a braid that looked as if it hadn't been combed out for several weeks. She wore a grimy white t-shirt, equally grubby jeans, and black Converse low-tops without socks or laces. She looked about my mother's age, but the shoes made me think of someone younger. Maybe it was the rough look of her skin, tired-looking and brittle, that made her seem old.

"Why are you sleeping here?" Her voice was rough, matching her skin, as if her body had been wrung dry and there was no moisture to keep her skin supple or lubricate her vocal chords.

"I don't have to tell you," I said.

"What's your name?"

"What's yours?"

"Pauline."

"Like mine."

"Your name is Pauline?" She sounded very excited about the possibility of having the same name.

"No. It's a boy's name turned into a girl version. I'm Alexandra."

"Nice to meet you." She smiled and wiggled my foot.

"Please let go of me."

She did.

"Do you have anything to eat?"

I didn't answer. It was starting to creep into the front of my brain that I was in over my head. I didn't want to share my few granola bars and apples with her. That would for sure shorten the amount of time I could take planning my future.

"You do. It's all over your face."

As if to further give me away, my stomach growled. Loudly.

Pauline laughed. "Jesus says you should share."

"He's not here."

She laughed again. "I'm famished."

"I don't have very much."

"Why are you sleeping in the park?"

"Because."

She nodded as if this explained everything.

I wriggled up closer to the top of my sleeping bag. I pulled my arms out of the comforting interior and rested them against the nylon exterior. It was damp. At least the moisture hadn't soaked through. I shifted into a sitting position.

"It's not safe out here," she said.

"No one can find me."

"Someone can always find you."

"This is a good hiding place."

"I found you. And eventually you'll have to pee. Get more food. Or just see something more interesting than branches and a small piece of sky."

I hadn't thought much about peeing. I hadn't thought about taking baths, either. Suddenly, I realized this was not going to work. I had nowhere to go and no plan.

"I know you have food," Pauline said. "You should share it. I'll get more later and share with you."

"How can I believe you?"

"You have to trust people sometimes."

"Do you?"

"No. You're a smart kid. But I'm really hungry. I might pass out."

"If I give you food, I'll get hungry."

"Not give, share. I'll return the favor."

I didn't see how that was possible, but I did like having company and if I shared an apple, she'd hang around longer. I reached into my backpack and pulled out an apple.

She slid a pocket knife out of her jeans and onto her leg as if she'd known all along I had an apple to share. She cut the apple into chunks and arranged them on the sleeping bag.

As I looked at the knife blade, glistening with juice and bits of white flesh, I pictured her hand moving only a few inches, plunging the blade into my neck, or between my ribs. I pulled the sleeping bag more tightly around me. Pauline smiled. One of her teeth was missing which made her seem less friendly than she had only a moment earlier. The knife wasn't very large, but neither was I. Her smile lingered for too long, and I felt she knew what I'd been thinking, that despite her insistence that I needed to trust her, I was moving toward being even more suspicious, imagining terrible possibilities.

She picked up a piece of apple and put it in her mouth. She chewed with her mouth open, and I heard my mother's voice explaining why that was rude. She put another piece in before she was finished with the first, and then a third.

I grabbed two pieces and stuffed them in my mouth. I didn't want her to eat more than her fair share, and obviously shoving it in fast was the way this was going to work.

"You're a good girl," she said. "A kind girl."

I smiled, not showing my teeth, maybe feeling a bit of social decorum that didn't want to flash my straight, clean white teeth at her and make her feel bad about the gap in her own smile.

"How long 'er you planning to sleep in the park?" she said.

"As long as I need to."

"Little girls can get stolen, ya' know."

"I know."

"Aren't you scared?"

"I don't want to talk about that." I put another piece of apple in my mouth and chewed vigorously.

"You should be scared."

I wasn't sure if she was trying to frighten me or expressing her own fear. Until she'd shown up, I'd thought I was well hidden. If I'd woken to a man crouched on my sleeping bag, I would have known immediately I was in danger. But women didn't steal children, did they? I'd never heard of it. My parents and siblings had told me plenty of stories of children gone missing, of terrible things done to them, of ugly murders. They'd whispered about bodies cut to pieces, or left to rot in the woods or in basements of run-down houses. But the perpetrators in these stories were always male.

She picked up the four remaining apple pieces and

shoved all of them into her mouth at once, gnashing them in her back teeth. The space inside her mouth was so filled with apple she couldn't bring her teeth together in the front.

"You had more than I did," I said.

"Don't keep score," she mumbled. "Judgment belongs to the Lord." Apple juice dribbled from the side of her mouth. The knife was still in her left hand. The blade pointed at her own ankle, but the sun was moving higher and it glinted off the tip and exposed the tightened muscle in her forearm. The slightest flick of her wrist could bring the knife to my throat. I swallowed.

28

Jen situated herself on the sofa beneath the painting of a woman. It was such a horrendous piece of artwork. The woman's blonde hair and red dress were beautiful, but her body was painted without the covering of skin, exposing bone and blood veins and muscle, the skull, and her nearly free-floating eyeballs. Jen hated it. Every time she entered the apartment building cocktail and coffee lounge, she asked herself why they'd chosen it as one of only a few pieces of artwork. They wanted to provoke discomfort, that was the only explanation. Alex loved the painting, and that love made Jen worry that Alex wasn't quite as nice as she seemed.

Still, Alex was a person you wanted to be around. Even if she had some strange ideas and unusual tastes. And you had to be thankful for a woman who didn't judge you for being a hooker. There were probably five women on the entire planet who were that accepting and understanding of how your life could veer off course and you didn't realize it was happening until it was too late.

This was Jen's fourth night in a row hanging out alone in the lounge, hoping to see the cretin who'd emptied his bladder onto the homeless woman. Jen had seen him and his girlfriend in the lounge before. Several times. All she needed was another look to verify who his girlfriend was, and cement the woman's appearance in her memory. Then she could set about finding a way to talk to her about the disgusting man she was seeing.

Sitting here night after night, drinking three or four glasses of wine, was cutting into her working hours. The dent was compounded by the cost of the wine. But something had to be done. No one seemed to care about that woman sleeping on the pavement. What would it be like, to not have a single human being who knew where you were, who wanted to make sure you were okay? What would it be like to be completely out of money, your possessions reduced to what fit into a backpack and a garbage bag?

She was on her second glass of red wine, some sort of Cabernet blend. It was okay, but after two glasses, her taste buds dulled and all she tasted was alcohol.

Across the room, where the staircase from the lobby merged onto the second floor, she saw him. Without his overcoat, he didn't seem quite as imposing. Still tall, but not as broad, and he wasn't particularly muscular. His face was smug, his lips protruding in a constant look of disdain. Beside him, his girlfriend was weighted down beneath his proprietary arm. It was draped over her shoulders, closing too tightly around her neck.

The woman wore gladiator sandals, a strange choice for a cold evening, a short silky black skirt and a red flowing top. As they moved into the room, the shimmering red toenails of a fresh pedicure explained why she'd chosen sandals when the temperature was in the low fifties, accompanied by a steady drizzle. Her hair was cut in a blunt line to her shoulders and she had thick bangs. She looked as if she'd stepped off the pages of Cosmo.

Jen was surprised she hadn't remembered her in more

detail. She was the sort of woman who stood out in a room, even when that room was filled with women who might also be found in Cosmo. The set of her shoulders proved her confidence, yet her face looked kind. She glanced around and smiled at people as she passed them on her way to the bar.

The woman touched the cretin's arm, turned, and walked toward the hallway leading to the restrooms. Jen stood, grabbed her purse, and began walking quickly toward the restrooms.

Inside the bathroom, the woman stood at the last sink, leaning forward, daubing something on her cheeks.

Jen walked to the sink beside her and set her purse on the counter. The moment the leather touched the granite, she realized the counter was covered with a thin layer of water. "Ew." She grabbed her purse. "I hate it when someone gets water all over." She glanced in the mirror, waiting for the woman to catch her eye.

"Me too." The woman turned to the towel dispenser. She yanked out two towels and handed them to Jen.

"Thanks." Jen wiped the bottom of her purse and stepped around the woman to drop them into the trash. "I'm Jen, you live here, right?"

"Yes."

She'd hoped for more, but she wasn't going to let social subtleties rob her of what might be her only chance. "What's your name?"

"Lizzy." She reached into her purse and pulled out a tube of lip gloss. She opened it and began spreading it across her lower lip.

"I met your boyfriend last week," Jen said.

Lizzy touched the foam-tipped wand to her upper lip. "So?"

The clipped tone sounded like the conversation was headed toward a sudden conclusion. She should slow down, smooth it over with nice chit-chat, but she wasn't sure where to take it so she plunged forward. "Does he live here too?"

"Why do you care?"

"Just being friendly."

"Sounds more like being nosey."

"Sorry. I didn't mean to."

Lizzy smiled.

Nothing like saying *sorry* to change the atmosphere. Even if she wasn't at all sorry. People felt obliged to be nice when you took the submissive position, like a dog lowering himself before a dominant animal.

"Why are you interested?"

"I was just curious."

"He doesn't live here." Lizzy dropped the lip gloss into her purse and pulled out a hairbrush.

For having just arrived at the lounge a few minutes earlier, Lizzy seemed to have a lot of repair work to do on her appearance. To Jen, she looked perfect already. Was this need to re-polish the boyfriend's doing, or just Lizzy's habit?

"I don't know you, and I'm not trying to be rude or..."

"Or what?"

"I just...have you seen that homeless woman sleeping outside our building?"

"Yes. Gross. I don't understand why security doesn't get rid of her."

"She's not hurting anyone," Jen said.

"She doesn't belong here. I hate it when they do that.

This city is turning into a giant cesspool."

"They need to provide more shelters."

Lizzy turned away from the mirror. She shoved the hairbrush into her bag and hung the strap over her shoulder. "Why?"

This was sliding in the wrong direction, but it was too late. Jen felt the chance of winning Lizzy to her side and getting her to exert influence over her creepy boyfriend slipping out of her grasp. She should have known that criticizing a woman's boyfriend was never going to work. Even if Lizzy was bothered by some of his behavior, criticism made a woman rush to defend her man, turning all flaws into admirable, lovable qualities.

"It's terrible that people have to sleep on the sidewalk. We should be helping her."

Lizzy took a step closer and widened her eyes. They seemed to jitter in their sockets. "It's not our fault she's too lazy to get a job. People should help themselves. She thinks she can sleep wherever and show up for free food and lounge around all day. I work my ass off and so does Scott. We don't need to come home to that shit. She smells like piss. It's disgusting, it makes our place look like a dive."

"But…"

Lizzy held up her hand, thrusting it toward Jen. "I don't want to hear it. People need to stop thinking someone else is going to take care of them. Who do they think they are? Wanting to suck money out of me when it's their own fault they're in that situation? Why should I pay for it? And why should I have to smell her every time I come home from a nice dinner?" She stepped to the side and started toward the door. "Thanks for being a downer. I need a glass of wine."

She flung open the door and walked out.

Jen turned and looked in the mirror. Her face was drained of color. She looked terrified and she wasn't quite sure why.

29

Saturday afternoon was clear and sunny. I'd gone for a long run that morning — six miles — but still wasn't keen on sitting inside Lorraine's apartment drinking tea and eating cream puffs, even if only for an hour. It was a day meant for walking outside, or at least sitting on the balcony with a glass of wine. The only thing keeping my mood up was the fact that I was interested in seeing the design features inside the classic building, the size and layout of the apartment Lorraine owned. Against logic, I hoped to get a peek at the entrance to the second floor.

I was tempted to dress in a more sedate style to mirror Lorraine's appearance. But after considering her eagerness to invite me inside to alleviate her loneliness, and her comment that I was the daughter she'd longed for, I backed away from that inclination. I opted for jeans and a black sweater. Sure, I wanted to get her comfortable with me, to let down the iron walls surrounding her knowledge of the woman on the second floor, but not so comfortable that she developed a craving for drinking tea with me every Saturday.

It's difficult to get something without giving. Most human interactions expect, and are built upon, fair exchanges. You compliment me, I'll offer one back. You treat me to lunch, I'll do the same. You confide in me, I'll tell you my secrets. You defend me and remain loyal and I'll have your back. You give me an orgasm, I'll reciprocate, maybe. I was giving her an hour or so of companionship, which seemed like a fair exchange for admitting she knew more than she was saying about the woman on the second floor.

Lorraine met me at the main door and ushered me into a lobby filled with plants. An arrangement of three armchairs was clustered in the back-left corner. They had a musty appearance, suggesting no one had sat in them since 1968. On the right side of the room was an opening to a staircase and beside it, the gold doors of an ancient elevator. I should have realized Lorraine wasn't in a condition to trudge up and down two flights of stairs every time she left the building. The elevator would zip us right past the second floor and I'd see nothing of the cloistered woman's apartment.

We got in and she pushed the button for three.

The elevator opened into a small alcove with a single door. A narrow window looked down on the street and a painting of Coit Tower hung on the opposite wall.

Lorraine put her key in the lock and opened the door into a vestibule. There was a second door opening into the living area.

I'd expected her apartment to reek of perfumed body powder, gardenias, maybe. I'd imagined too much furniture, a thermostat set too high, tabletops cluttered with knickknacks and shelves overflowing with framed photographs of faraway family members and dead friends.

I was right on only one point.

The temperature was pleasant, and the decor was modern. The living room was quite spacious, three of the walls were painted ivory. The fourth wall, with doors that led to the kitchen and dining room, was a light blue. Artwork was minimal, a few paintings in unpretentious frames, and several large photographs of the city. The furniture was comfortable and muted, as if she wanted the entire apartment to give off an air of quiet — a blue and gray sofa, two pale blue armchairs, and a coffee table made of ash with a large glass bowl in the center. The end tables had simple lamps with stark shades.

The only thing I'd been right about were the photographs. They were crowded into built-in shelves on either side of the fireplace. There was something odd about the subjects of the photographs, but I couldn't make out what bothered me because they were too far away for me to absorb the details.

Lorraine took my coat and gestured toward the sofa.

I sat down and when she went into the kitchen I leaned forward, straining to look at the photographs. There were three shelves on either side of the fireplace. The middle shelf of both sections overflowed with four-by-six prints in wide black frames. Just as I was about to get up and walk closer, Lorraine returned with a silver tray. The tray held a white ceramic teapot and two white cups and saucers, not the delicate, fussy floral china associated with an elderly woman.

"I should have asked what kind you wanted," she said. "I wasn't thinking."

"Whatever you made is fine."

"It's blackberry, but I can make another pot."

"Blackberry sounds delicious. I've never had it."

She poured tea into the cups and set the pot on the tray. "Let me get our sweets." She hurried into the kitchen and returned so quickly, it seemed as if there might be someone standing just out of sight who'd shoved the plate into her hands and given her a nudge, propelling her back to the living room.

She put the plate of cream puffs beside the tray and darted back to the kitchen, returning with two small linen napkins. She handed one to me and settled in the adjacent armchair. "I'm so glad you could come over," she said. "I haven't had a guest in a long time."

"Thank you for inviting me." I took a sip of tea. It was good. Maybe I could find my way to becoming a tea drinker. It wasn't something I'd ever considered.

"It's not too strong, is it?"

"Perfect."

She smiled and settled back in her chair. "Have a cream puff."

"In a minute. I'll enjoy the tea first."

She talked for several minutes about the boutique where she volunteered, telling me about petty struggles for power among the volunteers and even the people who donated goods for sale. One man who carved tiny, wooden models of cars, painting them with delicate precision to capture recognizable makes and models, was furious that his display had been moved out of the front window.

When his wife was volunteering for her shift, he went to the shop with her and moved the floppy stuffed puppies and kittens off to the side and rearranged his vehicles in the center spot. Each time he returned, he found his vehicles moved back to an interior shelf.

"But it's all for charity, why does it matter?"

"Some of the artists are very attached to their work," she said. "They want to feel their sales are contributing the largest portion. They're very competitive."

I took a sip of tea. It didn't sound all that different from sales reps fighting over lucrative contracts for millions of dollars, or marketing managers trying to make sure their concepts were the ones executives raved about, thus securing their position in the hierarchy. It's never surprising to hear that people behave in similar ways in very different environments, but this was more amusing than most.

"Tell me about yourself," she said.

I told her about growing up in Oregon with four siblings. I described our Victorian house but skipped over the Victorian behavior of my parents — suffocating rules, especially for women, that came from another era but were melded nicely into a somewhat modern religious sect. I described my years drifting through college classes, finally leaving without a degree, but retaining a little bit of knowledge about a wide variety of subjects.

"Degrees are over-rated," Lorraine said.

"Are they? I think not having one has held me back in my career."

"And what career is that?"

I gave her the Twitter-length version of project management.

"Really, the most satisfying career for a woman is raising children," she said. No room for argument. Stated as a fact that was well-known.

I smiled. I had no interest in arguing with her.

"You don't agree?"

"I didn't say that."

"You said nothing. And you're such a polite young woman, I know that saying nothing means you disagree. Violently."

The cream puffs were small enough to fit the entire thing in my mouth. I picked one up and ate it. As I chewed, I leaned slightly to the left, trying to see around her. Whatever was wrong with the photographs nagged at my mind like a fly trapped behind a window screen.

"If you don't want to talk about it, that's fine." She smiled. "When you have children, you'll see what I mean."

"Do you have children?" Her wistful comment about the lack of a daughter had made me assume she didn't.

"Yes."

I waited.

"A son. He lives in San Francisco, which is nice because I can see him every week. He owns a private technology company. *Bio*-technology. He's always correcting me on that." She laughed softly. "I'll have a dinner party soon, and I can introduce you. He's very successful." Her eyes looked warm and alive, the sharp bird-like look faded.

Was she hoping to set us up? It seemed an odd thing to do, she hardly knew me. That son must really be something.

"Wouldn't that be nice?" she said. Her lips parted slightly.

I ate another cream puff and smiled vaguely. While I chewed the airy pastry and pleasantly unsweetened cream, I nodded toward the shelves by the fireplace. I swallowed the sticky stuff. "You have a lot of photographs. Are they family? Friends?"

She reached toward the cream puffs, then moved her hand without taking one.

"It's unusual to see so many in black and white," I said.

"But so easy to produce black and white now, with a computer."

"So did you take all of them?"

She laughed. "Not all of them." She changed the subject back to her volunteer work, which she went on about for fifteen or twenty minutes, through a second cup of tea for both of us. I ended up eating four cream puffs.

When I stood to go, I walked around the coffee table in the opposite direction from when she'd first offered me a seat. I stopped by the photographs on the left side of the fireplace. Before I could study them, she came up close beside me and ushered me toward the vestibule. She thanked me for my visit and insisted we do it again. Soon. She rode down the elevator with me and waited while I crossed the lobby and went out into the fading afternoon light.

As I stood outside on the top step, it came to me what was wrong with the photographs. They were all women, and all nearly the same age. Twenty or thirty photographs, maybe more, of women in their late twenties to mid-thirties.

I closed my eyes and tried to imagine who they might be.

30

I walked slowly down the steps, pausing on the last one. All those photographs of women hovered in the back of my mind. They couldn't all be relatives. The images were recent, the hair and clothing styles up to date, so they weren't pictures of her friends when they were younger. Why would she have so many friends and family members, all female, all in the same age range? It made no sense. My head ached trying to figure out something I couldn't even guess at.

My phone vibrated. I pulled it out of my pocket and saw a message from Isaiah. He suggested dinner and sex. He ended with a crying emoji and a complaint that Damien would get my company overnight. I laughed, texted back, and slid the phone into my pocket. I took a step down onto the pavement.

The door opened behind me.

"Good afternoon."

I moved to the side and looked up.

Frank stood on the landing. "What are you doing?" he said.

"I had tea with Lorraine."

"Ah." His expression didn't seem surprised, more resigned, although why he had any particular reaction to that information, I had no idea. "And where are you headed now?"

"Home. I mean, back to the place where I'm house sitting."

He nodded.

I looked up at the window to see if the woman would make any gestures.

"Don't do that," he said.

"It's a habit."

"I warned you," he said.

"You *warned* me?"

"It's best not to encourage her."

"I don't understand what's going on."

"There are a lot of people in this city with too much money, who possibly should be locked up, but their money allows them to live among the rest of us, and…"

"And, what?"

"She's a very disturbed individual. I already told you that. It's best to ignore her. I don't understand why you want to stir up trouble."

I leaned on the balustrade and folded my arms. "I'm not stirring up anything."

"You keep looking up there. And you're letting Lorraine sink her hooks into you. Don't think it's not obvious what you're doing."

"I drank a cup of tea with her."

"Would you have had tea with an old woman, a complete stranger, if you weren't trying to get inside the building, trying to satisfy your morbid curiosity about a sad situation?"

"You seem awfully concerned about what I do or don't do. Why does it matter so much?"

"I'm trying to help you."

"Why?"

"Because I'm a decent human being."

"So you do know something about that woman on the

second floor."

He shook his head. He tugged on the brim of his hat, pulling it just low enough so that I could no longer see his eyes, making his sharp, straight nose more prominent and somewhat rat-like without his eyes to soften the angles. "You should keep to your luxury condo and stop loitering out here. It's not done in this neighborhood."

"Someone will call the police?"

"Anything can happen."

"It sounds like you're threatening me."

"Nothing of the kind. Just trying to be a gentleman. An art that's sadly lost." He walked down the stairs until we were on the same level. He placed his left foot on the sidewalk and hesitated.

"Why won't you tell me what's going on? Is she a murderess or something?"

He shook his head. "You're stubborn."

"No, I'm curious. And you're making me more so. Acting as if there's some big, dark secret."

"As I said, just warning you. Ignore it at your own risk."

He turned and started toward the corner, walking with slow, careful steps to compensate for the steep incline of the street.

I wanted to run after him. I was probably making something out of nothing, but they were both so dramatic about it. I had to find out what the big secret was. I had to know why they insisted I not encourage the woman's behavior. But encourage what?

I stepped into the street and surveyed the woman's window. The drapes were pulled behind the sheer curtains. It was possible the barest opening was there, something that was too subtle to be seen from my angle and distance, an opening that allowed her to watch me. Or, even someone else sharing the space with her, letting her know when I was out there.

But why? I couldn't understand why she wanted to attract my attention or why it was so terrible to encourage her. If she was mentally unstable, did encouraging her cause her to have a fit, something horrific that disturbed the neighbors or required outside intervention. Something that disrupted the routine of their lives? Did she scream and carry on? Her movements had seemed graceful and languid.

I wished I had my cigarettes to occupy me while I waited.

31

Back up in Tess's condo, I took another shower before dressing for dinner with Isaiah. It felt as if my very skin ached, straining to figure out something that was impossible to figure out. I should have made a vow to stop thinking about it entirely, to demonstrate some self-control. I could certainly do without the smoking for a few weeks. I didn't need to ever set foot on that sidewalk again. In fact, I could go running along The Embarcadero near work and shower and change at the gym. Or at my own apartment. The bird didn't need me keeping him company through breakfast. He just needed to be fed and to receive reassurance from my consistent, if occasional presence.

I dressed in black skinny jeans and a black top that scooped nearly to my waist in the back. I put my ankle boots with tall, narrow heels by the front door beside my leather jacket and a tiny black purse, just large enough to hold my phone, ID, a credit card, and lip gloss. And two twenties. The homeless guy who grabbed me was right about that. It suggested he knew women better than Steve did, for all his posturing.

Damien was already making noises, murmuring sounds that might have been normal bird sounds or the miming of an unconscious expression he'd heard muttered by Tess. Any minute a human voice would call out to me, asking about mango and apples.

I stabbed earrings into the holes in my lobes, ran my

fingers through my hair, and turned off the bathroom lights. I went into his room and took away the plate from his breakfast.

Thank you.

"No problem," I said.

I put the plate in the dishwasher, got out a new white plastic picnic plate from the stack designated for him. I cut up apple chunks and broke off half an ear of boiled corn on the cob for him to gnaw on. I arranged the food on his plate and took it into his room. I placed it on the floor. He climbed down from the perch and closed his beak around a piece of apple.

I emptied his water dish, washed and refilled it, and put it beside his dinner plate. I settled in the armchair across from him, per Tess's instructions to keep him company. I couldn't imagine he liked an audience watching him eat. I surely wouldn't want someone observing me without any distraction from food of their own, watching how I picked up each piece, placed it in my mouth, chewed, swallowed. My throat tightened as it would if I were being studied that closely, food lodging in my throat because the passage had narrowed, squeezed too tightly around something I hadn't thoroughly chewed.

Damien seemed perfectly fine with an audience.

After several minutes of silence, punctuated by nothing but the beak on plastic, I crossed my legs. "I had tea with Lorraine this afternoon."

Tea.

"She's a very strange woman."

Tea. Blackberry tea.

A shiver ran down the tender skin on the insides of my

arms. Clearly Tess had spoken to him about drinking blackberry tea with Lorraine. Repeatedly. That was all. He wasn't going to start going on about cream puffs. I laughed.

He laughed as softly as I had. He moved away from the apple chunks and began gnawing at the ear of corn.

"Does Tess sit here and talk to you?" I pulled my lower legs onto the chair, wedging my feet and bent knees between the arms.

The bird didn't respond.

"Only delusional people believe animals speak to them. I suppose animals have non-verbal ways of communicating — tail wags and purring. But they don't actually have two-way conversations. I know that." I laughed in a strange tone that sounded nothing like my own voice. "But it's unsettling, hearing you speak. You articulate the words so clearly. And it seems like you know what we're talking about. It's not possible. I know it's not possible, and yet here I am, talking to you. To be honest, it's nice, knowing you won't repeat what I say."

He was going hard at the ear of corn, although he hadn't eaten much of it. The kernels were mangled, pieces of corn scattered across his plate, but it seemed to be more of a plaything than a meal.

"I wonder if she's said anything about me."

He stopped attacking the corn cob and straightened. He tilted his head to the left.

"Does that mean she has talked about me? I wonder what she said."

What she said.

I laughed. "You can't tell me, can you."

What she said. He picked up a piece of apple and closed

his beak around it.

"Obviously she talked about Lorraine. She had tea over there too. I wonder if she was trying to find out about the woman on the second floor. She never mentioned it to me. Did she tell you about that mad woman, writing in blood?"

What she said.

"Yes, I get it. Mimicking is the extent of your intelligence. I shouldn't expect you to tell me Tess's secrets. She's a very private woman. I expect she talks to you so she can keep it that way. Maybe that's why she wanted a pet. She doesn't trust me all that much after all. Although she let me stay here, so maybe it's not a complete lack of trust, just extreme caution."

Dangerous woman. Dangerous woman.

"I said *private* woman, not dangerous woman."

Dangerous woman.

"Who's a dangerous woman? Is that what she said about me?"

Dangerous woman.

I leaned closer. I wasn't entirely clear if he was saying dangerous or delicious. Was I filtering it through my own train of thought? Both words are a mouthful, for a bird. I was pretty sure it was dangerous. What had she said to him? Or was that a phrase he'd known for ages and it had nothing to do with Tess? "Say it again."

He squawked. *Dangerous woman.* He dragged out the word so it was clear he was definitely saying *dangerous.*

I felt as if I had a balloon swelling inside my neck, the pressure was growing, as more and more helium was pumped in, too much for the thin, rubbery walls to hold, and any moment it would explode. I couldn't understand why the bird was repeating that phrase, why the woman smeared her blood across the window, why I was half-mad myself with needing to know what was going on.

Maybe she was trapped in an abusive relationship, crying out for help. Maybe her husband hit her and she used the blood as her only available tool. Maybe she was slitting her wrists, not brave enough to make a final, fatal cut. Just a thin slice that allowed her to see the effects of the self-inflicted wound, but too afraid to die. Neither Lorraine nor Frank had mentioned whether anyone else lived on the second floor. My impression was that she lived alone, but I didn't know that.

I went into the bathroom and brushed my hair as vigorously as I could, trying to scrape the thoughts out of my head so I could enjoy my dinner and sex with Isaiah.

32

Since our standoff over the envelope he never gave me, Steve had been texting me every day. Sometimes two or three times each day. It made me wonder how his customer meetings were going, whether he was holding the phone between his knees, under a conference table, tapping out messages to me while an important point was being made and he missed it completely. Texting all day didn't seem like senior executive behavior, but what do I know.

The messages were tame, asking about my day, listing the customers he was meeting with, comments on the previous weekend's pro golf tournament, even notes about the weather. It was weird. It seemed as if I was dealing with a junior high school kid. Was he trying to flirt and failing? Did he think his inane messages were intriguing to me, luring me into feeling connected to him? Were they just a flood of trivia aimed at making me forget his stupid behavior on a dark street, the unfortunate revelation of his weakness in the face of a moderate physical threat?

I responded to every third message. This delay, of course, made him send them more frequently. He used his company-issued phone, as did I. Did it ever cross his mind that he might not want a record of this flood of chatter, something that, put in the right context, could be interpreted in a way that made him look bad? The messages might appear to be harassment of a very subtle type, or simple mis-use of company property. No one actually checked the personal versus corporate use of our phones, but we were supposed to keep the personal to about twenty percent.

Many women would have cut him off by now. He obviously didn't have a job offer. He was after something else, some sort of flank attack on Tess. But my curiosity is an uncontrollable, unmanageable thirst to see how situations will play out, to follow various threads of human behavior like a dog on the hunt. I smell it and I keep chasing it, wherever it leads. I can't stop. Nothing diverts me. I have to reach the end.

On Friday, the message that all the others had been leading up to arrived.

Steve Montgomery: *I have customer meetings in Chicago the week after next. Why don't you join me and you can experience a sales call first hand. Decide if it's for you.*

Alexandra Mallory: *I don't have a job offer.*

Steve Montgomery: *Since when are you so proper?*

Alexandra Mallory (wondering how this thread would appear if it were seen by HR, or worse, somehow found its way to a public forum, as executive emails sometimes do): *Nothing's changed. You said you had an offer for me, and you don't.*

Steve Montgomery: *We can discuss it over dinner tonight.*

Alexandra Mallory: *Been there, done that.*

Steve Montgomery: *We got sidetracked last time.*

He was the one who got sidetracked, he always was.

Alexandra Mallory: *What is there to discuss? It's a number with a dollar sign in front of it. Either I'll like it or I won't.*

Steve Montgomery: *Fair enough. Drinks.*

Alexandra Mallory: *Okay.*

We met at the same bar.

I was already seated on a stool near the door, a brass bar

that ran from the floor, up and over into the wood counter at my right. On the one hand, the setup had the potential for making me feel trapped if Steve moved in too close. On the other, it was a barrier preventing others from crowding up so that I was completely swallowed by warm skin and the smell of aftershave and alcohol-laced breath.

To his credit, Steve placed the envelope on the bar before he even took his seat. I was already sipping a martini. He ordered a scotch on the rocks.

I picked up my drink and took another sip.

"Go ahead and open it."

I picked up the envelope, ripped it open in a rough, awkward fashion across the top, leaving a tear like ragged flesh cut by a dull serrated knife. I pulled out the single sheet of paper and unfolded it. The page was blank. I dropped it on the bar. "This is bullshit. If you just want to meet for drinks and dinner, if you're trying to flirt with me or something, stop talking about job opportunities and career growth." I picked up my drink and took a long swallow.

He laughed. "You don't get the metaphor?"

"Nope." I took another sip. Drinking so quickly wasn't a good idea — pure, uncut alcohol racing into my bloodstream — but I was tired of being the loser in his games, losing because the rules were constantly changing. My curiosity was suddenly dissipating. I no longer cared so much how he was planning to disrupt Tess's equilibrium.

"You aren't even curious?"

I shook my head. I put down my drink and moved the swizzle stick around the perimeter, watching vodka and vermouth flow across the olives. I lifted the stick out of the liquid and studied the olives.

"You really don't get it?" he said.

"I don't get it."

"You're spoiling the fun."

"Is this a serious discussion, or something that's supposed to be fun? Because I'm not here for fun."

"Oh. Excuse me. So serious." He laughed and swallowed scotch, letting an ice cube fall into his mouth. He spit it back into the glass. "It's a blank sheet of paper because you can write your own paycheck."

"That's lame. And difficult to believe."

"I thought you'd appreciate a little wit."

"I'd appreciate a bona fide job offer. Which I thought you were making. It seems like you just want to jerk me around. I have no idea why you're even talking to me."

"Settle down." He finished his drink and raised his hand at the bartender.

His glass was removed. A clean glass appeared, ice was dropped in, and silky golden liquid was poured from the silver spout, running over the cubes like blood spilling on ice. I thought of the woman writing on her window.

He took a sip. "I'm serious. I think you're bored working for Tess. And underutilized. Aside from the fact that sales commission is equal to hustle, there's no thrill like closing a deal. And I know you know that." He winked.

I ate one of my olives, very slowly, rolling it around inside my mouth, sucking all the vodka out of it before I chewed and swallowed.

"So how about Chicago?"

"I have other obligations the next few weeks. I can't leave the city."

"What obligations?"

"Personal."

He nodded. He looked at the wall lined with glass shelves, bottles of alcohol stacked up toward the ceiling. A disaster of glass and liquid in the event of an earthquake, which was a very real possibility in San Francisco. "Next time, then."

He put a fifty-dollar bill on the bar, poured the rest of his scotch into his mouth in one presumably burning gulp and put the glass on the bill. "See ya'." He slid off the stool and was nearly at the door before I turned around to watch him leave.

My head felt woozy, more from his bizarre behavior than from the martini. I turned back and ate the second olive. I still had half my drink and one more olive. I might as well relax. At least the drink was putting a fuzzy blanket over Steve's erratic chess moves.

33

Diagonally across the street from the Edwardian building was a bench. It sat on a small outlet that bulged into the street, bordered by concrete, filled with grass and small flowering shrubs. Because I was tired of standing on the sidewalk, I invited Isaiah to drop by and sit in the micro park, observing the building with me.

He sat beside me, his gaze drawn to Tess's building, admiring the sleek lines and the potted trees on the roof garden, mature enough to be seen, even looking up from the street.

I removed a cigarette and held the pack out to Isaiah. He shook his head. He always declined, but I kept offering, to be polite, I suppose. Or maybe, a subtle test to see whether he really didn't smoke or to see if a certain situation might cause him to give in, like some people only smoke when they drink.

I lit my cigarette and blew out a stream of smoke.

"So *why* are we sitting here?" he said.

"It was getting awkward, standing in front of their steps all the time. This isn't a part of the city where someone hanging around in front of a building looks normal, waiting to meet for dinner or drinks. They're a very private group."

"The whole street?"

"I don't know about the others, but the occupants of number four-thirty-six certainly are."

"Why are you so obsessed?"

"I just am. Something is off."

"Like what?"

"I don't know." I took a drag on my cigarette and crossed my legs. "That's the point."

He settled back and stretched his legs out. "So I'm your prop? To blend in, avoid a ticket for loitering?"

"Do they really give tickets for loitering?"

"Based on the amount of money represented inside most of these buildings, I'd say it's a good possibility. Where there's money, cops are more devoted servants of the public."

"Well I don't think of you as a prop. I thought you'd be interested, I thought we could just talk."

He took my free hand. "I always like talking. But it doesn't stop me from feeling like a prop."

I smiled. He was looking across the street so I don't think he noticed.

We were quiet for several minutes, me smoking, Isaiah turning his head this way and that, studying the eclectic mix of architecture, and the old city atmosphere of the street, despite the several modern buildings.

"Why do women obsess over things?" he said.

"Is that what women do?" I dropped my half-finished cigarette on the ground, stepped on it, and lit another — an extravagant gesture that was probably lost on him, but it steadied my nerves in the face of his stereotyping.

"More than men, in my experience. Women are like hounds. They fixate on something they can't do anything about and then they think about it, talk about it, let it bleed into every corner of their lives."

"I wasn't aware I was obsessed."

"Watching that window every day qualifies, I think."

"Do you?"

"Jen, too."

"What do you mean?" I inhaled carefully and let out a long, thin stream of smoke. He was such a perfect guy in so many ways, so undemanding. He hadn't constructed any boundaries to fence me in. Good looking, liked to hike, and run, sort of. He was a great lover, and witty and interesting to talk to. He was building a career around food!

"All she can talk about is that guy peeing on the homeless woman."

"Well it's horrifying. It's hard to get an experience like that out of your head."

"Not really."

"It wouldn't nag at you, urging you to do something about it? Not wanting people to be able to do whatever the hell they want, as long as they aren't caught, or as long as they do it to someone who can't fight back?"

A woman wearing a puffy white ski jacket and jeans came out of another Edwardian building next door to Lorraine's. She had a spindly coffee-colored dog on a leash — a Chihuahua, maybe. The dog pranced down the sidewalk as if she knew exactly where she wanted to go. She probably did.

"I think there are things you can accomplish in the world, and things outside of your control. And it's healthier to focus on the things inside your control."

"So I'm wasting my time trying to figure out what's wrong with that woman?"

"Probably."

"Yet, you're sitting here with me."

"Do I really need to explain why that is?" He let go of my hand and put his arm around my shoulders.

The dog stopped abruptly in front of Tess's building. It

turned, looked at us, then back at the building they'd just passed. She let out a single, piercing bark. The woman tugged gently on the leash and the dog turned and continued on her way.

As if the dog's bark had alerted her and me at the same moment, the woman appeared at her window. She'd opened the curtains, leaving a six- or seven-inch gap. She was standing close to the glass, naked. Her breasts were pressed against the window, flattened into disks of bloodless flesh.

I felt Isaiah watching too, as if all of us — the dog, him, me — felt her presence before we'd seen her, all of us turning to look.

"Freaky," Isaiah said. "I wonder why she's doing that."

"See what I mean? And now you're curious."

He squeezed my shoulder and continued staring.

It wasn't that her pose was erotic. It was more disgusting than anything provocative, as if she wanted to melt her body into the glass, not that she wanted us to admire it or that she hoped to arouse or offend us. She just wanted us to look. She wanted to absorb the attention of every living being on the street.

34

Jen sat in the lounge watching Lizzy and Scott. It turned out Lizzy and Scott came in several nights a week for a glass of wine. She wasn't sure why she'd never noticed their regular presence. She supposed it was Scott's inhuman behavior that now made them stand out from the crowd of other well-dressed men and expertly made up women.

Scott and Lizzy liked hanging around the piano when jazz was featured, urging the pianist to play songs that didn't fade as elegantly into the background — loud, dramatic pieces that left everyone staring at the piano, forgetting the threads of their conversations.

The wine on the table in front of Jen was her third glass. It wasn't a good idea to confront someone after so much wine, but she had to tell Lizzy about the disgusting behavior of her boyfriend. Surely, if Lizzy knew what he'd done, she'd be horrified.

Treating a human being like a toilet was not okay.

Since Scott didn't live in the building, it was Lizzy's responsibility to make him stop, to make him apologize. It was impossible to believe that Lizzy would excuse what he'd done, that she'd have the same lack of compassion and sense of right and wrong that the security manager had. Anyone with even a tiny heartbeat would be horrified. The fact that he'd done it, that he'd even thought of doing it, said he was a horrid, cruel man. Maybe Lizzy already knew that and didn't care, but maybe she was blind to what he was really like. Jen had been blind to Jake's cheating. Willful blindness was common. You overlooked things, you forgave. This was unforgivable.

First, she had to get Lizzy away from Scott. And second, she needed to find a way to cut through the bubble wrap surrounding Lizzy, allowing her to blame the homeless woman for her own predicament.

It was a few minutes past seven, the time the pianist normally stopped, but he was still going. Lizzy and Scott were the only two standing near the piano. Every time the pianist lifted his hands from the keyboard, moving to close the cover, Scott stuffed a bill into the oversized brandy glass on the bench.

The music was a pleasant background most evenings, and it wasn't clear why those two felt it needed to dominate the lounge, why they were so fascinated by it. If jazz was that important to them, why didn't they download some tunes of their own? Maybe this was another example of Scott's cruelty. He simply wanted to force the man to keep playing so he could feel good about controlling another man, and controlling what a room full of people listened to.

Jen picked up her glass and took a sip of wine.

The pianist finished the song and lowered the lid in one swift movement.

Scott stuffed a bill into the glass. The pianist dug it out and handed it back to Scott.

Jen couldn't read the denomination of the bill, but it didn't look like a one. She stood and stepped around the table. She left her wine glass where it was. She didn't need any more. As soon as she confronted Lizzy, or the two of them, which might be the only choice, she had to arrange her Uber to meet a client. He was an older guy. This guy was always very quick, already naked and wearing a condom when she arrived, which she appreciated. But he wanted to get his money's worth, so he insisted she stay until the end of the hour to cuddle with him.

Cuddling was the worst. She had no desire to touch any of them beyond what was absolutely necessary. And when it was late, there was a danger of falling asleep as she lay beside one of them. Cuddling made her feel like they possessed her, that she had no control over her life or her body, even her soul. There was something about cuddling that made her feel they wanted to possess more of her. She truly didn't have any control over her body, but for some reason, it was the holding and touching afterwards that shoved that fact in her face.

She crossed the room and stopped a few feet away from Lizzy.

Scott glanced at her. His face was blank, not even a tremor of recognition. It had been dark when she'd caught him and spoken to him, but still. She supposed she'd hoped he felt some sort of regret and that seeing her might stir it up, some unconscious connection between her presence and his buried guilt.

"I'll pay you to keep going," Scott said.

The pianist shook his head. "Can't. I play at another bar. I'm already late."

"Maybe we should head over to his next gig," Lizzy said.

Scott squinted and shoved his hands in his pockets as if he needed several minutes to consider this because it was such a complicated solution to the problem.

Jen moved closer. "Hi, Lizzy."

Lizzy fiddled with her earring — a twisted silver wire that

was shaped into coils in front of and behind her lobe. "Hi."

"I wanted to talk to you."

"About what?"

"Just...I..."

The pianist's face relaxed at the interruption. He lifted his hand toward Scott and backed away. "Thanks for the tips. Greatly appreciated." He turned and walked quickly toward the stairs and disappeared down them.

Scott glared at Jen. "A friend of yours?" He didn't look at Lizzy when he said it.

"She lives in the building."

"I'm standing right here," Jen said. "You don't need to be talking about me."

They stared at her but neither one spoke.

"We've met before." She looked at Scott

He shrugged. "Don't recall."

"You were pissing on the homeless woman out front."

"Oh, you." He snorted. He put his arm around Lizzy. "I'll take care of this. Go make yourself pretty so we can head out to dinner."

Lizzy's makeup was smooth and fresh-looking, her eyes lightly smudged with neutral shadow, her mascara luxurious and moist. Her hair hung in a silky curtain around her face, brushed back just enough to reveal the unusual earrings. There was nothing to be done to make her prettier.

Lizzy slid out from under his arm. "Don't be talking about nasty things while I'm gone." She smiled at him as if they were talking about going to a topless club, not about him urinating on a human being.

As Lizzy walked away, Scott took Jen's upper arm.

"Let go."

"You need to stop harassing me or I'll file a complaint. Understood?"

"I'm not harassing you."

He let go of her arm. "And don't ever speak to Lizzy again."

"You can't tell me who I can talk to."

"When she's my girlfriend, I can."

"Does she know you decide who she can talk to?"

"She likes me to watch out for her. She loves that I have her back." He moved away. "I'm done talking to you."

"What if that was you, forced to live on the street? Can't you put yourself in her place?"

"I would never be in that situation. Those people are druggies and drunks and they don't belong here."

"Well peeing on her isn't going to make her go away."

"Did you feed her? That's part of the problem. It's like stray cats — they never leave after you give them food."

"She's a person!" Her voice was shrill and too loud. Several people at a nearby group of chairs turned to look at her. "You can't treat her like this!"

"Get a grip. If you keep shrieking, you'll be sleeping right next to her."

She didn't think, didn't consider what might happen or why she was doing it. She didn't want to know that people like him existed. She raised her arm and slammed her fist into his shoulder.

He grabbed her wrist and twisted her arm behind her back. "This is a nice place," he said. "Watch out." He tightened his grip twisting her skin around her bones.

Tears rushed into her eyes and dribbled out. She felt mascara pooling beneath her eyes. She'd have to return to her room and fix her face before she went out.

"Talk to me or Lizzy again, or touch either one of us, and I will file a complaint. You're lucky I'm not doing it now. You'll be out of this place before you can take a piss yourself." He let go of her arm and hurried across the lounge, seeming to know by instinct that Lizzy would be emerging at that moment from the hallway leading to the restrooms. They started down the stairs.

A few people were staring at her, but no one spoke or moved to get up.

Jen found a seat and flopped into it. Instead of relief that he was gone and that he hadn't hurt her more, that no one had called security, part of her wanted to chase him down the stairs. Tears flowed out of her eyes. Her face was drenched.

35

Isaiah and I didn't discuss what we'd seen in the window. What was there to say? The *why* of her nakedness and the cause of her desperate need to keep our voyeuristic eyes on her, were unknowable. We could ask *why* throughout our entire dinner. We could lie in bed and debate our own speculations instead of enjoying each other's bodies. Nothing would come of it.

Two days later, I went for a run before dawn. The empty streets and the darkness steadied my thoughts. My footsteps seemed more solid, a comforting presence. I ran fast down the hills, feeling my body right at the edge of plummeting forward beyond my control. It was better than a blast of caffeine.

When I reached the bottom of the hill, I turned right, running on flat sidewalk, my soles crunching occasionally on brittle leaves, the sound echoing like broken shards of fine glassware. I thought of the bowl on Lorraine's table, and remembered my surprise at her modern, spacious decorating style. Everything about her appearance had suggested her apartment would be equally archaic. Her clothes and hair were classic, it wasn't as if she was fussy-old, but she definitely looked like a woman from another era.

Rounding the next corner, I encountered more fallen leaves, covering the sidewalk and piling in the gutter as if sweeping hadn't been attended to in several weeks. I slowed, unsure whether there was a layer of soft wet leaves beneath, glued to the ground after a drizzle, and then covered by another stratum — the earth rebuilding itself right on top of the sidewalk, ready to send my feet skidding away from me.

I cut across the street and ran four more blocks, headed toward a small park with a view of the bay. I skirted the edges of it three times, watching the trees emerge from the darkness as the sun spread light, if not its actual presence, across the sky.

When I reached Tess's street again, the streetlights still glowed valiantly, making sure they had a smooth hand-off to the sun before blinking out for the day. I slowed to a walk. As I reached the entrance to her building, Frank came walking down the steps of the building next door. I continued past Tess's entrance, waiting for him to notice me.

He looked up and nodded. His pace didn't change perceptibly, as if he'd expected to see me, although that wasn't likely at six-thirty in the morning. Then I wondered if he'd planned to leave early to avoid running into me.

I waved.

He touched the brim of his hat.

I walked up to him.

"Good morning," he said.

"Headed to work?" It was all I could think of to say. At his age, and having enough to afford the apartment he occupied, I couldn't imagine him needing to clock in at an office every day.

"Yes."

"Oh."

He winked. "I surprised you."

I smiled. "A little. Where do you work?"

"I teach film at UC San Francisco."

"That sounds fun."

"I never spoke of it in those terms, but yes, I enjoy it." He smiled. "Film Noir."

"Is that why you wear a fedora?"

He laughed.

"I understand now why you kept insisting that woman in your building is looking for attention."

He pushed his hat up and closed his eyes for half a second. "I told you…"

"I know, but she was naked."

He closed his eyes again. He wiped his hand over his face, pulling his cheeks toward his mouth. He suddenly looked much older than I'd originally thought, ancient, despite his perfect posture, well-fitting overcoat, and the hat.

"You seem like you're in pain."

"It gets tiresome."

"Does anyone live there with her?"

"Why are you so interested? Don't you have a job? A social life? Things to do?" He glanced down at my shorts and running shoes. "Other interests?"

"She's obviously disturbed, and she has my curiosity. It seems like you and Lorraine know more than you're saying."

"That's in your head. Besides, it's none of your business. People around here like to be left alone."

"Yet, she likes attention."

"If she wanted inquiries into her life, she'd come out of her apartment."

"I suppose." I stretched my arms behind me, clasping my hands. Standing still after a longish run was going to make my muscles freeze up.

"Well, soon your friend will return and you'll go back to

your life, and you'll forget all about this. And she can live out her sad, lonely existence."

"It seems like you don't care what happens to her, or what's wrong with her."

"She has her life, I have mine." He stepped around me. "I need to catch the cable car."

I said good-bye. He nodded, but said nothing, walking quickly, never turning to look back.

I went to the lamppost and began stretching.

I would not forget all about her when I moved back to my own place. This would continue to haunt me. Besides, I still had a few more weeks before Tess returned.

I'd meant to ask Frank who occupied the apartment on the top floor. Maybe it didn't matter. Despite their insistence I ignore the situation, they were my best chances at finding out what was going on. Although being granted access to the building and getting to the second floor might be more probable from someone who wasn't aware of my obsession.

36

Portland

Pauline twisted her pocket knife this way and that, watching sunlight, filtered through the trees, glint off the blade. At first I thought she was just playing around with it, but after a few minutes of this, I knew for sure she wanted to frighten me.

"Such a pretty little thing," the woman said. Her voice was almost a growl.

Did she mean the knife, or me?

She brought the blade close to my lower leg and pressed the tip into my jeans until it poked through the fabric. It didn't hurt, but I couldn't understand what she wanted from me. Was she planning to stab me? Take my small collection of coins? Something else? The knife was too small to kill me without quite a lot of stabs.

"It's not safe out here. Not at all." She smiled, although it was directed more at the knife than at me.

I didn't say anything, trying to think what I'd do if she actually drove the tiny blade into my flesh.

"You could really get hurt. Where are your mommy and daddy? Aren't they worried?"

They probably were, but I was thinking about what she might do, not my parents' worries.

"Why would you run away from home? Oh!" She snapped the blade closed and clutched the knife in her fist.

She looked at me. "Maybe they aren't worried at all. Maybe they're cruel. Monsters, even. Maybe they hurt you more than you could possibly be hurt out here, alone, with no one to protect you." She opened the knife again.

I stared at her.

"You don't talk much."

I said nothing.

"You're a very disturbing child."

I didn't blink.

"Why are you staring at me like that? Scared, are you?"

"No."

"You should be."

We sat for several minutes in silence, maybe longer. Maybe almost half an hour. Time didn't seem to be moving. My stomach didn't grumble and I didn't have to pee. The air was still and the birds had stopped chirping. The only movement was the slow spreading of light as the sun rose higher in the sky.

Pauline stared past me, holding the knife pointed up, her arm muscles tensed as if she planned to strike the minute I made even the smallest movement.

Every few minutes, I heard the soft tap of a leaf falling to the ground. My legs grew stiff and slightly numb from sitting with them straight in front of me. The weight of her body prevented me from moving them without her noticing and perhaps cutting short any possible escape by suddenly plunging the knife into my shin.

In a low voice, as if she was talking to herself, she said, "Have you ever cut yourself?"

After a moment she spoke again. "Probably not. You're too young. Although children do everything at younger ages now." She pulled up her sleeve and turned her arm so the underside of her forearm was exposed. It was covered with scars, and a few more recent cuts, split with dried blood. She dragged the knife blade across her pale skin, slicing it open. Blood rose to the surface and spilled over the sides of cut flesh.

I winced and closed my eyes.

"Open your eyes, Miss. You need to see this."

I shuddered. I kept my eyes closed.

"Now. Open them."

"I don't want to."

"Open them!"

"I don't like blood."

She laughed. "How can you not like blood? It's what keeps you alive."

"I don't like to see it all wet and running out of things."

"Things?" she laughed. "Open your eyes or I'll make you."

I imagined how she might make me and opened my eyes.

"That's better. It's not so bad. Cutting your skin makes you feel better. It gives you power."

"It's gross."

"Well everything about the body is gross — sweat, shit, pimples, blood, rashes, warts, piss, digestion, boils. Blood is the cleanest part. It's pure."

I shuddered again.

"The tough girl isn't so tough. Cutting is blissful."

"You have scars."

"So? In the end, there are all kinds of scars — wrinkles, age spots, blemishes." She drew the blade across her arm again, just below her elbow joint. Blood spilled out and several drops ran down her arm. They dripped onto my sleeping bag.

"Want to taste it?" she said.

"No."

"Why not? It doesn't taste bad."

"It's icky."

She laughed.

I tightened my jaw, wanting her to go away. Maybe she would bleed to death and that would be it. But the slow release of life would take a long time, and I didn't want her blood all over me. This was more unsettling than the way she'd turned the knife as if she was considering stabbing me, more frightening than asking me if I was scared.

I couldn't think of a way to make her leave me alone. I felt more trapped than I did during my father's lengthy prayers or Bible readings. I was forced to watch the things I said even more than I had to during my evening prayers when my mother censored what should and should not be said to god. "I wish you would leave me alone."

"I asked you to share, I'm still waiting."

"I gave you some of my apple."

She shook her head. "Not enough." She made another small cut in her arm. Her skin was smeared with blood now. My stomach clenched and relaxed, turning into something loose and soft.

"Do you want to try it?" She held out the knife, wet with blood.

"No." My mouth twisted as my stomach shoved apple back up into my throat.

"I don't have any diseases, my blood won't hurt you."

"That's not why."

"Then, why?"

"I just don't. I already told you."

"You're scared."

"I'm not."

"You won't be scared once you do it. If you feel any bad things, if you feel bad about where you live, your parents, whatever they did to you, this will make you feel better. Nothing hurts after you do it." She smiled.

I thought I saw blood in the crevices between her teeth.

37

San Francisco

I sat on the bench across the street from the woman's apartment. I lit a cigarette and thought about Pauline holding me captive in my hideout, cutting her arms and dripping blood on my sleeping bag, pleading with me to join her sick activity. She'd gone out of her way to upset me, to force her own pain into my life. The memory had risen to the surface for obvious reasons. Was the woman in the second-floor apartment also a cutter? If scars crisscrossed her skin, they wouldn't be visible through a window.

It was ten-thirty on a Wednesday morning. My usual Wednesday morning meeting had been cancelled. All my other work could easily slide to the next day. Or late that afternoon. Steve's text messages had gone suddenly quiet and it was best not to be in the office in case he made a personal appearance. If I went into the office at five, it was unlikely he would be prowling the halls, ready to pop his head up over the edge of my cubicle without advance notice, demanding attention and another pointless drink or dinner.

I needed to figure out my next move. The blank sheet of paper he'd given me was ridiculous. Did he recognize that? Did he really think I'd find it clever and funny? It wasn't possible to *write my own paycheck*, he just wanted to mess with me. He didn't want to give a real offer until he knew where I stood — a classic standoff. The problem was, I didn't know myself where I stood.

The heavy drapes and the sheers were both pulled shut. The closing of the drapes made the whole thing seem even more like live theater. And it truly was a drama. I felt as captivated as if I were sitting in a box seat on opening night for a wildly popular Broadway show. Eventually the curtains would part and she would appear at the window.

If she truly never left the apartment, looking out the window was her only way to keep from going mad with the lack of human connection. No matter how hermitic a person is, no matter how much she enjoys her own company, occasionally she needs other, non-virtual lives touching her own. I took another drag and blew out the smoke, watching it rise in front of my face then drift away.

As I lit my second cigarette, the curtains and drapes parted simultaneously. The woman wasn't visible, but I felt her watching me.

A few minutes later, she appeared. She wore a white satin robe tied with a sash that was looped into a huge bow. Her long blonde hair covered the sides of her face and hung down the front of the robe. A white cloche hat with a pink ribbon was pulled down as far as it would go, so all I could really see was her nose and mouth. Still, I felt her eyes on me. Her shoulders rose, stopped, and then fell, as if she'd released an enormous sigh. She moved closer and touched the tip of her nose to the glass. She remained like that, seeming to not move at all, for five or six minutes.

We were both holding our breath. Smoke drifted around me and the ash grew longer as my cigarette went un-smoked. I let out a tiny puff of air.

Suddenly, she slammed both her hands against the glass.

Her arms were extended, palms coated with blood. She dragged her hands down the glass, leaving thick streaks of red. As her hands grew level with her shoulders and then moved lower, the blood didn't thin to a light smudge. It seemed as if it was steadily pumping out of her hands.

I swallowed and took several puffs from the cigarette, keeping my attention glued to the window even though the blood made my stomach sway violently. I could no longer see her face or the white hat because she'd straightened her arms, pushing away from the glass. That, and because the smears of red that covered nearly half the window. I wondered if the blood was staining her white robe.

She was best ignored, her neighbors had insisted.

Now, I wondered if all this was only for my benefit. Had my presence pushed her into some darker place where she was doing things she wouldn't normally, simply because I was watching? She had an audience and my very presence caused the acting out, making her who she was. Maybe, when I wasn't watching, as Frank and Lorraine had learned, she disappeared into the depths of her apartment. When there was no observer, there was no blood or nudity or any other aberrant behavior. She existed in her own world, alone and content.

Like Schrödinger's cat, without me observing her, the mad woman might not be mad.

Frank had learned that. Lorraine knew that.

But I couldn't tear myself away. I had to see what she would do, I had to know what she wanted because I couldn't imagine being sealed inside a collection of rooms, never encountering the outside world except through cables bringing TV and internet into my vacuum-sealed space.

38

The woman moved away from the window, leaving it smeared with blood. After she'd been gone for fifteen or twenty minutes, I decided I definitely wouldn't go into the office. I dashed across the street, up to Tess's condo, and grabbed a warmer coat and a scarf.

While Damien shouted about a *dangerous woman*, interspersed with squawks and shrieks of laughter that sounded like he was also going mad, I threw together a turkey sandwich with mayo and lots of lettuce. I shoved it into a plastic bag, and put the sandwich and two bottles of water into a small canvas bag I found among an assortment of potholders in Tess's kitchen drawer.

The elevator crawled its way to the ground floor. I hurried across the lobby without responding to the perfunctory — *Have a nice day Ms. Mallory.*

I settled on the bench and looked at the window. It was wiped clean. I gritted my teeth, regretting that I'd let physical comfort prevent me from seeing part of the drama. I took a bite of my sandwich, watching the window.

Surely she couldn't be locked inside against her will. If there was another person, a controlling husband, or even a kidnapper, she wouldn't be allowed near the window. Such stories emerge from time to time — young women snatched on their way home from school and locked up for years. But they aren't held in multi-million-dollar apartments in upscale neighborhoods of world-class cities. They aren't allowed any access to the outside world — no form of communication and no visibility. They aren't given the freedom to stand in front of a window and create performance art with their body and blood.

I ate the sandwich slowly. I planned to remain on the bench until Frank arrived home from UC San Francisco. Even if he didn't know or couldn't say the why of it, I had to get him to tell me the other things she'd done, the things that made him give me that directive in such a strong tone, as if he could influence the situation. As if he was trying to protect me.

For the rest of the day, I sat in a dreamy limbo state, occasionally smoking.

The sun slipped behind the buildings and the temperature dropped quickly. It was the kind of cold that eats through fabric, worms its way into your bones, turning them to sticks of ice so you never get warm. I'd assumed Frank taught at the University every day, but with an obscure topic like film noir, maybe he only had classes two or three days a week.

I opened the last water bottle and drank half.

The curtains remained open but there was no movement. If the woman was watching, she was very still about it.

The sky had lost all of its blue by the time Frank appeared, walking from the corner toward his building. I stood and crossed the street. He touched the brim of his hat and gave me a grim smile.

"Can I talk to you for a minute?" I said.

He tightened his smile and shoved his hands in his coat pockets.

"I don't mean to be annoying…"

He gave a single nod of his head. "Or meddlesome."

I laughed. "I just don't understand what's going on up there." I lifted my chin toward the building. "I'm concerned."

"I've already told you, people around here like to conduct their lives without interference. Especially her."

Something about the way he said *without interference* sent a chill along my spine.

"It doesn't bother you that a woman is smearing blood all over the window? That she stands there naked?"

"Stop looking at her."

"I'm not offended that she's naked, I'm wondering why you don't seem bothered that someone living forty or fifty feet from you might be severely unbalanced. She could be dangerous." I didn't think she was, but I had to say something to get a reaction out of him. He was acting as if this were the most normal thing in the world.

"You really need to mind your own business." He took a few steps away from me.

"This sort of is my business since she wrote a message to me the first time I saw her."

He laughed. "A message."

"Yes."

He shook his head. "There's no message."

"Actually, there is. The message I'm getting is there's a disturbed woman living on this street who might need serious mental health intervention and the people nearest to her are being negligent about the threat to the neighborhood."

"She's not a threat."

"How do you know that?"

"I know."

"Then what are you not telling me?"

"I'm tired. I've been teaching and reading papers all day."
He turned toward the staircase.

"I wonder if I should call social services."

"Don't do that."

"You and Lorraine are hiding something."

"I would be very careful with Lorraine, if I were you."

"Is that a threat?"

"She has a lot of money."

I laughed. "So? You seem to be doing okay in that area."

"More money than you can imagine. And people with
that kind of money do as they please. And they get others to
do what they please."

A light mist started to fall. The door opened behind him
but he didn't seem to notice, because he didn't turn to look.

"You make her sound ominous. She's a nice old lady.
Very dignified," I said.

His voice was loud, angry, maybe...or frightened.
"There's such a thing as too much dignity." He straightened
his shoulders and adjusted his hat as if to argue with what
he'd just said.

"What do you mean?"

"You can have too much of a lot of things — money,
dignity...even love. That's all I'm going to say." He turned as
Lorraine stepped out. He bowed slightly, moved around her,
and went into the building. Once again, I'd gotten diverted
from asking who lived in the apartment above his.

I felt like the woman standing near her window, slamming
my bloody hands against a thick sheet of glass.

39

As Lorraine moved out of the doorway, her face appeared frozen. She wore a smile that said she was pleased to see me, but beneath it, was something brittle that looked about to shatter. She nodded at Frank, but said nothing to him.

The lightly falling mist faded into cool, damp air.

Lorraine descended the stairs as if she was making an entrance into a ballroom. "Such a nice man," she said.

I nodded, still trying to sort out what he'd said.

She grasped the lapels of her blue wool coat with her gloved hands. The leather was so thin and soft, it looked like a second skin, not bunching under her knuckles like most leather, but molding smoothly with the curve of her fingers. She pulled the coat up so the collar framed her jaw, hiding the tendons and thin, papery skin of her neck. "A real gentleman."

"He is."

"What was he going on about?" She smiled.

"Nothing much."

"Oh, come now." She smirked. "He was very keyed up."

There was no harm in telling her. He hadn't asked me to keep it to myself or suggested it was a secret. But the fact that she'd been watching us bothered me. She seemed to think she had some right of access to my life, or his. Maybe both. "Just chatting."

She smiled more gently. "So secretive. Or, just your usual gracious self. It's almost as if you come from another era."

"That's what I think about Frank. And you."

"Somehow I don't believe that's a compliment. It means you think we're old."

"I didn't say that at all."

"It's what you meant."

"Don't tell me what I meant." I softened my tone. "It's a way of being that has nothing to do with how many years you've been alive."

Her eyelids fluttered slightly. Her eyes were glassy, whether it was from the chilled air or something else, I couldn't be sure. "Very kind of you," she said.

"It's the truth."

"I came out to invite you to dinner." She smiled, the same brittle look that was more angry than friendly. "I know you don't have plans because you've been sitting here all day long. So cold outside. You're a very persistent woman."

"I have to…"

"I'd really like you to join me. I'll be devastated if you say no. Such an insult, to pretend another engagement."

Nothing to do all day did not at all suggest I had no plans for the evening, but she'd woven the two things together in her mind. I didn't have plans, but I had the feeling that accepting her invitation indicated something I didn't intend to communicate. She wanted something from me. Maybe all three of them did. The building was indeed filled with people from another era, thirsty for a connection to modern life and they'd all fixated on me as their means for entering a new world.

"Who owns the other apartment in your building?" I said.

"What do you mean?"

"There's the lobby and four floors." I held up my hand and raised one finger after the other. "There's the woman on the second floor, you, Frank, and…?"

She let go of her coat lapels and let it fall back into place. "Oh. That's not important."

"I'm curious."

She smiled. "It's not good to let our curiosity get the best of us. That's something you would have learned — in another era." She glanced at my jeans and boots, my slightly damp coat. "Why don't you change your clothes first."

"I haven't agreed to come."

She pressed her lips together. "I thought we were friendly. Maybe I mis-read you."

"Just because I'm not coming to dinner doesn't mean we aren't friendly."

"If you had other plans, you would have mentioned them immediately. So that's absolutely what it means."

It was a leap of logic that I didn't care to argue about any further. "I would like to have dinner with you."

"Lovely." She didn't smile. "Run home and change into something nice." She stepped inside the building and instead of letting the door close gradually under its own weight, giving me a chance to argue, she pushed it shut.

I walked to the edge of the sidewalk and looked up at the second floor window. The woman stood there, looking down at me. For the first time, I had a good look at her face. Despite her extremely long, somewhat ragged and unkempt hair, she appeared to be about my age, possibly a few years older. Her lips were parted slightly, her expression unsmiling. I couldn't really see her eyes, but they still managed to give the impression of hunger.

I lifted my hand to wave. Immediately, she stepped away from the window and a fraction of a second later, the sheer curtains swung closed.

It wasn't clear what Lorraine expected me to wear for dinner. Since we were eating in her apartment, I certainly wasn't going all out with high heels and a cocktail dress. I put on a pair of navy silk pants and a loose sleeveless top of the same fabric. My hair was still damp from the mist, so I wove it into a short braid. I touched up my eyeliner and added lip gloss.

Although it seemed as if Lorraine had manipulated me into agreeing to dinner, what she'd done was given me another chance to pry out information about the woman living below her, and to get a closer look at her odd collection of photographs.

Lorraine's apartment was pleasantly warm, a fact I appreciated after sitting on a cold bench for most of the day. The dining room held a table for six. It was already set with an array of glassware, and dinner, salad, and bread plates, soup bowls, and a full basketball team of sterling silver cutlery. I could tell it was sterling because the tine of one fork was tarnished on the inside edge where it's hard to polish.

One place setting was at the head of the table, the other to its right. She held out the chair at the subordinate position and I sat down.

She proceeded to wheel in a silver cart with course after course. First was a light shrimp bisque served with a glass of champagne, followed quickly by a salad of mixed greens, cherry tomatoes, and almonds with a creamy Italian dressing. Served with the salad was a fresh roll and soft, unsweetened butter. Next came a small serving of spinach and mushroom ravioli in a tomato sauce laced with chili peppers. The main course was a broiled lamb chop — cooked perfectly — new potatoes in their skins, and carrots paired with a Zinfandel.

Throughout the meal, she talked about San Francisco. She told stories about its history that included events in her lifetime, as well as detailed accounts of the earthquake in 1906. She followed this with tales of haunted parts of the city — from the prison on Alcatraz Island to the San Francisco Press Club to a young woman fleeing an arranged marriage who was said to haunt the Nob Hill area. She was well-versed on the history of the Castro district, and talked about that quite a bit as well.

She didn't seem to expect much conversation, just a pair of attentive ears.

Several times during the meal, I glanced behind me, through the living room to the entryway, half expecting the arrival of the son she wanted to introduce me to, but I didn't mention him and neither did she.

Dessert was chocolate mousse and French roast coffee. After opening a second bottle of wine, she served an assortment of cheese and fruit and nuts. I raved over every course, stunned that she'd prepared it all herself, and served it at a satisfying pace, nothing overcooked or growing cold before we ate. More stunning was that she'd done all this not knowing whether I would accept her invitation.

When she finally wound down during her fourth or fifth glass of wine, I nudged my own glass gently to the side. "Dinner was delicious. Thank you."

She smiled and bowed her head.

I moved my chair out from the table.

"Do you have to leave? Already?"

"I do."

She folded her napkin and placed it on the corner of the table. "All right then. We'll do this again. Soon."

I didn't mention that I wouldn't be living next door for much longer. No sense spoiling her plans after such a terrific dinner. "You're an amazing cook."

"Thank you."

I stood and pushed in my chair. She remained seated, so I leaned slightly on the back of the chair. "I can't stop thinking about all the photographs in your living room. Your friends."

"Why?"

"It's so unusual — they're all nearly the same age."

"It's the age when a woman is at her best, don't you think?"

"What do you mean?"

"Her early thirties. She's no longer silly and filled with ridiculous plans. She knows who she is. Yet she's still without wrinkles and gray hair, her body is in fine shape."

Her comment was not only odd, it didn't answer the question. "So, you only take photographs of your friends when they're in their prime?" I laughed. "All of them look recent."

She smiled. "They're important to me."

"Who are they?"

"Women I care about."

"No men?"

She shrugged. "I have photographs of my son…"

She stood and walked around the table. She took my elbow and ushered me through the living room, moving quickly past the photographs.

"It was good of you to come. I enjoyed our conversation."

"So did I."

She still had my elbow. With her other hand she reached for the doorknob. "I'll see you soon. Thank you."

I thanked her, again, which seemed more appropriate than her thanking me. I supposed she really was lonely.

Standing in the elevator, I realized I hadn't had a moment's pause in the flow of words to dig any further for information about the woman on the second floor. Had she filled the time with captivating stories to keep me from opening my mouth? It hadn't seemed so contrived while she was talking, but I couldn't stop thinking that was the case.

40

Even with all of that rich food and wine working its way sluggishly through my body, I woke at five a.m. I got up and dressed for a run. It would not be my peak run of the week, but there's a lot to be said for consistency, and I try to be consistent with running — at least four days a week, ideally five or six. My attendance at the gym had been irregular since moving into Tess's place, so running was doubly important.

I hate sensing that my body is losing its edge. A few days without lifting weights and I feel my muscles softening, their tough, tightly woven fibers turning to spongy lumps of flesh, preventing me from moving with grace and a sense of my solid presence in the world. When I don't run, my blood moves more slowly, my heart develops a dull, heavy beat. Nerves wrap themselves around each other, growing so taut they're ready to snap. I can hardly sit on the couch and watch a movie because my body is screaming at me to keep it alive and moving, crying to use the various pieces as they were meant to be used.

I checked Damien's water and he glared at me. He hadn't liked it the night before when food was placed in front of him without my expected company. It was a strange desire, shared by Damien and the woman in the window — they longed to be watched. The bird really was very lonely, locked up in an empty condo all day and many evenings. His life was the ultimate expression of human beings exerting their dominance over the natural world, bringing wild creatures into their homes so the human could satisfy fleeting desires for companionship or entertainment.

"I'll chat with you tonight," I said. Hearing myself talk to him with real regret was too much. I laughed, and he echoed the sound.

Bad girl. He bobbed his head at me, crown feathers extended as far as they would go. *Bad girl.* He didn't climb off his perch or even glance at the plate of fruit.

I drank a glass of water. I tucked the key in the interior pocket of my running pants, selected Chopin for my sound track, and hooked the phone and earbuds in place.

The elevator was empty, as it almost always was. For a building with over thirty homes, the entire place was strangely silent. I rarely encountered another resident in the lobby, and I was the sole occupant of the elevator about eighty percent of the time. When a neighbor joined me, conversation was usually non-existent. What was it about home ownership that made them so standoffish? In my high-rise of rental apartments, everyone chatted in the elevators. Maybe the lounge really did foster a neighborly atmosphere. I'd thought it was a gimmick — something they could list on their website as an enticing feature, not terribly useful. That, and a way to make a few more bucks.

Of course, it might simply be that I was a stranger here. Perhaps the neighbors all knew each other and I stood out like a cactus in a garden of lilies.

The security guard greeted me and I waved at her. I tapped to start my music and went outside to begin stretching. I walked to the curb and grabbed the lamppost. It was slick with the residue of fog. I put both hands on it to get a more secure grip and pressed the ball of my left foot against it to stretch my calf muscle. When I was finished with my lower legs. I wiped my hands on my pants and grabbed it again, taking my foot in the other hand to stretch my quads. As I did, I turned slightly.

The street light cast an irregular oblong shape across the sidewalk and up the side of the staircase leading to the lobby of the Edwardian building. Two men stood on the middle step, heads bent toward each other. I turned back the other way. A large white sedan was parked at the curb, a spotlight attached to the roof on the driver's side.

I performed a perfunctory stretch of my other leg and walked toward the staircase.

One of the men turned. "Can I help you?"

"What's going on?"

"Homicide. Please don't come any closer."

My body was blocking the light to the staircase. I moved to the right and saw a huddled form lying on the bottom step. I gasped softly. "Who is it?"

"Don't know yet. Why are you out at this hour?"

I jogged in place. "Going for a run."

"Not a good idea when it's dark."

"I'm fine."

"Then you need to move on."

"Is it a woman?" I glanced at the second story window. I couldn't see anything in the darkness.

"Male."

My stomach tightened and my body was suddenly icy cold despite my leggings, shirt, and hoodie. "Frank?" My voice came out in a whisper.

"Miss. We don't know who the victim is yet. Please leave the area."

"What happened to him?"

"No more questions."

The other man spoke. "Two gunshots. Did you hear anything?"

I glanced at the fortress where I was living. Had I heard any sounds from the street since I'd started staying there? Maybe the chattering bird drowned them out, but he wasn't talking and laughing constantly. I couldn't remember even the hiss of faraway traffic, or a siren, for that matter. I shook my head.

"Probably two or three hours ago," the second one said. "You sure?"

"I think the building is pretty solid."

"Gunshots are louder than you think."

"I didn't hear them."

They nodded, both of them looking like they wanted to ask more, slightly suspicious of a woman jogging before sunrise, maybe, or thrilled that they already had someone who knew the occupants of the building, eager to probe with questions, thirsty for information as cops tend to be — whether it's relevant or not. Just endless curiosity. Maybe they weren't so different from me.

I took a few steps closer.

The first detective held out his hand. "Stay back."

I looked at the huddled form and saw the ridge of hair where the fedora had rested. That, and the long, slender fingers, long arms and legs. I had no doubt it was Frank.

"Who reported it?" I said.

"What's your name?" the first one said.

"Alexandra."

"Full name."

"Alexandra Mallory."

"And you live there?" He jerked his head toward Tess's building.

"I'm house-sitting." I wanted to know what happened, wanted to understand what was going on, but I didn't want to get sucked into talking to detectives. The less information I ever have to give to law enforcement, the better.

He pulled his phone out of his pocket. "Phone number? Apartment number for the place you're staying? Home address?"

I gave him the information, deeply regretting having gone a step too far. Still, I wanted to know what happened to Frank. Dead. The idea was just starting to make its way through the corners of my mind. Such a nice man, and such strange things he'd said to me the last time we'd spoken. Only a few hours ago, a little over twelve. It seemed like longer.

He was such an interesting man. Dignified, intelligent, but so aloof. I thought about his constant warnings, and our last conversation. I thought about his strange comment that sometimes you can have too much money, and even more strange, too much love. Most people would not agree with him.

Who would shoot him? Someone trying to break into the building? A place that was oozing money and surely had not only first-class electronics and jewelry, and very likely significant amounts of cash. The whole neighborhood gave off that feel.

"Someone will call if we have more questions for you."

"Okay."

"Carry on with your running." They turned so their shoulders were almost touching and began speaking to each other in a strange, intimate cadence. I could hear the rise and fall, the starts and stops of their conversation, but couldn't make out a single word.

41

Jen had bitten seven of ten fingernails to the quick, trying to think of a way to make that disgusting man pay for what he'd done. Trying to think of a way to stop him from doing it again. Trying to think of a way to make sure the homeless woman was left alone.

There were no solutions to any of those problems, thus the gnawing, as if digging into her own flesh for answers.

More than any other time, more than drifting in the shadows of the city — knowing she had to keep herself hidden, knowing she was considered trash, not having a normal social life or really any friends, having no legitimate job connecting her to the rest of the human race — this one thing had made her see how awful her life was.

Until now, making money had been her primary goal, her only goal. She'd hardly paused to think about her life once she found a place to live after Jake dumped her on his front porch and locked the door. Earning a living had consumed her ever since she set herself up in an online community to solicit men who wanted sex without obligations.

Paying rent and bills, eating and staying safe occupied every moment of her life. The edges of her world were narrow and she realized now she had lived like an animal — all instinct. No different from the woman on the sidewalk except that Jen had regular meals, a warm bed, privacy, and a bathroom.

Now, she felt like that groundhog, popping its head out

of the earth after a long winter spent shivering below ice-frosted soil. She saw her vulnerability. She had no common threads to connect with the people who should have been her peers. She had no influence with the building management because she needed to avoid drawing attention to herself. She had no resources to help that poor woman and no ability to stop the injustice. Utterly helpless and forced to watch, ashamed of her helplessness.

All she could do was walk past the woman every night, smelling piss. Even if she wasn't absolutely certain it was there, she smelled it. The odor was so strong, her knees buckled, her vision blurred, her brain swam around as if it couldn't find the inside of her skull.

The whole thing made her want to cry…all the time. When she was with a client, she thought about the woman. She had dreams about her lonely, frightening life. Horrid, ugly dreams. In one dream, Scott and the security manager, and several other faceless men, urinated on the woman while Lizzy stood to the side, applying lip gloss, watching. In one dream, Jen had been huddled on the ground, trying to sleep on the cold, hard pavement without a sleeping bag, wearing nothing but a thong and a camisole. Scott began pissing on her, his urine unexpectedly cold. She woke shivering, frantically slapping at her body to see if her skin was truly wet.

The lounge was packed tonight. She sat in an armchair, facing a small table and an empty matching chair. She'd chosen this seat because it was the farthest spot from the grand piano. Scott leaned on the edge where the piano opened to display the strings and hammers. Lizzy was nowhere in sight.

Jen had been watching him for nearly twenty minutes. It didn't seem possible that Lizzy had been in the restroom the entire time, but it didn't make sense he'd chosen the apartment lounge as a place to hang out if she was working late or at a club with her girlfriends.

Jen sipped her beer. Wine was good, but it was too expensive. She could make beer last longer, keeping her less tipsy and giving her something to do to justify her presence, watching him laugh and annoy the pianist.

She reached forward and plucked two pretzel rings out of the bowl of pretzels and mixed nuts. She ate them and took a few more sips of beer, then placed the bottle on the table beside the nuts. Best to slow down or she'd be forced to buy another. She might lose her seat, crossing the room to the bar. He might see her.

The evening belonged entirely to her. None of her regular clients had booked, and she hadn't been able to find anyone new. She was choosey about the messages she responded to, relying on her gut to tell her when a guy seemed too aggressive or too entitled. Entitled was the worst. Sometimes there were other little warnings bells. She couldn't always say what set them off, but she obeyed them without question. It was better to have a lower income than end up beaten and bruised, or worse.

It was always a battle inside her head — knowing she needed money, yet craving the freedom of her life belonging only to her, knowing she had nowhere to go and no one to answer to, if only for a single evening. She leaned back in the chair and closed her eyes.

When she opened them, Scott was sitting across from her. She jerked upright and recalled the cold wetness of her very life-like dream. Sneaking up on her like this was further proof of the kind of man he was. She picked up her beer.

"You had no right to complain to security about me," he said.

She felt her face go slack. After making her feel like she was the one with a problem, the security guy had actually talked to Scott? She had no idea what to say.

"It's an effective deterrent," he said.

"What?"

"Pissing on bums is an effective deterrent. They find other places to sleep."

"Are you serious?"

"Yup." He took a long swallow of his beer and put it on the table with too much force, making her bottle and the bowl of nuts jitter slightly.

"What's wrong with you?"

"What's wrong with them is a better question. In any other period of human history, people who couldn't take care of themselves died. Eaten by wild animals, starved to death. The herd was thinned to worthwhile, contributing members. We coddle these losers and as a result, they're multiplying. It's a scourge."

"We should care for each other. A lot of homeless people are veterans. They fought for our country. And lots of homeless people were abused as children and got into drugs to numb the pain."

"Suffering doesn't absolve you of responsibility. Look at you. You must work hard for your money, if you can afford to live here." He glanced up toward the glass ceiling that soared four stories above them. He looked back at her and took another swallow of beer. "What do you do?"

"None of your business. I don't even want to talk to you."

"Kind of touchy."

She stared at him, wishing he'd disappear.

"On the rag? Or do you have a shitty job and someone is subsidizing your rent? You know you don't really belong here, so you're embarrassed to tell me you're a waitress or a housekeeper or whatever."

She pressed her lips together.

"Worse than that? Hmm." He glanced across the room. After a moment he turned back. "Can't think of much worse. Come on, what do you do? Doesn't it piss you off to work long hours and then you're forced to pay a huge chunk in wasted taxes to support these losers?"

Jen picked up her beer. She put her mouth around the top of the bottle but didn't drink. She should get up and walk away. There was no rule of politeness that required she stay and listen to his disgusting viewpoints.

"Oh. Maybe you don't pay taxes? Bookie? Drugs? New fields for women. Maybe you're a feminist breaking new ground." He laughed.

"I really don't want to talk to you," she said.

"Well you won that one. You're not talking. I'm trying to be friendly, to patch things up between us, for Lizzy's sake." He grinned in what he surely intended to be a boyish, charming way, but just made him look more evil.

A year ago, she wouldn't have believed there were evil people in the world. Not really. Maybe people that lacked a conscience, or people who were corrupt, but they still probably had some redeeming qualities. Of course there were people like Hitler and Mussolini, but those were so far outside the norm. Freaks of nature, really. In general, most people were good. She still believed that, but she worried the percentage was much less than she'd always thought.

She stood.

"Hey, where are you going?"

"I wanted to have a nice evening. Alone." She turned and walked toward the stairs. A bowl of Pho would make her feel better.

42

The day after I had a glimpse of Frank's body lying on the front stoop, I was in a fog all day. I entered data into spreadsheets. I created PowerPoint slides that displayed colorful, intricate charts revealing insights from my data — which projects were on track, which were behind, which were chronically late. I dialed into two conference calls. I wasn't in charge of either meeting, so I muted my desk phone and half listened, scrolling through Twitter, holding my phone on my lap so anyone sticking their neck up and peering over the walls of my cubicle wouldn't immediately notice. Not that they cared. Everyone did it. Facebook. Twitter. Online shopping. Browsing reviews on Yelp, trying to decipher whether the horrid comments about a restaurant you're considering were written by perpetual cranks, or had some validity.

It's so difficult to know what's real sometimes.

Of course I assumed Frank's murder wasn't random — a break-in or a gang bullet gone astray. The Russian Hill neighborhood was not an area with a lot of gang activity. And sure, armed robbery was possible, upscale neighborhoods are attractive targets, but they're also areas where security cameras and sophisticated alarms proliferate.

After work, I went back to Tess's and mixed a martini. I sat on her balcony, wrapped in a yellow cashmere blanket, and watched the sun sink behind the buildings, the state of numbness continuing. It was the unexpected nature of his death that created the white-out condition in my mind. Although, murder is always sudden, so maybe that was a ridiculous explanation for my mood.

Contrary to how it should work, as the martini wove its way through my blood vessels, the numbness faded.

For all the time I'd been watching and thinking about the woman next door, I'd been on her side, so to speak. I assumed she was trapped by some force beyond her control, trying to send a message or at least make a connection outside the narrow confines of her life. Even telling Frank she might pose a threat, I didn't really believe that. I simply wanted to provoke him. Despite their efforts to persuade me otherwise, it had seemed obvious that the woman was trying to convey a desperate request for help.

Now, I wondered if it was something else.

Just because everyone insisted she'd never left the building, much less her apartment, didn't mean it was the truth.

Was it possible Frank had been afraid of her? I tried to remember the things he'd said. Mostly he'd emphasized not encouraging her behavior. But why? I'd thought he was simply disgusted. Maybe I'd read that wrong.

I ate one of my olives.

Considering these questions was pointless. I was making things up and trying to connect slivers of information that were very likely not even related to each other. Everything he said was either cryptic or repetitious. I could resume my post across the street, but with detectives crawling around, that would have to wait for a day, at least.

The temperature was dropping. Even with the cashmere blanket and the soft cushion of the chaise lounge beneath me

I was shivering. I took one more sip of my drink and stood. I set the drink on a metal table. It made a rough, scratching sound, like something buried in the earth trying to claw its way out. I tossed the blanket over my shoulder and pulled the canvas cover over the lounge chair.

Inside, Damien was angry.

Bad girl! Bad girl! Delicious mango! Bad Girl! Between phrases, he laughed in a tone that made me think of a ghoulish creature in an old horror movie. I guess he didn't like me prioritizing a cocktail over his dinner.

I took another sip of my drink and cut up some mango and strawberries for him. I put the plate on the floor near his perch and settled into the chair across from him. I wasn't hungry yet. In fact, I was pretty sure I'd be treating myself to a second martini before I thought about scraping together the contents of leftover takeout containers for my own dinner.

Bad girl.

I held the martini glass with both hands, arranging my fingertips around the rim. I studied the bird, waiting for him to climb down and begin eating. He'd been so worked up about it, as if he were half starved. There was a small dish of seeds that sat beside his perch all day, so he should never be fainting from hunger. And clearly he wasn't. He didn't make a move toward the fruit. He didn't even go for a sip of water. He continued repeating that phrase, laughing, his crown feathers standing in their usual posture of terror.

"I thought you were hungry," I said.

Bad girl. He opened his beak. His worm of a tongue waggled inside his mouth. He shrieked and shook his head.

This went on for nearly ten minutes. My glass was empty, the last olive eaten. I desperately wanted another martini.

Sitting there waiting for him to eat, spoiling my own evening, was ridiculous. I stood and left the room.

The bird began shrieking so loudly, it made my eardrums ache. I went into the kitchen and put my glass on the counter. I poured vodka into the shot glass and dumped it into the shaker, followed by half a shot of vermouth. I got out the olive jar and spooned out three large olives, stabbing them with a black plastic spear. The bird continued to shout, mostly incoherent sounds. When he did seem to form words, the noise was so raucous I couldn't decipher what he was saying. I went to the window and looked out at the glistening lights. I took a sip of the martini. I set the glass on the counter and covered my ears. The membrane-splitting sounds were slightly muffled. I returned to his room. He still hadn't touched his food.

I went back to the kitchen, took another sip of my drink, and pulled my phone out of my pocket. It was about two in the afternoon in Australia. I had no idea what Tess was doing with her days, but I hoped her phone was as close by as it was when she was working. I sent her a message.

Alex: *Damien is a bit wound up and he won't eat. Just checking the range of normal behavior.*

My martini glass, olives included, was empty and I was standing in front of the open fridge, the bird still shrieking, when the phone vibrated.

Tess: *Have you been spending enough time with him?*

Alex: *Define "enough".*

Tess: *It's on the instruction sheet!*

I hadn't looked at the instruction sheet after the first day when I checked the meal-preparation guidelines. I went to the drawer where I'd tucked it out of the way. She'd clearly spelled out that he needed to be aware of my presence at least an hour in the morning and another hour in the evening. Added to this, he needed additional interaction on weekends. It didn't have to be scheduled, but he needed that extra time. I sighed.

Tess: *Hello? U there? Did you even read it?*

Alex: *Of course.*

Tess: *Let him sit on your shoulder. That usually soothes him.*

Alex: *He's making too much noise, my ears can't take it.*

Tess: *Your ears will be fine. He'll settle right away.*

I didn't want the bird on my shoulder. I carried my phone and a banana to the bird's room. He stopped shrieking and tilted his head to one side. He eyed the banana. I held it out. He turned away and laughed in a sad, slightly bitter way.

I put down the banana and walked over to him. The phone vibrated in my hand.

Tess: *Well? Is he okay now?*

I lowered my shoulder. The bird reached out one foot, thick scaly skin and deadly claws touching my body, a thin piece of cotton the only thing between my flesh and his rage. He placed his foot on my shoulder. I held my breath. He paused for what seemed like minutes but was probably seconds. He moved the other foot over and settled his body against the side of my head. He started murmuring...*delicious mango.*

Alex: *Shoulder worked.*

While she was engaged in texting with me, thanks to her demented, demanding pet, I decided to ask about the woman next door. She'd never mentioned anything unusual about her neighborhood, but why would she? I couldn't imagine her loitering in the street, studying her neighbors in the same way

I had. It was more likely she rode the elevator from her floor to the underground parking most of the time and rarely even passed through the lobby. She might go months without stepping outside onto her street. Still. Every bit of info I could pick up had the potential to help settle the questions picking at my brain.

Alex: *Have you ever noticed the woman on the second floor in the building next door?*

Tess: *The nut case?*

Alex: *I guess you could say that.*

Tess: *What about her?*

Alex: *What's the story?*

Tess: *No idea. She's an exhibitionist. Ignore her.*

I felt myself deflate slightly, only then recognizing I'd nurtured an extravagant hope for the revelation of some fascinating secret that would explain everything.

Alex: *Damien seems fine now.*

Tess: *Good. Don't ignore him. He needs company. He gets lonely.*

Alex: *Yup.*

She texted a series of tropical emojis. I lowered myself and the bird close to the floor. He hopped off my shoulder and began devouring his dinner as if I'd deprived him of food for hours.

I went into the kitchen. Instead of leftovers, I boiled a handful of fettuccini and heated up some pesto sauce. I opened a bottle of Chardonnay and poured a glass. Damien didn't comment. Although it seemed slightly unappetizing, I decided to bring a tray into his room and eat my dinner while he finished his. Maybe he'd have more information than Tess.

43

Damien settled down and I poured a second glass of wine. I sat in the darkness in Tess's sunroom. I looked out at the city lights and turned my thoughts to Isaiah in an attempt to rid myself of the circular stream of questions about the people next door.

So far, Isaiah and I been talking and laughing, watching movies and hiking, eating wonderful food, and enjoying pretty amazing sex for more than a month. It was close to a record for me.

I'm not opposed to having a guy longer term, permanent even. Maybe. That's an enormous maybe. My history of serial lovers was due to men liking me on the outside but being less than thrilled with my view of the world and my desire for lots of space. Huge amounts of space. I require lots of time alone and I get very irritable when a man interprets that to mean I'm hiding something, aka seeing another guy at the same time. *Seeing* as in fucking. That's what they're mostly worried about.

Most guys also tend to grow unnerved by what they consider my cold, selfish attitude. I can't help it if I'm ruled more by instinct and practicality than I am by feelings. I have passion, I think, but I don't have sentimental feelings and I don't feel responsible for other people's feelings. That's insane. How can you affect how another person feels?

I don't spend too much time or effort censoring myself. I know who I am and what I want and I don't need reassurance, or to pretend I'm someone I'm not just so people will like me, whatever that means. As if anyone can control who likes them. Or so they'll consider me a good person. Whatever *that* means.

It's funny how any behavior outside the societal norm, whatever that may be in any given area of life, in any given historical time period, is looked at with suspicion, criticism, and downright paranoia. If someone in the corporate world chooses to get a tattoo sleeve they might as well end their career right then, or else sweat through five months of the year in long-sleeved shirts and jackets. Yet a biker without a tat or two is looked at with equal suspicion.

All those instinctual drives to keep the herd behaving in a similar fashion have taken thousands of years to even recognize and who knows how many thousand more before they're overcome. Besides, most people don't want to overcome those drives to orchestrate the behavior of others. I suppose the problem is rooted in widely different opinions regarding which behaviors should be approved and which should be shunned.

My behavior often falls outside the norms of how women are supposedly expected to, and want to interact with men. Women are supposed to desire belonging to one half of a committed couple that shares a home and most of their meals, and if not children, pets or a business venture, or a cause. Women are supposed to want to care for a man and lean on a man and want a man all to herself. It's not that I have polyamorous tendencies, I just don't feel the need to possess another human being. And possession is how it often looks to me.

Jewelry and ceremonies announcing that you're in it for

life don't get you anywhere. Not really. It's an illusion. And it can become such an oppressive weight, sucking all the fun out of everything.

I certainly don't want to be possessed.

I like companionship and interesting conversation and laughing. Lots of laughing. I like eating out and seeing shows and hiking and running. Sometimes, that's enjoyable with a man. Other times, it's more enjoyable alone, lost inside my own head.

I don't like obligations or expectations. I don't like having to tell someone where I'm going at any particular hour of the day.

So far, Isaiah seemed to be on the same page. That wasn't surprising. A lot of men like to have sex and good times without any detailed definition around which parts of their day belong to another person.

The problem is usually that space thing. When you don't need them, suddenly they start needing you. It's a little confusing, to be honest.

Isaiah was an only child so maybe he was used to getting his own way and had the same desire for space as I did. His father was never in the picture, not even a name on Isaiah's birth certificate, not even the bare minimum gift of a last name. Parker was his mother's name. When Isaiah was a child, he'd asked his mother where the man was, when they would meet, why he didn't want to be around Isaiah. Endless questions, to hear him describe it. She never answered a single one and eventually, when he was nine or ten, he gave up.

As an adult, he had no inclination to track the man down. He said he could take a hint. Why force yourself into the life of someone who obviously isn't interested?

I agreed with him completely.

Isaiah had known when he was thirteen that he wanted to be a chef. His mom was a registered nurse and did a pretty good job supporting their family of two, but culinary school wasn't in her budget. So Isaiah went to a junior college and worked part time. When he finished the two years, he spent several more years working as a server in a waterfront restaurant in Sausalito, across the bay from San Francisco. It wasn't exactly cheap living in the artistic, exclusive town, but he loved the restaurant, and he loved looking across at the city skyline and imagining himself living on the other side of the water, getting trained to live his dream.

He was obsessed with cooking. Since I'm obsessed with eating, I liked being around him. He took me to fantastic restaurants, but he hadn't done any cooking for me yet.

The kitchen in my studio apartment had a small cooktop and an oven large enough for a lasagna pan and that was about it. The preparation area consisted of two square feet of counter space. It did nothing to inspire him to cook. Not to mention the lack of utensils and pans and bowls he'd come to consider essential. At the culinary school, he had enough stuff to open his own little chef supply shop.

Tess had a magnificent kitchen. And although she didn't do a lot of cooking, she'd managed to acquire quite a lot of fancy instruments just in case she somehow was overcome with a food preparation frenzy, and the associated skill appeared like it does with those people who wake from a coma and speak a language they've never learned.

I desperately wanted him to come over and cook dinner for me. The exercise with the bird proved the lobby attendants were not going to bend the rules.

I stared out at the glittering, softening lights, feeling quite blissful with my glass of wine and the silence. But I did want to think of a way to get Isaiah inside of her condo.

44

The next time I saw Lorraine it was raining. She was carrying a huge black umbrella. She gave me a tiny wave and kept walking, heading downhill toward the corner.

Watching an eighty-something woman juggle an oversized umbrella along slippery pavement was both unsettling and slightly amusing. It wasn't something that should be laughed at, but the umbrella seemed to be carrying her along. I couldn't understand why she hadn't called for a cab.

I hurried after her, pulling my own umbrella close to my head, hoping I could duck beneath her more enveloping shelter once I was close to her side.

"Do you have a second?" I tried to insert my wet umbrella under hers. They overlapped, causing water that was running down her nylon covering to drain onto mine and cascade over the sides.

"It's a miserable day for standing around chatting."

"It was so awful — what happened to Frank," I said.

"Yes." She kept moving.

"Are you going somewhere?"

"Obviously."

I couldn't invite her for coffee in Tess's place, but inviting myself to her apartment seemed odd. I wanted to know what the detectives had said to her. It seemed strange they hadn't been in touch with me. I guess they figured since I'd heard nothing, I had nothing to contribute. "You can't chat for a minute?"

"Alexandra, it's pouring rain. And I have an appointment."

"Maybe later?"

"Later when?"

"Or, how are you getting to your appointment? Are you taking the cable car? I could ride with you." It made no sense that someone with the resources she had would take a cable car, that she'd walk in such weather, but here she was.

"I'm only going two blocks."

"To where?"

"That's none of your business. I'll see you another time." She walked quickly, sure-footed in a way that showed misplaced optimism about the condition of the pavement.

I kept pace with her. "Did the police talk to you about Frank? Did you hear a gunshot, or anything? Do they have any suspects? Did they talk to that woman on the second floor? I can't imagine she would be able to avoid them if they had questions for her."

Lorraine shook her head. "You sound like an excited child. It's not nice to be so interested in a murder."

"I just want to know what happened. He was a nice man."

"Well we likely won't know what happened. Most crimes go unsolved."

"Do they?" That was definitely the case for my crimes, but I wasn't sure that was true in general. She said it with such authority. It seemed as if she didn't really mind whether or not his murder was solved.

"I really need to get going." She walked faster.

"Be careful. You don't want to slip."

"I've been walking on San Francisco hills in wet weather

all my life. I'm not going to slip."

I wasn't going to point out that she may have done it all her life, but she'd had more supple bones and stronger muscles during all those years of hurrying through the city on foot. "So they don't have any suspects?"

"Not that I'm aware of."

"They talked to you?"

"Yes. But I couldn't provide any information. I didn't hear a gunshot. And it's not as though I have intimate knowledge of what's going on in his life, his comings and goings."

"Did they talk to the woman on the second floor?"

She shrugged. Her umbrella tipped back slightly and rain splashed onto her shoes. "Now look what's happened."

"I can walk with you. And hold the umbrella for you," I said. "Will that help?"

"No. I'll talk to you another time." She began walking quickly down the hill. The rain pounded the sidewalk with too much force to run efficiently into the gutter. I could imagine her shoes beginning to hydroplane. I pictured her feet, advancing ahead of her body, throwing her torso backwards, the sopping wet umbrella catching the wind and yanking harder until she fell on her back, all her bones, drained of marrow and meat after eighty years, snapping like the stems of crystal wine glasses.

I walked alongside, lengthening my stride to keep pace with her rapid movement. "I can't imagine him having enemies. Would a student who earned a *B* instead of an *A* gun down a professor?"

Lorraine stopped and turned. "Frank was not the charming gentleman you think he was. First, he was not a professor, he was a run-of-the-mill teacher."

"Is there a difference?"

"There certainly is."

"But he was so polite and…"

"Not everyone who dresses sharply and wears a hat is a worthwhile individual."

What she said was the truth, although it depends on the definition of worthwhile. Often, it means someone who has similar beliefs and a lifestyle that mirrors your own. "What do you mean?"

"I mean it's possible he had enemies. And now he's dead. And unless the police are more clever than they've indicated so far, the killer is likely to remain hidden forever."

"It's not so easy to shoot someone and get away with it."

"I don't know why I'm even discussing this. It has nothing to do with either one of us."

"Did he have children? Do you know who inherited his apartment?"

"Why are you intruding where you don't belong?"

Frank had insisted she was not the person she seemed to be and now she was saying the same about him. It was an old and tired story. People love to talk crap about each other.

I hear it at work all the time. One co-worker complains about another. You listen without comment and they assume you're all-in with their viewpoint. Then the object of their rage drops by with a complaint about the other. No matter how much you try to divert them, to not get engaged, they don't notice your non-response, going on as if they have to pour out their aggravation on anything breathing or their brain will explode. They take a non-response as agreement, feeling secure in their imagined position of superiority.

I've heard it all my life. Even in the church where I grew up being warned of the evil of gossip, they loved to verbally inspect the details and dark corners of each other's lives.

"Do you think that woman on the second floor killed him? He seemed a little afraid of her, maybe."

"Why on earth would you think that? Besides, she hasn't been out of her apartment for years." She began walking again.

I tried to follow, but she moved with surprising speed and when I spoke her name, she didn't turn or even give a parting wave. I suppose that was difficult with both of her leather-gloved hands clutching the handle of her umbrella.

45

Portland

Pauline's grin became more gruesome as the sun rose higher and her face began to perspire. Sweat pooled on the small, soft patch of skin below her nose. Sweat lined her lips so she appeared to salivate over the idea of persuading me to make deep, bloody gashes in my skin.

I tried inching away again, but the weight of her body held me in place. My feet were getting pins and needles from the pressure she put on my lower legs.

"You need to do it," she said.

"I don't want to."

"It's better than Vicodin for taking away the pain."

"What's Vicodin?"

"God's little gift to lift your brain into the clouds where you can float for a few hours without hurting."

"From the cuts?"

"Oh, honey. You are such a child."

"Of course I am. I'm ten." I regretted telling her my age. It seemed like the less information I gave her, the better off I'd be.

She laughed. "The pain of a few cuts is nothing. Nothing compared to what life delivers, the longer you live. Just you wait. Whatever it was that made you pack up your itty-bitty sleeping bag and a few apples will look like a picnic when you're my age."

I stared at her.

"Pain in your body is bearable, for the most part. No matter how violent the torture. The main thing is, it eventually stops, and then it fades over time. The cuts scab over, the bruises disappear. The broken bones knit themselves back together. But pain right here…" she slapped her chest, "…that pain gets worse! It never stops, and it eats you alive."

I scratched the back of my head, feeling as if ants might have found their way into my hair while I was sleeping. A tremor of tiny little feet seemed to run all across my scalp. The more vigorously I scratched, the more they scrambled, scattering everywhere so it felt like I had an ant stomping its feet at the root of every single hair. I lifted my other hand and used both to make their way across my entire head, nails clawing frantically.

"Scaring you?" She laughed.

"No. It felt like ants in my hair."

"It's the fear. It turns itself into something recognizable so you can deal with it. The terror of what the world does here," she slammed her fist against her chest, "That's impossible to understand. So we escape to things we can wrap our heads around — ants and spiders and snakes, rapists and gangs and terrorists."

She wasn't making any sense. There had to be a way to get rid of her. Maybe, cutting myself would satisfy her and she'd leave me alone with my granola bars and my *Fear Street* book. "Why are you here?" I forced myself to lower my hands to my lap, to let my scalp shudder and tremble and tickle. I wouldn't let the sensation drive me to look as crazy as this woman pinning my legs to the ground. The itching would go away. Wasn't that what she'd just said? Pain in your body takes care of itself, eventually.

"I live here," she said.

"In the park?"

"In Portland."

"But where in Portland?"

She waved her arm over her head. "Everywhere and nowhere. Now, should we get down to the cutting?"

"Why do you want me to do something so icky?"

"I already said. It will make you feel better."

I hadn't told her I was feeling badly. I couldn't understand why she was so determined to have me join in her disgusting habit. She was just like my father, wanting to force his habits on his children — long hours of prayer, Bible reading. He wanted us to like the same food and TV shows and books that he liked. While I watched her playing with the blade of her knife, I started to understand that every adult wanted to coerce children into doing things their way.

The sun was now hitting my sleeping back with its full force. Between it and the heat from her body, my legs were on fire. I wiggled, trying to tug them out from under her hip.

"Where are you trying to go?" she said.

"You're hurting my legs."

She smiled. "You need more stamina, if you want to live on your own."

"Can you move?"

"We're having a nice talk. And it's comfortable."

"Not for me."

"I'm not moving until you take this knife and try it out."

"Why? I don't know why you want me to do that."

"I'm trying to help you. Help you get rid of the pain."

"I don't have any pain."

"You wouldn't be out here sleeping in a park, completely exposed to so many awful things if you didn't have pain. You're lucky I found you. If a man had seen you — do you know what a pedophile is?"

I shook my head.

"It's a man that wants to touch little girls and little boys in a bad way. And sometimes they regret it, and they slit your throat, or strangle you, or stab your heart. Is that what you want?"

I shook my head.

"It's very dangerous out here."

"It's a nice park."

"Sure it is. When you come here with your mommy and daddy. But you don't like them, do you? That's why you ran away."

I shrugged.

"Didn't your parents teach you more respect? To answer questions when asked?"

"Maybe."

"You're one weird kid."

"I don't think I am."

"Trust me, you are. So why did you run away? What's so awful at home that you'd rather risk all kinds of ugly things done to your body instead of staying in your nice house? With your very own bedroom?"

"How do you know I have my own room?"

She looked down. "Your parents can afford to buy sleeping bags for children. And expensive backpacks. You have nice teeth, and teeth don't get that way on their own. Someone made you brush them every day, took you to the dentist. Should I go on? There are all kinds of clues, if you really look at a person."

My feet had gone completely numb. I tried wrenching my legs from beneath her. She hardly seemed to notice my writhing.

"Are you going to tell me? Why you took off?"

There wasn't anything she could do with the information. It wouldn't give her any power over my life. At least none that I could think of. "I don't belong with them."

"Do they beat you?"

"No."

"Father or brother sneaking into your bed and putting his hands all over you?"

"No."

"Why don't you belong with them?"

It was too complicated.

She seemed to enjoy bothering me and she acted as if she had all day to sit on my legs. Maybe several days. She was probably bored and I was her entertainment. She wanted to make me afraid of being cut, and she was annoyed that I wasn't afraid.

"Does it hurt in here?" She put her hand to her heart again. Then, she lowered it and pulled the blade out of the narrow slot in the handle.

"No."

"Well something hurts or you wouldn't be sleepin' in the park."

"Nothing hurts!"

"Liar." Without changing her expression or really shifting her position all that much, she grabbed my arm and drew the blade across. It was a very gentle movement and I felt nothing. Blood bubbled up in a thin line. I closed my eyes, not wanting to watch it ooze out of my body.

"That's what you get for not tasting my blood." She laughed hysterically.

It seemed as if I was growing faint, but I couldn't open my eyes. Not with knowing my blood was draining out of my vein, right there in front of me.

46

San Francisco

It was ten-thirty in the morning when Jen woke. She hadn't gotten home until one-thirty the night before and was too wound up to sleep, so she'd had a rather large glass of wine, followed quickly by a second glass, and watched a movie that she'd already forgotten the name of.

She picked up her phone and checked messages for hook-up requests. There were three. Decent enough guys. She tapped a quick response to accept their suggested meeting times and then opened her regular messages. Nothing new. Before she had time to second-guess herself, she typed out a message to Alexandra.

Jen Miller: *Want to meet for Pho after you get off work?*

She tucked the phone under the pillow and tried to close her eyes, but they had that jittery feeling they got when she was super wide awake, and even closing them for a moment took too much effort. They seemed to pop open on their own. She might as well get up, but the day stretched before her, empty and bleached with a sameness that made her want to smoke a joint just so she had a chance of falling back to sleep, erasing the day entirely. The phone buzzed and she pulled it out from under the pillow.

Alex: *Sure. What time?*

Jen Miller: *Whenever you can.*

Alex: *Six-forty-five?*

Jen tapped a thumb's up and got out of bed. It amazed her how a few words exchanged with Alex made her feel like a real person. It almost seemed as if she had a friend, and she'd lost most of those. Not that her former friends knew exactly where she was or what she was doing. They hadn't turned in disgust and dumped her for becoming a hooker. She hadn't given them the chance. Their disappearance from her life wasn't really their fault. She'd deleted her Twitter and Instagram accounts.

After a while, a rather short while, they didn't notice she was slowly disappearing from Facebook. She stopped with the thumbs up and the laughing and crying faces. She checked in once a day, then once every few days. She received fewer and fewer alerts, no one messaged her or tagged her in photographs. She'd hidden her birthdate, so they all forgot about it. No one really knew when your birthday was unless you made it visible. Then, Facebook reminded them so they could dutifully write *Happy Birthday* with a cake or a gift emoji.

She took a shower, eager to dress in normal clothes — jeans and a white sweater and low-heeled boots. Six-forty-five in the evening was a long time away. She blew her hair dry and made coffee. She sat at the bar and drank two cups of coffee and ate three slices of whole grain toast with thick, glossy-red strawberry jam, the bits of strawberry like clots of blood.

There had to be something she could do, somewhere to spend the day besides sitting around her apartment thinking about which slutty outfit she should wear to her ten o'clock appointment tonight.

She put on her coat and rode the elevator to the first floor. She walked through the lobby, the only person at this time of day when everyone else was at normal jobs. The echo of her boots on the marble floor seemed to fill the entire space. The guard at the desk looked up, nodded, and went back to texting.

She shoved open the door and stepped out onto the sidewalk.

Now that she was out, she felt she could breathe, but she had no idea where she was headed. She glanced toward the alcove just past the bank of doors leading to the lobby. The homeless woman wasn't in her usual spot, but Jen was rarely outside before mid-afternoon, usually later. It was likely the woman packed up and left before the sun was even up, to avoid being chased away.

She turned and headed toward The Embarcadero. Even if there was no real destination, at least she could go for a long walk. It was something to do, and it would make her hungry for lunch, unlike lying around watching TV all day did. Most days, that's exactly how she spent her time. The result was a steady flood of snacks and soda, so she never had much of a real appetite for lunch, and sometimes not even dinner. Then, she'd be starving late in the evening and end up gorging on a hamburger and onion rings. The only healthy thing was the occasional turkey sandwich and her bowls of steaming Pho.

Thinking about her shitty diet made her want to cry. She walked faster, hoping the cool air biting at her cheeks and brushing across the surface of her eyes would make the tears evaporate. Her whole life made her feel shitty.

She crossed the street to the wide sidewalk that ran along the edge of the bay, past the Ferry Building, toward the Exploratorium. She shoved her hands in her pockets and kept her gaze on the pavement, not wanting to meet the eyes of anyone she passed, especially women dressed for work, people with places to go. Groups of women smiling and heading out for lunches in nice restaurants where they left large tips. They simply scribbled their names on the receipts, not even thinking about what the credit card bill might look like at the end of the month.

When a man handed four one-hundred dollar bills to Jen after an hour of sex, it seemed like a lot of money. But the rent in her tiny studio was outrageous. It was worth the price to feel secure, to know that no one knew what she did or assumed they knew just because she lived at a certain address, but it meant cutting corners on clothes and food and entertainment. The cable connection and the internet, included in the rent, provided her only entertainment. That, and her trips to the apartment building lounge where she tried to stick to beer and ate too many of the free snacks. Of course, the pretzels and nuts weren't really free, they were also buried in the cost of the apartment along with those lovely security people who kept her safe, but had to be avoided.

She felt a hand on her shoulder. She jumped to the side, stepping on the toe of a man trying to weave around her after her sudden move. "Watch it." He hurried on before she could even see his face.

The man touching her shoulder was only an inch or two taller than Jen. He wore a dark gray suit and white shirt, but no tie. "I know you," he said.

Jen smiled cautiously, only the suggestion of pleasure.

"You remember." He laughed. "Sir Henry?"

Oh. Right. The guy whose fantasy involved receiving a knighthood, who liked to talk dirty in a very bad British accent, and insisted she call him *Sir*. There wasn't any rough stuff with it, so she didn't mind. She'd mostly been embarrassed for him. She'd seen him three times and remembered clearly. She'd thought he might become a regular — one that made her yearn for it to be over out of sheer boredom, but who at least never made her feel afraid.

"You remember. I can see it in your eyes."

She gave him a minimal smile. "Yes."

"I lost your number. Can I get it again?"

She looked around. "It's better to book…I don't think this is a good place…"

"It's fine. We could be colleagues catching up."

She glanced down at her fairly expensive, yet scuffed and slightly faded leather boots. Her jeans from the Gap.

"You look great. Lots of tech workers dress like that. Don't worry." He took her elbow and maneuvered her off the path to a gravel area near a concrete bench.

Of course he wasn't worried. The men never had to worry. She was the one with the face that might be recognized. She was the one the building security noted coming home long after midnight most nights. Not that the security manager would be out wandering along The Embarcadero. He stayed close to the building he was responsible for. But still, at some point he took a lunch break.

It didn't matter what the odds were, she was nervous. Always thinking about it, and even when there was no risk, the constant thinking had created a small pool of paranoia in the center of her gut making her view *everything* as a risk. Thinking about it often made her think of it more, and it had grown into thinking of it all the fucking time. Always looking over her shoulder, always worried she'd be recognized. Trying to alter her looks slightly so some of the hotel desk clerks and security guards didn't begin to notice she visited too often. She never arrived with a man, but the arrival itself was a red flag.

Her skin felt clammy. She glanced behind her again.

"So can I get your number?"

"Sure."

"Why are you whispering?" he said.

She coughed. Her throat felt tight. She coughed harder. "I don't know."

"I don't suppose you have a card."

She laughed.

"Didn't think so."

She glanced toward the buildings across the street. The usual flow of foot traffic passed in front of them. No one was looking her way. Why did she feel so anxious? It was the time of day causing her heart to beat too fast, and standing in plain view on a street where she didn't belong.

He pulled a business card and pen out of his coat pocket. "What is it?"

As she spoke, he scribbled her number on the back of the card and drew a misshapen heart in the upper left corner. "That's how I'll remember you."

"Okay."

"Anyway, good to see you. I'll call."

"It's actually better to book online, you…"

He shoved the card and pen in his pocket. "Don't have time to write down a web address right now. Good seeing you." He leaned forward and kissed her full on the lips. Then, as if that hadn't attracted enough attention, he grabbed her ass with both hands and squeezed hard. "Sir Henry is ready."

She held her body stiffly, hardly breathing, unable to turn to see how many people were staring.

He let go and smacked her ass. "See ya'." He walked away, strode, really, as if he'd just conquered her world.

Taking a casual walk was no longer appealing. She should crawl back to her three-hundred-square-foot apartment and hide her face like the cockroach she was. And for that matter, why was she so damned worried about the woman who'd been pissed on? She needed to worry about her own life and make sure she didn't end up in an even worse position. She couldn't be sticking her neck out to save someone she didn't even know. If the woman didn't want to be pissed on, she needed to move.

Jen turned.

A few yards away, Scott stood near a hot dog vendor. He was staring straight at her. He didn't smile or nod or give any suggestion of recognition, but she knew he recognized her. And she knew he'd seen the whole thing.

47

I was a little early leaving to meet Jen for Pho, but I was done with work and hanging around a Pho place was more appealing than huddling within the inadequate walls of a cubicle. I'd told Jen six-forty-five to be sure I wasn't late. A buffer is always good. Besides, I figured I could find a table and get settled in.

Jen's addiction to Pho was hard to understand. I enjoy it every few months, but Jen chose it as her default meal. She ate Pho three or four nights a week, maybe every night. She couldn't seem to think of any other type of food. Maybe the broth was comforting to her.

As I walked toward the elevators, desk lights glowed in most of the cubicles. People were huddled up to their large screens, working silently, some wearing headphones to make sure they signaled *no interruptions*. Often, five to seven in the evening was the only time to actually get work done. The days overflowed with meetings. Meetings gave birth to meetings, so many with questionable value — constant status updates, updates to the next level of management who then updated the group above them. The larger the company grew, the more meetings required to keep everyone marching in the same direction, or even knowing what the hell was going on.

I pressed the button for the lobby.

"Hi there Miss Elusive."

I turned. Steve stood a few feet away, arms folded across his chest, shoulders back. Possibly the self-confident pose was trying to compensate for his hair. It was painfully short from a recent haircut that had gone a little too far. Most of the male execs did a good job of obsessively trimming their hair every few weeks so there was never a sudden change in appearance. They cared for their hair like they did their cars — always polished — but unlike their cars, maintained to avoid attracting attention. The sheered back and sides made him seem younger.

I smiled and said *hi*.

The elevator dinged and the doors slid open. I stepped inside.

"You can't escape that fast." He followed me into the elevator. The doors waited patiently for half a moment too long. They finally eased their way closed, as if they'd wanted to give us a last-minute chance to escape.

"Time for a drink?" he said.

"I have plans."

He leaned against the wall and stretched his legs out, crossing them at the ankles and folding his arms. It was a lot of effort for a pose he'd have to unwind within thirty seconds, maybe less.

He unfolded himself and shoved his hands in his pockets. "I'm going to put myself out there." He laughed and looked up at the ceiling. "Our dinner ended badly. And our meet-up for drinks wasn't much better."

"No worries."

He looked at me. "I shouldn't have let that homeless guy assault you. I'm sorry I didn't protect you adequately." He let out a puff of air. "There. I said it. Not easy for a man to admit."

"I don't need protection, so it wasn't a problem."

The bell chimed and the doors opened. We stepped into the lobby and moved away from the elevator, although at that time of day, no one was waiting to go up.

"He assaulted you and I didn't..."

"Not the first time."

"Do bums do that a lot?" He looked genuinely shocked.

"Depends on how you define *bum*."

"Well it caught me off guard. And I should have come to your defense."

"It really isn't necessary. I can take care of myself."

He stiffened. "You may be the tough little feminist, but some jobs require a man."

"What jobs are those?"

"Jobs that demand strength. Beating off an attack like that."

"I've found that thinking one step ahead is more effective than brute strength."

"Why do you call it brute strength?"

"Because that's all it is. Muscle and bone. Taking care of yourself requires more mental strength. Surely you know that from your career."

He ran his hand through his too-short hair. "I'm trying to apologize here."

"And I'm trying to explain I don't need protection. Or an apology."

He stared at me, his gaze hard and his expression impossible to read. It could be interpreted as angry, insulted, or threatening. But there was no threat. I could take his job offer, or not. Assuming a real job offer existed.

A part of me felt an intense desire to try something different. Working in sales, where I'd actually be challenged to learn something new, was appealing. But I also have a streak of laziness. In my current job, I didn't have to drive to appointments across the city or in the south bay. In this job, I was only occasionally required to give up my evening hours. In sales, it would be a given that I'd spend evenings preparing strategic conversations for customers I'd be meeting the following day.

More money. Pushing myself to be more than I was, versus decent money and a boss who was wowed by me, most of the time. The other part of the equation was a man I really did not want to work for. A man who turned my stomach. It was fun chatting with him, seeing whether I could keep him confused and off balance, but not a man I wanted to spend a lot of time with.

He continued staring at me.

I smiled.

"Tess said you're difficult to manage."

The skin of my face grew cold and my smile hardened. My stomach caved, disappearing for a moment. I took a slow breath. He'd only said it to throw me off course. His view of manhood was *rescuing hero*. He needed me to know he wasn't a failure. He needed me to know he had power. I hadn't buttered up his ego, so now he was out for me. Was there a core of truth in what he said, or was it a total fabrication to frighten me into going to work for him? Was this my gut revealing my decision then? My instinct telling me that money and career growth were not worth letting a man like this be the one deciding my day-to-day fate?

"Surprised you, didn't I."

I didn't say anything.

"You're not as slick and secure as you thought. It's a

shock, knowing your boss talks behind your back. Knowing she discusses all her employees' strengths and flaws with her peers. You see, we're a management team. We work for the good of the company overall. And Tess…" He stopped.

I waited for half a minute. "And Tess, what?"

"That's all. I just want it to be clear where you stand."

"And where is that?"

"You can't play us against each other."

"I'm not." Truly, I wasn't. Maybe a little, but not in the way he seemed to think.

"I'm not stupid, Alex. And neither is Tess."

"I never thought you were."

"But maybe easy to manipulate." He smiled. "No need to respond to that. If you're interested in an entry-level position in sales, let me know. I still think you'd be good at it. But if not, no *worries.*" He turned and strode toward the doors leading to The Embarcadero. He didn't look back.

48

It was a triumph of Jen's willpower that she was still meeting Alex for Pho. A very large part of her would have preferred to strip off her jeans and sweater, stuff her body into sweatpants and a fleece coverup, and smoke half a joint. She would watch TV and eat Doritos until it was time to go out in high heels and scratchy, tugging, pinching lingerie that looked awesome and made her feel like a roast tied with string.

But Alex had agreed to meet and not showing up wasn't an option. Texting that she was canceling would require an explanation. If it was true that vulnerability was the key to good relationships, maybe she could tell Alex everything she was feeling, even the awful stuff, and they would become real friends. It seemed like they were halfway there already.

She couldn't wear the jeans that *Sir Henry* had smacked his grubby hands all over, even though they'd been clean that morning. She dropped them in the laundry basket and chose a new pair.

The Pho place was a few blocks away, but it felt like ten, as she twisted her upper body this way and that, straining her neck looking for Scott, certain that he was following her, that he'd been following her earlier. She reached the restaurant and pulled open the door. The steamy warmth of the interior wrapped around her and she felt slightly less anxious. She gave one last glance over her shoulder and stepped inside. Alex was already seated at a table beside the front window.

Alex smiled when Jen sat down. Jen felt her own face

respond, and her shoulders return to their normal position.

They ordered beef pho and a liter of sparkling water to share. Alex poured a shot into each opaque plastic glass and lifted hers in a toast. Jen tapped the rim of her glass against Alex's. Sparkling water splashed onto the back of her hand, bubbles tickling her skin. "Oops." She licked it off and took a sip. "What are we toasting?"

"Whatever. Pho, I guess," Alex said.

"Dinner with a friend." Jen gave Alex a tiny smile and took another sip.

Alex smiled, but she appeared to be looking past Jen. The sensation was intense enough that Jen turned, fearing Scott's sneering face.

No one was there.

They ate their soup, slurping and not caring if it sounded low class. Alex talked about the cockatoo and the man who'd been murdered in Tess's neighborhood.

Jen told her about two movies she'd seen, just released to streaming. She told her about running into *Sir Henry* and his grabby behavior.

"That is so wrong!" Alex said.

"I hate it when they see me in my regular life. It doesn't happen very often, and I guess I shouldn't be surprised, but I always am."

"It's like stealing."

"What can I do about it? It's not like I can flag down a cop." She laughed and refilled both glasses. She thought about mentioning Scott, but what was the point? Sitting across from Alex, the paranoid thoughts, whispering that Scott had guessed all about her, faded into tiny bubbles like the ones dissolving across the surface of the water, no longer popping and shooting up pinpricks of carbonation. "I wish I could stop."

"Stop…being a call girl?"

"Yes."

"Why?" Alex pinched her chopsticks around a thin piece of beef and put it in her mouth.

"Are you kidding? Because it sucks. Because I have no life, no guy, no job, no friends, no…I just exist."

"Are you not making enough? I bet you could raise your rates. There's a lot of cash flowing through this city. Especially around here. And you have class."

The compliment twisted inside, warming and disgusting in a way Jen couldn't separate. "But I hate doing it. I feel like I don't exist. I feel like every man is…I don't know. It's hard to explain."

Alex stared at her.

Jen shivered. There was something about Alex… sometimes Jen wondered if she had any feelings. Like her love for that creepy painting in the lounge, showing the woman's bones and muscles and the optic nerve where it attached to her eyeballs. She put her hands between her thighs, trying to stop their trembling as the memory of the grotesque image filled her mind. She'd assumed Alex would completely understand why she wanted to escape. Who thought the best plan for a hooker was to raise her rates?

"You don't answer to anyone. You make good money. You don't have to work long hours. A regular job is overrated."

"But in a regular job, everyone treats you like you're normal, like you're part of society. I'm like…I don't know. I don't fit in. I can't talk about anything."

"There are lots of things to talk about. Movies. Sports. Who wants to talk about work anyway? Most people who go on about their jobs at parties are boring."

"Maybe. I don't like being with all these men. I feel like they own my body."

"That's in your head. You own your body. You decide who, you decide the price, you decide the time and place."

"But so many. I feel…used." She felt her eyes filling with tears. She blinked and picked up her glass. The sparkling water was gone. "You really think it's not a horrible life?"

"There are worse lives. Living on the street. Not making enough to afford a decent place to live so you have to deal with rats and insects. Living in a marriage where you don't even get to think your own thoughts."

"Yeah."

Neither one spoke.

Alex leaned on the table. "Yes, having sex with a lot of men is not ideal. It would be better if you could choose a handful, maybe. Get them to pay much higher rates. But I'm telling you, I have a job that looks good on the outside, except there's this guy…and my boss. They act like they own you. I don't get to make any decisions about how I spend my time or whether I have to do the same stupid project over three times because they changed their minds about what they want." She swallowed the rest of her sparkling water. "I'm not saying there aren't downsides to what you do, there definitely are, but right now, not having to answer to someone in order to get money sounds fantastic to me."

Jen stacked the empty glasses and pushed them toward the window. "Want to come over to my apartment? For a drink or something?"

"I can't. I'm already really late feeding that bird. He'll be screaming his head off at me. I'm supposed to go right back there after work. He's on a schedule."

"Maybe another time." Jen felt as if her lungs were collapsing inside her chest. She would never have a friend. Not really. Her life was going to be one long dreary march through hotel rooms until she was too old. And then what? Alex was insane if she thought this was any kind of life.

"I was going to have Isaiah come to Tess's place and make a gourmet dinner, to show off what he's learned. Do you want to come too?"

"When?"

"I don't know. It's a bit difficult to get you inside, since visitors aren't technically allowed, but I'll work it out. Maybe Saturday? I'll ask him."

Only a few words, and now Jen felt her lungs re-inflating, filling her body with a warm flood of…contentment, maybe.

49

Although I prefer early morning runs, I didn't go out until nine the next morning. The rain had stopped, but low clouds hovered near the tops of the buildings and a sharp, bitter coldness clung to the air. I went out later because I planned to linger outside, waiting for the woman to make her appearance. I was certain she would notice me, as she stood behind the sheer curtains for most of the day, lingering.

I ran two miles. A shorter route than usual, but the woman in the window got my blood pumping far more than my feet pounding on pavement. Soon, Tess would return and any chance of finding out the woman's story would be ripped out of my hands.

Seated on the bench across from her apartment, I sipped water from my refillable container. I'd left it on the bench while I ran, hoping for the best, and it was still there when I returned. I snapped the top closed and held the container in both hands.

It was a good ten minutes before I saw a slight movement in the curtains. I thought I glimpsed two fingers sliding between the pieces of fabric, but couldn't be sure. Part of me wanted to stop being coy, pretending I was casually watching, and cross the street. I'd stand beneath the window and stare up at her with the same intensity exhibited when she faced passersby.

It wasn't that I was trying to hide what I was doing, at least not from her, but neither did I want to go out of my way to attract attention. She and I had an understanding, I felt.

I didn't want one of the detectives to return and ask what I was doing. I didn't want to risk another neighbor challenging me and end up causing problems for Tess.

I took a few sips of water and put my container on the bench. I crossed my legs, leaned against the hard, cold back of the bench, and waited. My hoodie and my rapidly circulating blood were keeping me warm, but soon my heart rate would return to normal and the chill would set in.

A few minutes later, both hands appeared, pressed flat against the glass. I saw the hazy outline of her shoulders and head, her long pale hair like a curtain itself, the ends falling past the lower edge of the window, suggesting her hair hung as far as her hips.

She pulled her hands back and the left one returned. She began drawing on the glass, using the same thick red liquid as before. She drew large, misshapen ovals. She pressed her hand to the glass and began wiping at the shapes until only a large smear remained. Below that, she traced her finger more slowly. There was more paint, or blood, than she'd used the last time.

Any rational interpretation would insist it was paint, yet there was something deep in the pit of my stomach that knew it was blood. I think there was something about the consistency, remembering the blood that ran down my arm when Pauline sliced it with her tiny knife. It was the only time I'd willingly watched blood run, and it has an unmistakable life and consistency of its own.

Had she put on her show for the detectives who were investigating Frank's death? I found that difficult to believe, but she didn't seem to concern herself with who observed her. If there was a breathing body in the street, she began her performance.

Simply knowing what she wanted was no longer my only goal. I was desperate to know whether the detectives had managed an interview with her. Of course, law enforcement has their ways, and their right to get the information they want. At least, they have the right to ask for it. Whether they get the truth, or even a lie, instead of cold silence is not in their hands. If they'd wanted to question her, surely they had.

Her finger moved slowly across the glass, dragging blood as if it were flowing from the tip of a pen. The symbol that emerged was a large, well-shaped question mark. A question mark that was almost seductive in its curves. The hand disappeared and nothing disturbed the curtains for quite a while.

I drank some water and looked away, letting my gaze go to the place on the front stoop where I'd seen Frank's corpse, still and limp as a pile of soggy, discarded clothing. Had Frank recognized the person who shot him? Had he been given a few minutes to consider that his life was coming to an end? I haven't usually offered that courtesy to people, but they've been deserving of death. Did someone view Frank as deserving of the same? Obviously they had. Or else they hated him. Or feared him. But who can fear a smart, sharply dressed, friendly gentleman nearing the end of his life all on his own?

There are lots of reasons for hate. I knew nothing about his personal life, and nothing more than a two-line bio about his professional life.

The curtains remained still. I was getting cold, a chill

seeping through my spandex pants, crawling through the fabric of my sweatshirt, lingering sweat making the cold deeper. I stood and waited several more minutes.

I was tired of being an observer.

I had to find a way to get inside that woman's apartment and meet her face to face. I had to find out what was wrong with her, and whether she'd heard the gunshot that killed Frank. Or, possibly, if she'd pulled the trigger herself.

She'd been crying out to me all along, and the only thing I'd done was sit and watch. Possibly, she was as frustrated with me as I was with her.

50

It was an obvious ploy, but I decided to buy a bouquet of gladiolas for the woman next door. If she answered the door, which was an enormous if, the soft white blossoms would catch her attention and open a toehold.

Based on her reclusive history, I expected no response. If she was held in there by someone stronger, even someone who was armed, someone who controlled her mind, she certainly wouldn't be answering the door. If she had access to the door, to a face-to-face conversation, why the antics in front of the window? It was also possible she was simply mad, sending messages from a world that existed only inside her own skull. In that case, maybe she would answer the door.

Tucked among the stems was a card with my name, phone number, and email address. I waited until dusk, hoping to avoid the mail carrier, any delivery people, and Lorraine. The occupant of the top floor still hadn't made an appearance, at least not that I was aware of. The entire structure was riddled with questions. Maybe that's why she drew a question mark on the window. That, or she was referring to questions from the detectives. Or a question about Frank's killer. It might be a question mark about me, or why this was happening in her life, whatever *this* was.

I climbed the front steps and entered the lobby. In most apartment buildings, someone has to unlock the door to admit you after you press a bell outside the building, or in the lobby. I wasn't sure if the lack of security was due to the age of the building, or they were just lax, most of them having lived there before the world became more crowded, and threats spilled over the edges of so-called bad neighborhoods.

I entered the elevator and pressed the button for the second floor. The ride was brief. The doors opened slowly and I was looking at her door, painted a glossy turquoise. I stepped out and moved to the edge of the doormat — a plain sheet of rubber with shallow grooves.

To my right was a small rectangular table. A glass vase stood in the center. The glass was clear with a semi-transparent dark pink interior that faded to gray where the glass fanned out at the top. The scalloped edges were nearly hidden by drooping stalks from a large bunch of wildflowers. Some of the wilted leaves clung to the glass with a touch of white furry mold along the edges. The small space stank of sour water and decay.

I knocked on the door.

The space was silent, and there was no suggestion of movement — footsteps or a person clearing her throat, even breathing — on the other side of the door. I pulled the gladiolas closer to my chest, feeling their blossoms like cool fingers touching my cheek. The flowers trembled as I shifted my feet, my knees stiff from standing in one position for several minutes. I coughed.

Moving the flowers to the other arm, I stepped onto the mat and put my ear up to the door. The silence was as complete as it had been from my spot a few inches away. I rapped on the door with the heel of my hand, causing a muffled thud that went nowhere. I stabbed my finger at the doorbell. There was no sound audible outside the apartment so I couldn't be sure it was working.

I set the flowers on the doormat. I slid the vase along the table to the end, which succeeded in knocking three dead blossoms onto the floor. I picked them up and set them by the vase. I placed the gladiolas on the table, wiggling the card so it was buried more deeply, hoping to ensure the only one who saw it would be the person who removed the cellophane.

Inside the elevator, as the doors closed slowly, I stared at the turquoise door, hoping at the last minute, it would swing open and I'd see the woman with the long, ragged hair. Nothing happened.

The lobby was empty and the street was equally deserted when I walked out of the building. I stopped beneath her window and looked up. The curtains as well as the drapes behind them were drawn. I waited for five or ten minutes, my neck growing stiff from holding my head at the angle required to see the window.

I don't know what I'd hoped for. Did I think she'd come to the window and wave down at me, shaking the bouquet to indicate she'd received it? She would throw away the rotten wildflowers, filling the vase in the hallway with gladiolas. As she arranged them inside the thick glass, the envelope would fall out. She'd unseal the flap, pull out the card, and see my name. She'd call me, or rush to her laptop or tablet and send me email, inviting me up for tea.

I laughed at myself, turned, and walked back to Tess's building.

Something was terribly wrong up there.

51

The sun was out and the air was warm enough to lounge around Tess's balcony without a jacket. I was sipping French roast coffee out of a thin white cup, enjoying the aroma as much as I did the taste.

I looked down at the sidewalk and saw a woman walking with precise, but rapid steps, careful of keeping her body protected from unwanted encounters with rough patches in the pavement, concrete planters, and the occasional person darting out from a building. Fairly certain it was Lorraine, I leaned over the railing to get a better look. As if I'd called her name, she lifted her chin slightly and I knew it was her.

It was ridiculous to continue thinking I could draw any information out of her. She was as stubborn as...she was as stubborn as I was. I laughed out loud. Through the partially open sliding glass door, Damien heard me and felt compelled to mimic my tone. I walked over and slid the door closed.

Despite her eager suggestion of more dinners, her wish that I might meet her son, her yearning to schedule regular dates for afternoon tea, she seemed to be avoiding me since Frank had been killed. Until that moment, her behavior wasn't making sense, but now it occurred to me that she might be afraid. She refused to reveal what the police had asked, but if they were pursuing any particular direction, they might have mentioned something that scared her.

After I finished my coffee, I went inside. I ate a banana and changed into a sundress and sandals. I grabbed my credit card and phone and walked to the flower shop. This time, I selected yellow roses. Twenty-four. The bouquet was enormous and extravagant, but I needed to get her attention in a big way. I needed another invite inside of her apartment.

I returned to Tess's like a rat, scurrying along the sidewalk, close to the buildings, eyes darting in every direction, hoping I didn't run into her. The impact would be deadened if she saw the splashy bouquet before I was standing outside her door.

I placed the flowers on the kitchen counter while I picked up clothes that had been tossed all over the guest room. I did the same with my cosmetic bottles and boxes and brushes spread across the bathroom counter. I watered the plants, which had missed their mid-week drink. They looked healthy as ever, so I didn't think Tess would notice what a poor caretaker I was. Of course, the bird might inform her of that, finding a way to let her know I'd stopped for Pho before giving him dinner, and that I hadn't spent the required number of weekend hours chatting with him. I vowed to do better with the plants and the bird.

Lunch was a roast beef sandwich on dark rye bread with alfalfa sprouts, tomatoes that were easy to slice paper thin with one of Tess's magnificent knives, and a light spread of mayonnaise on each slice of bread. I drank a glass of water, refilling the glass as soon as I was finished eating.

At two, I pulled a bottle of Syrah from Tess's wine rack and put it in a canvas bag that I hung over my arm.

Lorraine opened her door the moment I rang the bell. Either she'd seen me approach the building, or she was simply eager for company. She smiled and stepped back so I could enter.

"What gorgeous roses." She smiled, somewhat eagerly.

Inside, I handed the bouquet to her.

"What's the occasion?" Her voice was shrill, tinged with excitement and a hint of something like fear.

"Sympathy."

"That's not necessary. Frank…"

"He lived in your building for so many years. I know it's a loss, even if you weren't close."

"It is strange, not seeing him around. I'm surprised by how much I think of him." Her voice grew softer. "I didn't…" She crossed the room and laid the bouquet on the dining room table. She touched one of the petals. "They're beautiful. I should put them in water." She picked up the bouquet. It covered her chest and shoulders and half her face. She went to the kitchen and I followed. She took a vase out of the cabinet and filled it with water. I unwrapped the stems and trimmed the ends with a large pair of shears she provided.

When the flowers were arranged in the vase, I carried it to the living room. "Where do you want them?"

She pointed to an end table and I set them down.

"Should I open the wine?" I said.

"I don't drink wine in the afternoon."

"This is an exception, don't you think?"

"Why?"

"Toasting Frank's memory."

She didn't say anything.

"Do you know if there's going to be a memorial?"

"I haven't heard."

"Has anyone been by to check his apartment?"

"Not that I've noticed."

"It's so strange. Well, you and I should remember him."

"All right." She went into the kitchen again, returning several minutes later with two glasses, half full.

We sat on the sofa and tapped our glasses against each other. "To Frank," I said.

She smiled and took a sip.

"I'm sure there will be some sort of memorial."

She shrugged.

"You don't seem very interested."

"We weren't close."

"Would you go to his memorial?"

"It will probably be at the college. I wouldn't know anyone."

"Have the detectives been back to talk to you again?"

"You seem awfully interested in the details."

"He was murdered. It brings out natural curiosity, don't you think?" I took a sip of wine and put my glass on the table.

"You have an excessive amount of curiosity," she said.

"I do."

"It's not attractive." Her face was unsmiling, her lips drawn down, making her look old. When I'd first met her, I didn't think she looked her age, but now, she seemed ancient.

The room suddenly grew cooler than it had been. I glanced over my shoulder.

"What are you looking at?" she said.

"Is there a window open? It's cold."

"You're wearing a summer dress. That's why you're cold."

"But I wasn't cold a moment ago."

She smiled. "I think it's comfortable."

Despite her earlier hesitation, her wineglass was almost empty. I stood.

"Where are you going?"

"To get more wine." I went into the kitchen and returned with the bottle. I dribbled some into her glass. I paused. When she didn't object, I dribbled more. She still didn't say anything. I poured a bit more and set the bottle beside her glass.

I walked over to the shelf beside the fireplace and looked at the photographs.

"Again, your unattractive curiosity."

"I can't help it. And I'm not going to apologize for it." I didn't think my curiosity was that unattractive. Why display photographs if they're not meant to be looked at? I leaned closer to the shelf. The photos in the front were formal portraits with studio lighting. Behind them were several more similar shots. Farther back, almost hidden by those in front, were a number of candid shots. I moved closer.

At the back left was a shot of a dark haired woman outdoors on a cloudy day. Her hair blew across her face, but it didn't hide her annoyed expression. Her bangs were mussed by the wind, lifted to the side so her forehead was exposed. There was no mistaking those darkly-shadowed eyes and that mouth — it was Tess.

I straightened suddenly. I stared at Lorraine. She looked at me with a bland expression.

I returned to the sofa and sat beside her. "Does it feel creepy, living in a building with an unoccupied apartment? And another where there's a woman who's...unbalanced, I guess?"

"This is my home. I don't concern myself with the other

apartments. I'm not even aware of them except when I'm going out."

I took a sip of wine.

Her eyelids were drooping. She put her glass on the table. "I really should not have had a drink at this time of day. It makes me very tired." She leaned her head back on the sofa and closed her eyes.

I put my glass on the table and put the strap of my bag over my shoulder. I went to the shelf and waited for a minute or so. Her eyes remained closed. I picked up the photograph of Tess and slipped it into my bag. I walked to the door and opened it carefully. I turned the button lock in the handle and closed the door behind me.

52

The homeless woman wasn't sleeping beside the building when Jen went out to pick up something for dinner. It was early still — only seven-thirty — but it was long past sunset. Had they chased her away for good? Was she now sleeping on a street more commonly inhabited by homeless people, a place that was surely unsafe for a woman, especially a young woman, as her hands had seemed to suggest? Jen had never seen her face up close, the hat was always pulled low, only the tip of her nose showing. She'd only seen her when it was dark.

Jen's feet wanted to walk to the Pho place, already moving out of habit, but her stomach was suddenly tired of soup. A burger would be good. Or maybe a burrito. She couldn't remember if there was a burrito place within easy walking distance. She pulled her phone out of her pocket.

"Hey."

Jen tapped the restaurant locator app and typed in burrito.

"Hey, I'm talking to you."

Jen looked up, blinking as her eyes adjusted from the bright screen to the dim light that filtered out through the thick glass of the lobby doors. Lizzy stood a few feet away. She wore ballet slipper shoes, a short skirt, and a leather jacket. Her hair glistened with gel, combed back into a tight, sleek ponytail. In the darkness, the nearly colorless hair blended with the skin of her face, making her look bald.

"Hi. How are things?" Jen said.

Lizzy smirked. "You tell me."

"I don't know."

"Like hell you don't."

Jen slid her phone into her pocket. For some reason, she felt vulnerable holding it, looking for food, when it seemed as if Lizzy was ready to attack her. "What's wrong?"

"Don't be cute."

"I'm not being anything. I'm not sure what you're asking me."

"I'm asking you to stay the fuck away from my boyfriend."

"Okay. I don't really…"

"Who do you think you are?"

"What are you talking about?" Jen took a few steps to the side. Her stomach growled. She was starving and she had no interest in getting into a fight. Especially one that had no purpose that she could figure out.

"You act all moral and superior and you have no right."

"I don't think…"

"That homeless woman stinks. She's filthy and she doesn't belong here. At first I thought you were just being nice, that you were some kind of saint, but now…"

"She can't help that she smells. She doesn't have a place to shower."

"And whose fault is that?"

Jen smiled, hoping it would make Lizzy back off from whatever was making her so upset. "I feel so sorry for her. Don't you? She's almost our age, I think."

"I don't feel sorry at all. And I don't *feel* you have a right to go around telling other people how they should feel. Yeah, maybe Scott shouldn't have done that, but men pee wherever, and they aren't so private as women."

"Not on a person!"

"Well it's not that big of a deal. He was a little drunk."

"He knew what he was doing."

"You don't get to pretend you're Miss Pure and Perfect."

"I didn't."

"You tried to get him in trouble. And you tried to manipulate me into joining your crusade, or whatever it is. I know what you're trying to do. And you have no right."

"I feel bad for her. It's horrible to pee on a human being. Anyone who doesn't think that is sub-human."

"Is that right?" Lizzy stepped closer. She put her face within a few inches of Jen's. "What does it mean to be sub-human, as you so expertly call it?"

"Do you really think that's how people should treat each other?"

"I think classy people should treat each other with class. And I think the deadbeats should stay in their areas and not infect the rest of us. Or preferably, get their shit together. She's probably diseased. She could be dangerous. Like a rabid dog."

Jen had no idea what to say. Lizzy had obviously lived a pampered life. Her voice was warm and her smile seemed to say *let's be friends*. The outfits Jen had seen her wearing stirred up envy, but not a hateful kind of envy, more of a craving kind, a feeling of being impressed by her clever choices and good taste. Everything about her appearance said she was a good person, but Jen was shocked by her ugly view of humanity. She was like an avocado with smooth, glossy skin, firm and seemingly perfect. When you cut it open, the pale green fruit had gaping holes and mushy black decay. How could she be so downright cruel? She was the most ungrateful person Jen had ever met.

"Don't stand there with your mouth open, your tiny brain will fall out," Lizzy said.

"I don't know what to say."

"I'm not asking you to say anything. I want to tell you to keep away from Scott. He doesn't need your moral superiority and someone who does the things you do has no right to tell other people how to live their lives. That's all. But mostly, I don't want you trying to hook up with him. Is that clear?"

"Why on earth would I do that? He disgusts me."

"And you disgust me." Lizzy turned and began walking toward the corner. Before she reached it, a Mercedes pulled up to the curb at an angle. The passenger door opened, and Lizzy slipped inside. The door slammed shut, the car made a sharp U-turn, and sped up the street.

They knew. Scott knew. He'd told Lizzy. The whole time Lizzy was talking, something had been spinning inside Jen's head, making it hard to figure out what she would say next, and so she'd blurted out things she wouldn't normally. Scott had guessed her relationship with whatever-his-name-was. If she avoided Scott and Lizzy, if she never even smiled or said *hi*, if she didn't look in their direction, would they leave her alone? Would they forget about her?

She shivered and began walking toward the Pho place.

53

The gym is my go-to place when my brain is racing so fast I think it's turning into a whirlpool that will suck my conscious mind below the surface. Pushing my muscles to do what they were designed to do has a way of pulling those runaway thoughts back into place. It's also the breathing. Concentrating so your breath flows in the opposite direction of what your instinct tells you — contract the muscle, breathe out, relax it, breathe in — when what your body wants, is to gasp for air as you exert yourself. The blood rushing to my muscles, the concentration of performing a strenuous task, and the breathing lasso my thoughts and put them in order.

I was lying on my back on the bench beneath a barbell holding 139 pounds. My hands, sheathed in padded, fingerless gloves, gripped the bar. My eyes were closed and I was breathing slowly.

"Are you done?"

I opened my eyes. A woman stood a few feet from my knees, hands on her hips.

"No."

"Taking a nap?"

I laughed. "No. One more set. Just a minute." I lifted the bar off the rack and lowered it slowly, annoyed that I'd now forgotten what I was trying to think about, and slightly off balance because I needed one hundred percent of my mind on the 139 pounds and my breath, not skittering about searching for a lost thought.

After eight reps, my brain was still twisting around trying to recall what I'd been thinking about. I lowered the barbell to the rack and sat up. The minute I stood, the woman moved to the barbell.

I only gloated a little bit as she released the clips and slid twenty-five pounds of plates off one side of the barbell. I didn't wait to watch her balance the other side. I walked to the lat pulldown and settled on the padded seat.

Tess. That's what I'd been thinking about.

It was possible Lorraine had taken the photograph with Tess's knowledge, but Tess didn't appear to be looking directly at the camera, so maybe not. Her pose was casual. If she was aware of the picture, would she consider it none of my business to know why it was sitting in Lorraine's living room? And why on earth would Lorraine have her photograph, no matter if Tess knew or not? Was she some weird kind of stalker, taking pictures of young women? But half the photos were studio shots obviously given to her by their subjects. Who were they?

I did four sets of lat pulldowns and went to the squat cage.

By the time I'd finished four sets of twelve, a slick coating of sweat bathed the sides of my spine. I wiped at my upper back as best I could.

I stood facing the front of the gym where treadmills look out of floor-to-ceiling windows on the first floor, and elliptical machines line a sort of interior balcony that forms a partial second floor. Anyone passing by can see the entire guts of the gym. Of course their attention is usually drawn to those jogging and climbing on the machines just inside the glass, but it's easy enough to see beyond to the weight training area as well. The only escape from public scrutiny are the yoga studios and locker rooms.

The design sometimes made me feel like an animal in a zoo. Their existence is difficult enough, cut off from roaming through hundreds of miles of open space, forced to make do with pacing back and forth among a few trees and artfully placed boulders. All day long they endure unwanted human voices and cameras. We think they don't know they're being watched, but they do.

Had the woman next door to Tess become like a zoo animal? Perhaps she acted out because people were constantly staring in at her. She couldn't hear them, but she observed them looking up at her, then turning their heads to talk, criticizing her appearance, her behavior, her choice of a reclusive lifestyle.

I finished the contents of my water bottle and started toward the front of the gym, headed toward the women's locker room. As I passed behind an unoccupied treadmill I thought about the apartment security guy who had followed me for several weeks, the man Tess shot. Before she killed him, he'd been everywhere, making me feel the same as those zoo animals, always observed, unable to escape his interfering gaze, no matter how hard I tried to ignore him.

The memory drew me to look out at the street, expecting to see him, back from the dead. Or not really dead after all. In the way your mind can play tricks, I started to wonder if he really had died. She'd only shot him once. He'd fallen immediately, but we'd taken off so quickly, had we confirmed he was dead? What if someone did see us, or heard the shot, and instead of pursuing us, they offered help, preferring to save a life rather than exacting punishment?

As if my mind had truly conjured him, a man stood close to the window, staring directly at me — Steve Montgomery. He smiled slightly but made no gesture to greet me, confident I'd seen him, and confident that he'd caught me off guard.

With a single glance from a place he didn't belong, he'd advanced himself from entitled executive to full-on predator. What was wrong with the man?

54

Convincing Jen to hide in my trunk in order to sneak her into Tess's underground garage was easy. Convincing Isaiah was not. He resisted as if I'd suggested planting a pipe bomb in The White House.

"She doesn't want you to have visitors. The guy at the security desk was clear about that." Isaiah folded his arms as if he was personally guarding the integrity of Tess's building.

"She didn't mean you," I said. "I'm sure if I'd asked, she would have clarified."

"Then why don't you text her and ask?"

"I've already had to send her too many messages about the bird. I don't want to keep bothering her. She's supposed to be wiping out all her concerns, not having to think about anything. No responsibilities."

"I can cook dinner right here," he said. He waved his arm toward my kitchenette, only a few feet from the couch.

"You haven't seen Tess's kitchen. You'll die."

"I'm sure."

"Seriously. There's nothing you need that she doesn't have a tool for. And the counter space goes on forever. We'll have a fantastic meal. Her wine selection…"

"It's not right."

"I promise she won't care. Look what I'm doing for her. With that irritating bird."

"Then why did she say no guests?"

"She's worried about a guy at work. For no rational

reason, but she is. She's very focused on keeping him out of her life, so she over-corrected."

Jen was listening to our back and forth, already dressed to go, totally up for the excitement of being locked in a trunk, which was a bit weird. But she didn't get out much for fun, so I guess anything unusual that didn't involve sex with a stranger was exciting to her.

My plan was to drive to a luxury grocery store in Tess's neighborhood. Jen and I would follow Isaiah around as he selected his ingredients, then with the bags of food on the floor of my car and my moving boxes on the back seat, I'd help them curl up for a short ride in the trunk. Security checked to see that you didn't have unauthorized passengers, but they weren't so hardcore that they opened your trunk like border control agents.

"She won't even know," Jen said.

"That makes it worse." Isaiah spoke in a soft voice, but he raised his eyebrows like a teacher quietly delivering wrath disguised as disappointment to a cheating student.

I walked to his side and slid my arm around his waist, pulling him close so he could feel the warmth of my body. "After all this time, you've never made dinner for me. I want to see if you're at the top of your class." I looked up at him.

He rolled his eyes. "Your apartment…"

"It's too small. There's not enough room for all three of us to have an elegant dinner. Where are we going to sit? At the bar?" I moved away from him. "I'm really looking forward to it. And Tess is a generous person. Look at all the things she's done for me — the gym membership, letting me stay in her place. She bought me vodka and olives for martinis. You should see all the food she left for me, almost as if she expected me to have a guest or two, because I could hardly eat it all before it spoiled. She totally trusts me."

"And that's why you shouldn't betray her trust."

"You make it sound momentous and it's not like that."

"Then send her a text and find out for sure."

"Haven't you ever heard of begging forgiveness versus asking permission?"

"You're not the begging type."

I smiled. It's so lovely to be known. That might sound self-worshipful, but it's not. There is nothing as satisfying as knowing someone knows the thorns of your personality, understands it's your nature, and allows the authentic *you* into their world. I wonder if that's all that any of us are after — to be known, to hide nothing — no matter what our philosophical views or all of our quirky needs and demands we make on each other.

Everyone likes to be known. And understood. None of us want to be chastised for something that developed before we were conscious of it, and told it needs to be eradicated. That's what was wrong with my parents and their church and their views of humanity. Everything needed to be perfected according to their beliefs, and the things they judged immoral or selfish were to be ripped out. Your skin sliced open and bled out.

I put my arms around him and leaned my head on his chest. "I'm aching for your dinner and you will ache when you see this kitchen. Tess didn't want parties or one particular person. She said *Steve*. She just wasn't clear in communicating it to security. That's all. I promise. If she's angry, it's on me, not you."

For some reason, that softened him. I don't think that

meant he would be pleased to see me punished if anything went wrong while he skated free. I think he simply realized it had nothing to do with him. At least that's what I wanted to think he recognized.

Isaiah spent nearly an hour strolling along the aisles of the grocery store — the kind that sells fresh crab and then cracks it for you, the kind with an imported cheese section and a cheese connoisseur who makes recommendations, and you can find cheese that costs more than an Uber ride. The kind of store that has a sommelier in their wine department.

After all of his careful shopping, there were only three bags, which wouldn't catch the attention of the man guarding the entrance to the parking garage.

The two of them climbed into the trunk, hugging their thighs against their ribs. Now that he'd made his decision, all of Isaiah's concerns had evaporated and he was loving the clandestine aspect of our plan. It's another thing I like about him — once he chooses a course of action, he doesn't second guess himself or dwell on the past.

55

Portland

After several minutes watching the blood flow from the cut Pauline had made in my arm, I started to feel like the night sky was creeping into the sides of my eyes. My head felt like I'd just climbed off a merry-go-round and couldn't find firm footing. The apple I'd eaten earlier, now liquefied in my intestines, swam in mad circles.

Then, I couldn't take it any more. I leaned forward and shoved Pauline out of the way. While she was trying to right herself, I took the edge of my sleeping bag and patted the blood off my arm. I stood and kicked her hip. She cried out and tried to grab my ankle, but a skinny ten-year-old girl can out-maneuver a slack, middle-aged woman whose body is filled with the residue of drugs, the wiring in her brain shorted out, and scars lacing her appendages so she can hardly move without the welts and scabs tearing at her skin and making her feel as if her body might come apart at the seams.

I picked up my backpack and swung it at the side of her head. "Leave me alone."

She groaned in what I thought was a rather dramatic way. "I'm trying to help you."

"I don't need your help. I don't need any help at all."

"You'll live to regret those words."

"I won't." I grabbed the ends of my sleeping bag and

yanked it hard. She rolled off onto the gravel-encrusted dirt, moaning and complaining and whispering swear words as if she thought she had to say them softly to protect my innocence.

I shoved the sleeping bag into my suitcase, my feet into my tennies, and my arms through the straps of my backpack.

"Don't leave."

Blood was dripping down my arm again. The feeling of approaching darkness returned to the inside of my head. I put down the suitcase and pulled a tissue from the outside pocket. I wiped my arm and then pressed it over the wound. I picked up the suitcase with my other hand.

"I thought I could help you. Show you how to be rid of your pain."

I shoved my suitcase through the opening between the shrubs and crawled out after it, branches catching themselves in the straps of my pack and my hair, as if they too wanted me to stay.

"I wouldn't hurt you. I don't do those things any more."

I shoved my suitcase down the hill. This time, I couldn't take time to carry it with slow, awkward steps. Whatever it was she'd done, the urge might return. The sight of my blood might have stirred her up. I ran down the hill after my suitcase, the pack slapping my back.

By the time I reached another small park, the sun was directly overhead. It was unlikely I'd see a lot of people at this park because it didn't have a play structure. It was a small rectangle of grass with trees and shrubs and a single picnic table. My family passed by it every time we drove to church, but I'd never seen anyone playing there. It wouldn't offer me much protection, but I supposed as long as it was ignored, I could sleep under the picnic table and no one would see me from the street.

I spent the day sitting with my back against a tree, hoping it hid me from passersby. I patted at my blood until a scab began to form. I read my book and ate nearly all of my food.

The picnic table turned out to be a huge help because it rained that night. I hardly slept, watching for people driving by and glancing out of car windows, keeping my flashlight directed at the shrubs, half-expecting Pauline to reappear. I knew she hadn't followed me, but her ability to locate me when I'd been so well-hidden at the other park made me think she had instincts that were sharper than average.

In the morning, the sun came out again but the ground was sopping wet. I was starving.

Leaving my possessions under the tarp, mostly hidden by the picnic table, I took my damp, grubby body and my plastic bag of coins to a Quick Stop four blocks away. I was aware of a dirty clothes smell coming off my body, and possibly a sour smell coming out of my mouth, although that was hard to know for sure.

When I stepped inside the doorway of the Quick Stop, my oldest brother Eric was standing at the counter. He was handing the clerk a flyer with my picture on it. He turned and smiled as casually as if I'd walked out of my classroom at school. "There you are," he said.

To be honest, I was a little insulted that he wasn't more upset. But then, I hadn't wanted them to be upset, I'd wanted them to accept the fact I didn't belong in that family, and you can't have it both ways.

He folded the flyer and slid it into his back pocket. "Mom is freaking out."

I nodded.

"Where's your backpack?" he said.

"At the park."

"Well let's get you home."

"I'm hungry."

"You can eat at home. We can't waste time. I hate seeing mom cry like this."

"What's dad doing?"

He glared at me and I knew the answer. What else. Preparing one of his ingenious *punishments to fit the crime.*

One thing I have to say for my father, he believed one hundred percent in his view of god and the world. It was doubtful that he'd had a moment of worry or fear about my safety because he was always absolutely certain god was on his side. God was protecting his family and directing everything that happened.

On the walk home, Eric didn't say anything. He pulled the suitcase and I carried the backpack. I thought about the cut on my arm and wondered whether the knife had been clean, aside from apple juice and her blood.

Had her blood still been on the blade? Did it make its way into my veins and was now putting some of her life and her thoughts inside of me?

I'd heard of girls cutting themselves and mixing their blood to become blood sisters. I thought it was silly and sounded creepy to willingly make yourself bleed. But I wasn't sure if that was a real thing — if putting someone else's blood inside your body could change you.

At some churches, not ours, but churches my classmates went to, they drank wine and said it was the blood of Christ. They thought it changed them.

Of course, that wasn't really blood, but you never know. Blood is a scary thing.

56

While Isaiah prepared his feast, Jen and I sat on Tess's enormous balcony and sipped martinis. He cranked up a playlist of *The Smiths* and spread his implements out all over the granite counters. In the end, he used every one of the six gas burners on her stove.

The first course was cream of cauliflower soup served in shallow slate-colored bowls. It was so divine, Jen and I agreed that cauliflower was the most underrated vegetable on the planet. Next were tiny individual glass dishes of caviar served with a single cracker. The salad was arugula with three quail eggs and the meat of a Dungeness crab leg. After the salad, he poured the last of the Chardonnay in our glasses and told us to enjoy the sunset while he put out the main course.

He set Cabernet glasses by each place and poured in enough wine to last through the main course without interruption.

The dish he'd prepared proved the importance of going to a good grocery store. He served steak tartare with a soft mound of whipped potatoes with butter and glazed baby green beans.

The steak tartare was the best I've ever tasted. When you're eating raw meat, it better be high quality. And anyone who thinks meat doesn't vary in quality, hasn't eaten enough steak tartare.

Isaiah offered a toast to the gods of food and wine. We clicked our glasses gleefully, in a single ringing sound.

I told him he could open his restaurant immediately, no need for any more education.

He said the moment I had a quarter million dollars to lend him, he would do just that.

We ate in silence for a few minutes, letting the food melt across our tongues and around the insides of our mouths.

Jen cut a green bean in half and ate it. "I hate to be a downer, but I'm worried about the homeless woman outside our building," she said.

I sipped my wine. She *was* being a downer. I didn't want to sit in a glorious home, candles flickering, wine glowing, the city sparkling outside the windows, a gorgeous guy looking at me like he wanted me more than the steak tartare, and talk about a street person. Every street person became Pauline in my mind, mildly threatening, sad and confusing, but ultimately unstable and impossible to predict.

Jen would not let go of it. The degradation that woman had suffered was an awful thing, but I didn't understand why Jen thought she could do anything about it.

"I haven't seen her for two days."

"Maybe she found a place where she won't get pissed on," I said.

"I'm worried they did something."

"What do you mean?" Isaiah said.

Jen poked her fork at the steak. She cut a small bite and piled potatoes on top of the meat before she put the fork in her mouth. She chewed quickly and swallowed. "I don't know. Hurt her. Took her some place where she couldn't find her way back and she has no access to resources, or whatever."

"Who is they?" Isaiah said.

"Scott. Lizzy, maybe."

"Or she left on her own. I was serious when I said she found a place she wouldn't get pissed on. I'm sure she hated what happened more than any of us can imagine. Maybe she's in a better place."

"You make it sound like she's dead," Jen said.

Isaiah grinned, then glanced at Jen and changed his expression. He took a long swallow of wine.

"I wish we could do something to help her," Jen said.

"We can't," I said.

"How do you know?"

"Well first, she seems to have moved on, but even if she comes back, what can you do? You can't ask her to move in with you." I laughed.

"It's not funny."

"I know. I don't know why I laughed. But there are places that can help her, people who know how to do that, and people who know who can actually be helped and who can't. If she's an addict…"

"Why does everyone assume they're addicts?"

"They're usually addicts or mentally ill," Isaiah said.

"I feel like you're ganging up on me." Jen shoveled the rest of the potatoes into her mouth. She stabbed two green beans and stuffed them in with the potatoes. She nudged her plate away from her. Most of the steak tartare remained in the center of the plate.

I picked up my wine glass and took a sip.

"I'm really upset about it," Jen said. "It seems like no one cares."

"We care," Isaiah said, " but…"

"Caring means doing something," Jen said.

"She could be dangerous," I said. The image of Pauline's pocket knife, the easy way she sliced my arm, a flick of her wrist, a burst of red, floated behind my eyes.

"Why does everyone assume that!?" Jen said.

"Everyone?" Isaiah said.

"Lizzy said it. Alex said it. Most people think it."

I thought about the man grabbing my breast. Not dangerous, really, but definitely alarming. "Why are you so obsessed with her?"

"Because I care! I'm a fellow human being and I care about people who are shoved outside of society, people who had stuff happen and didn't realize how it would turn out." Tears began dripping down her face.

I stared at her, thinking about obsessions. They're everywhere, and no one really knows how they develop — me and the woman in the window, Jen and the homeless woman, Steve with Tess.

I ate my last bite of steak. "Let's talk about it another time. We don't want to spoil this fantastic meal. And dessert is…"

Jen stood up. "Food? I wonder when was the last time *she* ate a piece of steak? Or anything decent? She's not *dangerous*. She needs our help." She poked her finger in the center of her steak tartare. A thin stream of pepper sauce mixed with Worcestershire ran away from it, not unlike a stream of blood.

Damien, strangely silent until then, chortled. *Dangerous woman.* He chuckled again. *Dangerous woman.*

57

One of the detectives was leaning against the staircase to the building next door. He was just out of range of the streetlight. I stepped back inside Tess's lobby and fiddled with the shoelaces of my running shoes, trying to think. It was the second detective, the one who'd seemed slightly less stiff and dismissive, not as worried about breaking some rule regarding talking to a civilian, or talking about the investigation, or whatever the rule was that kept the other's lips twisted in a look of mild disdain.

I stepped back outside where I could see him around the edge of the entryway, but he couldn't see me unless he moved a foot or two away from the staircase. He wore a knitted dark blue cap pulled over his ears and black leather gloves. Neither seemed to be helping him withstand the weather because his nose was shiny red and he kept putting a tissue to it and blowing fiercely, stuffing the used tissue in his pocket.

The non-stop flow of mucous and his obvious discomfort seemed like a positive sign. Nothing like nasal misery to weaken a man's natural reticence. At the risk of acknowledging that some of my views have an obviously stereotyped gender-bias, in my experience, men are big babies when they're sick. I think it's a protective device for their macho exterior. If they complain that whatever they're suffering is far worse than any other head cold experienced by the human race, more serious than the flu, possibly life-threatening, because no one has ever experienced a sore throat quite like this or a cough so deep and all-consuming, then it's okay to not be in control. And sneezing and coughing are definitely forces that exert utter control over the human body.

A man who is sick feels weak. Possibly his ears are plugged, making him feel vulnerable to an attack he doesn't hear coming. He knows he's not at the top of his game, and he can hear the frail quality of his voice echoing inside of his head.

It's probably wired into their DNA over thousands of years. They can't help it, just like women can't help being drawn to make-up. Not all women, but a significant percentage, who like the idea of painting the thing closest to them. Who doesn't want sable bristles as soft as feathers, like an angel's fingertips, brushing across your cheeks? And in the end, all your rough spots are smoothed away.

I straightened and walked out onto the sidewalk. I used the lamppost to support myself while I stretched my legs and watched him turn three more tissues into soggy messes. I ended my stretching, walked up to the staircase, and greeted him.

He nodded and pulled a tissue out of his pocket. He held it over his mouth and coughed. "Can I help you?" His voice was rough and wet and he strained to get the words out.

"I met you when you found Frank's body."

He wiped at his eyes. "Right. Watery eyes, didn't recognize you."

"That's a terrible cold. How come you're standing out here when you're sick?"

"Just observing the activity on the street."

"Can't you do that from your car?"

"Harder to get a full view."

"What activity are you observing?"

He sneezed. I pulled a tissue out of my pocket and held it out to him.

He shook his head. "Thanks. I have a warehouse full." He pulled one out of his coat pocket and blew his nose.

I waited for him to recall my question. His eyes looked like they were turning to liquid. Maybe he was taking medication, making him more malleable, but also more lost in a mental fog. Those OTC things never really stop the symptoms, and then you either feel tired or amped up or slightly queasy or experience some other condition that further disables you. "What are you looking for?"

"He was killed between four and six a.m., so I'm observing what goes on around here at this time."

"Is that useful?" It sounded like a complete waste of time, but obviously he didn't see it that way.

"No one owns up to hearing a gunshot or seeing a damn thing. This will give me a feel for the area."

"Makes sense," I said.

"What's your name again?"

I smiled and pulled the zipper on my hoodie down to just below my ribs. "Alex."

He didn't push for my last name. I was glad to have dodged settling my full name in his memory. "Do you have any suspects?"

He shook his head. He didn't smirk or laugh at my use of the word *suspects* — it sounded corny in my own ears, but maybe the condition of his head made everything sound slightly off key.

"We'll get one. We almost always do."

"That's impressive."

"People let little things slip out, things they think don't matter."

"I can see that."

He didn't react to that rather lame comment either.

"Everyone in this building keeps to themselves," I said. "So I suppose that's why they don't notice much."

"Do you?"

"Do I what?"

"Do you notice much?"

"No more than average." That was a lie. I notice a lot more than most, possibly because I'm so curious and always listening to conversations that don't involve me, always looking to see what people will do next, always trying to keep my edge.

"Most people don't notice much. Unless it's something shocking," he said.

"Which a gunshot would be."

"Yep. All his colleagues — he was a professor at UC San Francisco — said he was the nicest guy you'd ever meet. Of course, that's what is said whenever someone is murdered. He was very well respected."

I thought of Lorraine insisting he was not a professor and being very eager to make the distinction.

"Did the neighbors agree?"

"For the most part."

"Oh? Not all?"

"The guy on the top floor said he was difficult. But didn't know much about him. The woman on the third floor…"

He paused. I wondered if his ingrained caution and law enforcement guidelines had crawled their way up from the soup flooding his skull. Then, he seemed to decide it was either too much effort, or didn't really matter since there wasn't much to say.

"She had a similar response."

That was a lie. I think Lorraine knew him fairly well, possibly better than she'd admitted to me, or she wouldn't have suddenly gone off on his professor versus teacher status as if he was putting on airs. For someone to get under your skin that easily, there's more of a long-term relationship. Those irritations take years to develop. She also knew enough to know he wasn't what he'd said. Whatever that meant. Unless it was simply another reference to the missing professor title, but I didn't think so. She was very precise in her speech, and she'd suggested those were two different comments on his character.

The detective removed two tissues from his pocket and began to blow an enormous amount of gunk out of his nose. As he tried to maneuver the sodden tissues, I turned toward the street, giving him some privacy for the messy job. When I turned back he seemed un-phased whether or not I'd been repulsed.

"Shouldn't you be home drinking chicken broth?" I said.

"This needs to be done."

"Oh."

We stood there for a few seconds. It didn't look like he was going to willingly give up information about the woman on the second floor.

Finally, I spoke. "What about the other woman who lives there? I guess she didn't know him well either? Didn't hear anything?"

"Funny you should put it that way."

"What way?"

"She *didn't* hear anything. She's deaf."

"Really?" I don't think I managed to keep the shock off my face. Of all the things he might have said, after the antics I'd seen, being deaf was something that had never entered my mind. "So did you bring an interpreter to talk to her?"

"We could have, but she doesn't answer her door."

"Isn't she required to talk to you?"

"Actually, no. Unless we get evidence she's a material witness."

"So you didn't communicate with her at all? How did you find out she was deaf?"

"Mrs. Clayton told us."

Despite her precise way with language, Lorraine always seemed to be hiding something, shifting the story slightly. She used her precise language to do it.

If it was a lie, was it really that easy to lie to them? I didn't think it was. Maybe if you were a certain kind of person. If you were a person who wore nice wool slacks and you were elderly and had lived in a pricey San Francisco neighborhood since before the detectives were born. Maybe. And more importantly, if you chose your lies carefully. It wouldn't work to lie about something large — such as an alibi. But maybe little things...things that seemed unimportant to them. Why would they question such a story? Unless it was true.

"So someone can refuse to talk to the police?"

"We don't think anyone who lives here was involved."

"Why not?"

"He was shot in the back. It looked like he was returning home. There's no physical evidence in the lobby or elevator.

It could be an angry student, we're pursuing that. Or he was mistaken for someone else."

I glanced up at the second floor window. The heavy drapes and the curtains were both closed. The glass was sparkling clean.

"Look," he said. "It's nice to break up the monotony talking to you, but I really need to pay attention to the neighborhood. I need to ask you to leave."

"No worries." I smiled. "Have a good day." I began a slow jog up the street. I kept the easy pace for the entire first mile, trying to sort through what he'd said. So many questions.

58

Each time I'd taken my spot on the bench across from the Edwardian apartment building, I'd noticed a brass plaque in the center of the back. I'd never bothered to read it. This time, maybe because the air was warmer than usual, the sunshine making the metal shimmer against the wood, I paused. It was a line from a John Lennon song, probably not a concept that originated with him, but expressed in a memorable way — *Life is what happens when you're busy making other plans.*

I lit a cigarette and settled down, positioning my back so the brass plate was between my shoulder blades. I exhaled and studied the window. The drapes were parted, the sheers closed. I drew smoke into my body and held it for a moment before releasing it in a long, elegant stream.

It occurred to me that part of the point of the John Lennon line was that we don't notice many things in the world because we're fixated on one thing, often not the important thing — making plans, trivial and important, rather than seeing what's happening right in front of our eyes. In my case, I'd spent so much time staring at that one window, I hadn't bothered to notice the others much.

The drapes on the fourth floor were all closed, now that Frank was never coming home. I didn't remember whether they'd always been that way. There was still no sign of anyone entering the apartment. Surely the man had a will. There must be someone who was thrilled to have a million-dollar apartment in a glorious neighborhood. Even if that person wasn't a blood relative, somebody should be looking the place over. Or at least it would be put up for sale.

I took another drag and moved my attention to Lorraine's apartment. The windows that were visible from where I was sitting had shutters rather than drapes. They were slanted so she was able to see out, but from the street, no one would see her.

The fifth-floor resident was still a mystery. How strange that all my loitering and lurking had never put me near the building when he was leaving or returning. His windows were covered by blinds — tiny aluminum spears.

I took a few more drags, looking at nothing in particular. I bent down to stab the end of my cigarette on the pavement. When I straightened, a man at the corner of the street caught my eye. He stood facing me, two buildings past Tess's on the opposite side from Lorraine's. I put my hand on my forehead to block the glare that my sunglasses didn't entirely shield me from.

There was something familiar about his stance. He wasn't moving, simply leaning against an elegant Spanish building. He was staring at me, although it's a bit of a stretch to think I could confirm that from a distance of several hundred feet, sun boring into my eyes. He crossed his arms over his chest, giving off an even more familiar air.

He uncrossed his arms and began walking up the street. When he reached Tess's building, my brain, slow to recognize him because he was out of context, clicked into gear — Steve Montgomery.

Now I was in deep shit with Tess. Isaiah had been so worried about breaking her murky rule, and somehow, I'd managed to break the one she'd been absolutely clear about. How the hell had he found me here?

He crossed the street and stopped a few yards away from me. "I didn't know you smoked."

I pulled out another cigarette and lit it.

"Aren't you going to say hi?" He stepped around the plants and sat on the bench beside me.

I was still seated in the center and there was plenty of room between me and the end of the bench, yet he sat so that the slightest movement on my part would press my thigh against his. Shifting to my right was out of the question.

I inhaled and blew out a thick cloud of smoke, directing it in front of him. I looked up at the apartment building and saw the woman. She was holding the curtain to the side, watching us. She stood motionless and I couldn't see her face at all. I hoped she didn't start spreading her blood across the window. I didn't need to get into a conversation about that with Steve.

"I wanted to know what your very important plans were that night we rode in the elevator together. I saw you go to that hole in the wall soup place."

I thought about the steady uptick in his creepiness factor.

"When you took off like a bat out of hell, I followed. And, here I am."

So, he didn't realize Tess lived here. After all, I was sitting on a public bench smoking. For all he knew I was visiting a friend, or taking a break from my boyfriend.

"I had you all wrong," he said.

I looked at him.

"Ah. She speaks."

I hadn't spoken, but I wasn't going to do it now.

I took a slow drag.

He shifted away from me. "Aren't you wondering how I had you wrong?"

"Not really." It was the truth. I no longer gave a shit what he thought of me. The guy was a freak and there was no way I would work for him. I didn't even want to be in his organization, a protective layer of management between us like…well, like a condom. Those things can break when you least expect it. He might be smart enough to run a global sales organization, smart enough to pull down a very nice six figure income with stock and bonuses to spare, but he was a Neanderthal in every sense of the word.

It's funny how you can bat a question back and forth in your mind like the longest tennis rally in history, then suddenly, someone misses a shot and the answer is so clear you wondered why it was ever a question at all.

"I thought you were different. A self-sufficient woman who knows what she wants. Hungry to get ahead, wanting to prove yourself and build a career. But no woman is really like that, is she?"

"What do you mean?"

"Women just want their creature comforts."

That was true, but there was no *just* about it. And it certainly wasn't unique to women.

"So you don't need a job at all."

"Why would you think that?"

"And not needing means not going for it." He gestured at Tess's building, looking up toward the top floor. "Which one is yours?"

I blew out a stream of smoke.

"So does Daddy pay for it, or your boyfriend? Husband?"

I took another drag, hoping he'd wind down soon.

"You certainly give a different impression, not like a rich bitch at all. Does Tess know about this? She must. She sees your address in the HR tool."

My cigarette was burning down fast.

He stood. Finally.

Still looking across the street, his gaze shifting to the Edwardian building, he said, "I still think you have strong skills. I was concerned about you, trying to give you a leg up. If Tess leaves the company, you're out of a job, you know. The company might find something for you, but anyone that tight with a senior VP, well most managers might not want you infecting their team with your sense of entitlement. Someone with a reputation of hard-to-manage." He laughed and shook his head. "But I guess none of that matters. You don't need a job. You are playing both of us after all."

59

For several minutes, Steve and I stared at each other. He, believing I was someone else entirely. Me, knowing he had it right the first time and now he was ignoring his instinct in his rush to reshape me into his tidy view of women.

"Smoking isn't good for you," he said.

A movement across the street caught my eye and I looked away from him.

"It's really annoying how you don't respond to people," he said. His tone was so petulant I wanted to laugh. I thought of Damien and imagined him mimicking Steve's whining voice.

The door in the Edwardian building was open. A man stepped outside. I stood.

"Where are you going?" Steve said.

The man coming out of the apartment building was tall and slim. He wore jeans and a white turtleneck with a coffee-colored suit jacket. The lower part of his face was dark with stubble, made prominent by the sunlight. My mind raced through the possibilities, floor by floor — a caretaker for the woman on the second floor, Lorraine's son, the man who had inherited Frank's apartment, the faceless man on the fifth floor. I stepped to the curb.

Steve turned. He moved up beside me, lifted his hand and gave a phony-looking salute.

"You know him?" I said.

"Yes. He's a customer. Owns a biotech company that..."

"Will you introduce me?"

"What made you so friendly all of a sudden? Will the boyfriend like you rushing across the street to meet a good-looking neighbor?"

"Will you introduce me?"

Steve bowed slightly and started across the street. I dropped my cigarette, stepped on it, and followed closely. "What's his name?"

"Slow down."

We stopped near the staircase just as the man reached the pavement.

"Hey, what brings you to this area?" he said.

Steve shook the man's hand and jerked his head toward me. "She works for me, lives right there." He jerked his head toward Tess's building.

I didn't correct the lie, delivered to make me squirm and throw me off my game. He truly had underestimated me, from the start.

"Barker Clayton, Alexandra Mallory."

I eased my breath out and tried not to let my thoughts bleed onto my face. Clayton. It couldn't be a coincidence. He was obviously related to Lorraine, and the right age to be her son.

I extended my hand and he took it, giving one firm shake before releasing it quickly. "A pleasure."

"Do you live here?" I said.

He smirked. "Top floor."

"I've met your mother." He lived in the same building as his mother? Two floors above her, and she hadn't bothered to mention that? What a strange woman. Especially since she'd been so clear about wanting me to meet him.

He gave me an obligatory smile.

There were so many things I wanted to know, but I wasn't about to dive into the topic of blood on the window and Frank's murder, not with Steve lapping up every word like dribbles of steak juice. "I haven't seen you around before," I said.

"Why would you?" He flashed a charming, teasing grin at me.

Steve nodded, as if he thought I'd made the stupidest comment ever.

A prolonged silence fell over the three of us. Well, prolonged from Steve's perspective because he leaped to fill the empty space. "We should meet for a drink."

"Sure," Barker said. "No relevant projects for CoastalCreative in the pipeline right now, but always good to keep the channels open."

"Absolutely," Steve said.

Again, the silence. I glanced up at the second floor, which had become my habit. It was very similar to Steve's unconscious head-jerking habit when he lied about who I was and my role at CoastalCreative, followed by his imagined story of why I was in the neighborhood. It's interesting how you can make stuff up and believe it yourself as long as no one dares to contradict you. Of course, some people make stuff up and the world screams contradictions at them, pointing out facts and truth, yet they persist in adhering to the stories in their own minds.

My parents and the rest of the members in the church where I grew up believe fervently, maniacally, that all truth about the world is written in the Holy Bible. Others believe differently, but there's no discussing it with any members of

Pure Truth Tabernacle. There's no discussion with *anyone* who has constructed their own view of reality. Maybe we're all mad, locked inside our own heads, no different from the woman imprisoned on the second floor. If we aren't raised in a prison of firm beliefs, we go on to create our own, brick by brick and bar by bar with what we choose to believe.

While the silence stretched, Steve and Barker began inching away from each other. Both wanted to end the encounter but they were unsure how to do it quickly and gracefully. It seemed they both believed they needed to say a bit more to be truly cordial. As we stood there, the curtains in the second-floor window parted.

The woman stood to one side, looking down at the group of us. Her face was contorted in a horrifying expression. She began to let loose a flow of invective, but it emerged soundlessly, her lips moving with fury. She began pounding on the window, muffled thuds that captured Steve's attention first, then Barker's.

"What the fuck is that?" Steve said.

"Ignore her. She's a nut case." Barker extended his hand. "Good seeing you. Shoot me an email and we'll have that drink."

Steve shook his hand. "Will do."

I felt I was in a surreal performance in which a woman was screaming to make herself heard while they conducted a casual business conversation as if she didn't exist.

60

For several days I hadn't gone into the office at all. No one missed me. I could do email on my phone and I'd manufactured laryngitis to give me a pass on conference calls. One snarky woman on Tess's web content team suggested I should still listen to the calls, it was still important to know what was discussed, and that I didn't always have to be the one talking. I sent a very pleasant reply to her email that it was best for me to lie down and drink tea and rest up. She didn't write back.

For the past day and a half, I'd done nothing but sit on that bench and smoke. I brought sandwiches for lunch and I stayed until the sun went down. Lorraine hadn't left her apartment the entire time. I was coughing regularly. The smoking had to stop, but I had to have something to keep me calm and focused. My pre-dawn runs had been brutal, but I forced myself to push hard, believing the air circulating with deep breaths would clear out some of the nicotine. We all adhere to the stories we tell in our own minds.

Just as the sun was going down, Lorraine came out.

I stabbed out my cigarette, popped a peppermint candy in my mouth, and hurried across the street, leaving my water container and half a sandwich on the bench. "Hi. I haven't seen you around."

"Are you stalking me?" She smiled. She seemed genuinely glad to see me, and genuinely teasing about the stalking.

"I am." I gave her a charming grin, not unlike Barker's, I

thought. I had no intention of mentioning that I knew he lived two floors above her. There was a reason she'd left that pertinent fact out of the details she'd fed me from her life while I devoured her incredible meal. I wasn't going to trip her up. Not with that. Not yet.

"I'm meeting an old friend for dinner," she said.

"I'll walk with you to the end of the block."

"How nice." She held out her arm for me to take it. Whatever had made her cranky the last time, was completely gone. Maybe she simply didn't like standing in the rain. Or maybe she was upset about Frank and felt helpless.

I'd upset her.

We walked past Tess's building. "I talked to one of the detectives investigating Frank's murder," I said.

I felt her body move against mine as she nodded. "They don't know anything," she said.

"No, they don't. It's sad. And frustrating. The detective said the woman on the second floor is deaf, so she wasn't any help."

"I don't imagine she was."

"I was surprised. You hadn't mentioned she was deaf."

Her arm seemed to stiffen slightly. "It's not important. Her behavior is so disturbing, I forget."

"That's understandable," I said.

She didn't respond and her arm remained stiff, making me suddenly aware of her bone wrapped in skin without much flesh, pressing into the bones of my forearm. I felt I had something very fragile in my arms and I needed to walk more carefully. "She must feel so isolated. I can't imagine what that's like."

"I'm thankful I still have all my faculties."

"So it came on when she was older?"

"Why do you ask?"

"You said you were glad you could still hear, and see…I assumed that meant something had happened to her…losing her faculties."

"Oh."

I waited for more, but Lorraine was as good as I am about keeping her thoughts to herself. I saw how that tendency would drive people mad, which I suppose is why I do it. I only had a few more minutes with her, unless I was going to walk her all the way to the cable car stop, or to her friend's house. "I really enjoyed my dinner with you. And tea."

"I'm glad."

"If it's not too rude to ask, I'd love to come over for tea again. You've made me a fan. I've never been a tea drinker. And those cream puffs…mmm."

She laughed. "I thought you were anxious to escape the company of an old lady."

"Not at all. You misread me. That happens to me a lot."

"I can see that."

I wasn't sure what she meant, but the tea invite was first on my agenda, so I didn't bother asking. "Would tomorrow be a good day?" I said.

"Yes."

We'd reached the corner.

"Four o'clock?" she said.

"Perfect."

"You don't have to work?"

"My schedule is flexible."

"Technology." She squeezed my arm gently, then released it.

"Yes, it frees you and traps you all at the same time."

"I'll see you tomorrow. At four," she said.

"Yes."

"It was nice walking with you. Everyone should have a female companion."

"A daughter?" I said.

She smiled. She lifted her hand in a little wave, and walked at a much faster clip, headed toward an area populated by single-family homes. I admired her constant walking. No wonder she was so in charge of her faculties, despite creeping toward her nineties.

Tea was a good first step, it didn't seem outrageous to invite myself for something so small. And once we were settled in her living room, I could work my way to a dinner invite with her son. With him, I'd have better leverage in extracting information about the woman downstairs.

It was almost laughable the way they pretended that woman wasn't really a problem, as if the TV were tuned to a reality show, the volume muted while they went about their business, occasionally glancing at the human drama being mouthed out in their unhearing presence.

61

Portland

My mother opened the front door and grabbed me as if Eric were the one who'd taken me away from her. She cried, her face pressed into my hair until I felt her tears soaking my scalp. Her body shook against mine and there was a faint sound of her teeth rattling in her jaw, threatening that her whole body was coming apart.

Several long minutes ticked past before she released me. Her face was so bloated and red, I had to close my eyes, not wanting to see the soggy, crumpled mess of it. Even as she loosened her grip on my wrists and allowed me to move away from her, the sound of her breath was heavy, broken by soft groans. I thought she was overcome with the terror of losing me, her mind filled with imagining abuse to my body ranging from simple cold and deprivation to brutal assault and worse.

That wasn't it at all.

"I'm so sorry. I'm sorry I didn't watch over you with the care you deserve. It's my only job. The one thing I'm supposed to be better at than anything else, and I let you get away. My precious daughter, one of the jewels of our home." She let go of my wrists. She took another step away from me and knelt on the hardwood floor. "I've failed to teach you what the Lord wants. I'm so sorry. Please forgive me."

I giggled. I didn't mean to. It was just so unexpected. And I didn't know what to say. No one had ever asked for my *forgiveness.* I was a kid! Why did she need forgiving? It wasn't as if she could attach herself to my side all through the school day. She couldn't handcuff me and lock me in a cage. Although my father had already made clear that sometimes, he thought physical restraint might be the best solution to dealing with a girl who refused to yield her mind to him and her soul to god.

"Say you forgive her," Eric said.

I stared at him.

"I think that's what you'll need to say."

My mother hugged my hips and pressed the side of her head against my belly. "You could have been damaged forever."

"I doubt that," Eric said. "She's made out of cast iron."

"Will you forgive me?" Her voice had dissolved to a whisper.

I had no idea what to say, but I certainly wasn't going to forgive her for not locking me up, for not tracking me twenty-four hours a day. She hadn't done anything that needed forgiving, except maybe getting on her knees like that. It was embarrassing and I wanted her to stand up. I grabbed her hands, trying to tug her to her feet, but she twisted them out of my grip.

"Will you?"

"She's not going to get up until you say it." Eric grinned. It was always hard to tell where he was coming from. His tone was often mocking but he always said the right words. I wasn't sure if the mocking got trapped in some weird filter that prevented it from entering my parents' ears, or if they chose to ignore it, happy that their words were parroted.

"I guess," I said.

Eric let out a short laugh, but my meek, confused answer was enough for her. She squeezed me harder, then pushed herself to her feet. She wiped her eyes and smiled at me as if I were the most amazing creature she'd ever seen.

The minute my father stepped into the entryway, I knew he'd already devised his plan for my punishment. He looked so pleased with himself. He didn't immediately mention how the punishment would fit my crime of running away. There were actually multiple crimes. I could already guess what they were — the crime of upsetting my mother, the crime of leaving the house without saying where I was going, the crime of going out alone, and the crime of ingratitude for all the things they did for me, all the blessings I'd been *handed on a silver platter.*

And the crime of being a girl.

I didn't see that then, but later, it was clear. At the time, I was vaguely aware of the discrepancy — that my brothers were allowed to take off on their bikes, disappearing for hours. They were allowed to stay outside after dark without parental supervision. But later, I saw that in my father's mind, girls could be raped and boys could not. Girls were vulnerable. Girls were not tough enough and strong enough to take care of themselves. There was a suggestion that girls weren't really clever enough to get out of compromising or potentially dangerous situations.

My father's weird punishment didn't directly address those issues. It mostly focused on the ingratitude and the idea of getting what I'd *asked* for.

No time was allowed to fill my groaning, grumbling belly. I was told to go get in the car. A minute later he eased himself behind the steering wheel. As we drove to the mall, he delivered a sermon about gratitude for the incredibly comfortable life I'd been given, for the deep love my parents had for me. The sermon was riddled with Bible verses. He parked outside Walmart and took my hand as he led me into the store.

We went to the sporting goods department where he purchased a two-person tent, a metal mess kit that fit together like a clever puzzle, and freeze-dried food designed for backpacking. We strolled through the store and he picked up several large jugs of water, toilet paper, a bucket, a shovel, and a child-size knitted cap.

I didn't ask what any of this was for. The image of what he planned for me was taking shape in my mind despite his cheerful silence.

At home, he piled the supplies at the foot of the stairs leading down from the back porch.

"You think you're too good for this house. You think you're capable of taking care of yourself. Ha!" He kicked the tent case. "You can set up the tent in the wooded area. It needs to be visible from the house. There are instructions on the packages for how to mix the food with water. You can relieve yourself in the bucket, or directly on the ground, but if it's on the ground, you need to dig a hole and bury it. We'll see you in three days."

He walked up the back steps and went into the house. I didn't hear the lock turn, but I had no doubt that it did.

I wasn't allowed any books or toys. I had a small flashlight and extra batteries that he'd dug out of a box in the garage.

During those three days, I learned I didn't need a book or toys to keep me entertained. I slept as late as I wanted and I didn't have to do homework or chores. I watched the birds and squirrels and I got to skip family prayers and Bible readings. He thought he was punishing me, but he didn't know I had the best three days of my life. The food was icky though.

Because they didn't see me for three days, the cut Pauline had made in the tender skin of my forearm healed without them noticing. The wound began to fade. Eventually it went away, but I never forgot the sight of my blood seeping out of my body.

62

San Francisco

Relieved to be done with the smoking for a while, and feeling the need to cleanse my body, I stripped off my jeans and sweater, pulled on yoga pants and a sports camisole. I fed the bird and changed his water, then rolled out Tess's yoga mat.

After twenty minutes of a sun salutation sequence, I was pleasantly warm and limber and purified enough to mix a martini. It was past seven and dark outside, but I wasn't quite ready for dinner.

As I pulled the vodka out of the freezer the bird announced — *Chardonnay time.*

I laughed to shake off the chill that came from his words. There was no sound of a cork coming out of a bottle to trigger his memory. How did he *know?* I mixed my drink and took a quick sip, then another to wipe out my fanciful thoughts about the bird. I settled onto the sofa in the sunroom, which I thought of more as a moon room since I was more often in there at night, letting the colorful blur of lights wash over me.

I took a sip of my martini and let my mind drift. After a few minutes, I put down my drink, opened my phone, and sent a message to Tess.

Alex: *Do you have a minute? Quick question.*

She responded immediately: *What's up?*

Alex: *Why does the old woman next door have a picture of you on her shelf?*

Tess: *How did you manage to meet her? Much less see her apartment?*

Alex: *She introduced herself. We chatted a bit, and she invited me to tea.*

Tess: *Stay away from her.*

Alex: *That's harsh. Why didn't you mention her?*

Tess: *I didn't realize you'd be lurking around my neighborhood.*

Alex: *I'm not lurking. I go running and take walks.*

Tess: *Well stay away from her. She'll start obsessing over you.*

Alex: *Why does she have your photograph?*

Tess: *I didn't realize she was taking it, and then she wouldn't delete it.*

Alex: *She has photos of a lot of women.*

Tess: *I felt sorry for her because she's old, she seemed lonely. Don't be fooled. She plays the lonely old lady card, but she's very passive-aggressive.*

Alex: *How?*

Tess: *She'll be sweet and then turn on you. Did she say you're the daughter she never had?*

Alex: *Yes.*

Tess: *She's obsessed with wanting a daughter. I think she latches on to a lot of women our age. You saw all the pictures.*

Alex: *I did.*

Tess: *She might be dangerous.*

Alex: *You can't be serious.*

I took a sip of my drink while I waited for what was turning into a lengthy reply from Tess.

Damien shouted from the other room. *Dangerous woman!*

I took a longer sip, my head floating on vodka. How

could the bird possibly know what I was thinking about? We were texting! He couldn't know, but...maybe Lorraine was the dangerous woman. Not the woman on the second floor. I pulled one of my olives off the stick and ate it.

Tess: *She's the type who wants to control everyone, even people she hardly knows. She has enough money to be very persuasive. And she has this weird, consuming FIXATION on not having a daughter. It's all she can talk about sometimes. It's sad, but scary the way she looks at you.*

I made the mistake of giving her my phone number. I was worried about her. She walks everywhere, and she's so frail. She started calling me all the time. Several times a day. After she called that day we were having coffee, I ended up blocking her. She would not stop talking. She wouldn't leave me ALONE. I felt bad, but she was smothering me.

Alex: *She's not so bad. I don't want to push her away because I'm trying to find out what's going on with that woman on the second floor.*

Tess: *Stay out of it. I don't want problems with people in my neighborhood. That woman is a nut case, that's all. Lorraine is different. She's a dangerous woman, I think.*

Alex: *I thought you were talking about the woman on the second floor when you said that.*

Tess: *No. Lorraine.*

Alex: *Is that why the bird* — I backspaced, and typed Damien. *Is that why Damien says "dangerous woman" all the time?*

Tess: *LOL. Probably.* She sent an emoji with a blushing face. Tess: *How's everything else? How's he doing?*

Alex: *He's doing great.*

Tess: *Good. Is Steve bugging you?*

I thought about telling her right then that I was done with Steve, but he still might provide a little leverage with her. I'd keep it to myself until she returned.

Alex: *Not too much. I'll let you go now.*

Tess: *See you in a few.*

Alex: *Yes. Cheers!*

I finished my drink, gazing at the lights.

Dangerous woman! The bird's voice ripped through my thoughts about Tess and Frank both suggesting Lorraine had too much money. Wanting a secure life myself, a spacious home, property, good food and wine, a chance to travel, I didn't see how too much money could be a thing. I didn't agree. Tess was over-reacting. The photographs were quirky, but they weren't dangerous. Lorraine was odd, inclined toward lying, hiding things about her downstairs neighbor, maybe, but dangerous? I laughed.

Damien laughed harder.

63

When Jen left the apartment a little after ten o'clock, the space where the homeless woman used to sleep was empty. Each time she went out, Jen walked over to the spot, studying the pavement. It was swept clean, hosed down, possibly scrubbed with disinfectant. They'd washed away every hair and skin cell. It was as if she'd plunged beneath the surface of a lake and now, the ripples were gone and it was impossible to identify the spot where she'd gone under.

Tears rushed to the backs of Jen's eyes when these thoughts rushed into her head. It wasn't the right state of mind for going to a four- or five-star hotel to meet a man who expected charm and smiles, a good mood and a chance to make his life exactly what he wanted for sixty minutes. She needed to be strong. She needed all her feelings wrapped up in a tidy bundle and placed on a hidden shelf. She needed to be someone else. But Jen imagined the homeless woman's heart was beating inside her own body, she felt as if she'd lost a friend.

A black Toyota Camry pulled to the curb. She walked across the pavement and opened the back door. The driver said nothing. She pulled her coat around her, yanking the sides hard as if she could close her heart in the same tight package as her thoughts. The car was overheated, but taking off her coat was too revealing. She pressed the button to lower the window. It remained in place. "Can you unlock the window?" she said.

"I don't want the windows open."

"It's hot."

"Take off your coat."

"It's too much trouble for a short ride."

He said nothing.

She took a deep breath and slumped down in the seat. She wished that she'd smoked half a joint, or had a drink before going out. She tried not to — it was risky. She needed to be fully alert, her instincts sharp and close to the surface.

Mike, that was her *date's* name, the only part of his name she knew, if that was even true, would probably offer her a drink. A shot, at least. They usually did. When it was their first time, they often needed several shots themselves to get over their discomfort. To forget they were paying a woman to sleep with them. A man wanted to blot out the assault on his ego. Part of her responsibility, part of what made men keep coming back to her, was that she did a pretty good job of helping them forget that insulting view of themselves. No one wanted to think he couldn't get sex unless he paid for it.

She always found a way to suggest it wasn't that they *had* to pay, it was that they paid to be relieved of responsibility and obligation. That was something worth paying for.

She wished she could buy the same for herself.

Her thoughts circled back to the homeless woman, gone from Jen's life forever. No one in the entire building had noticed her, except for the man who peed on her. In a few weeks Jen would hardly remember her. Then in two or three years, probably much less, if at all, she might as well never have existed. Tears flooded her eyes again.

Get a grip. She whispered the words to herself.

"What's that?" the driver said.

"Nothing."

"You're not high, are you?"

"What difference does it make to you? Isn't that why you're here? To take care of people who shouldn't be driving?"

"I'm not here to take care of anyone but me. And if everyone looked at life that way, the world might have made more progress by now. That's my motto — take care of yourself, and stay out of other people's lives."

She wasn't interested in a discussion with him, philosophical or political, and there was a suggestion in his tone of voice that this could veer quickly toward the political. Responsibility for the less fortunate turned political very quickly.

Alex and Isaiah didn't seem to think she should do anything to help that woman. Alex considered Jen's desire an obsession. Maybe it was. Maybe caring about people who were hurting, and feeling like it was your job to help, weren't the same thing.

"Here we are." The car pulled to the curb with a sudden turn of the wheel, leaving the rear still in the street.

Immediately someone honked.

"Chop, chop," the driver said.

"Thanks." Jen opened the door and slid to the edge of the seat.

"You take care of yourself now," he said.

"I will." She climbed out and slammed the door.

As she walked to the entrance, she thought about requesting another ride. She could start taking care of herself right this minute. Walk away from the hotel. Leave *Mike* waiting all night. He would then write a bad review on the website. Her shoulders and back grew cold at the thought of stopping this very minute. Not yet. She would take her time. It was better to carefully plan something that huge. But she was definitely going to start planning.

64

In an effort to give Lorraine the impression I was honored by her tea invitation, I wore a casual skirt with pockets and flat black shoes. I even put on nylons, which I avoid as often as possible. I picked a pale-yellow sweater with a scoop neck and added a string of pearls that rested on my collarbone. I left my hair down and went minimalist on the makeup — foundation slightly lighter than my skin tone, beige eyeshadow, and a bit of mascara. I skipped the lip gloss altogether.

I left the condo at quarter to four, giving me a few minutes for indulging my obsession.

It seemed to be Barker Clayton who had incited the woman's rage a few days earlier, but why? He seemed like a fairly innocuous guy, so there was obviously a history there. Neighbors can certainly get wound up with each other, fighting over noise and property lines, parking and pets, loud music and raucous parties. From time to time there are stories of neighborhood fights escalating to lawsuits, or violence. It's even less surprising in a large city where people literally live on top of each other.

Once again, as if she'd been waiting for me, the curtains parted, and the woman moved to the center of the window where I could see her clearly. Without any preliminary tracing of her fingers on glass, or simply staring out at me, she began gesturing wildly. She flung her upper body from side to side as if she was engaged in an offbeat modern dance. Her head jerked sharply and her hair swam around her shoulders and arms.

After a few minutes of this, she stopped and stared at me. Slowly, she raised her arm, bent her elbow, and pulled back three of her fingers, leaving the index finger straight out, and cocking her thumb at an angle. She made a chopping motion with her forearm, miming shooting a gun.

So...

Either her rage was boiling over at seeing Barker emerge from the building, making her want to shoot him, and she felt I needed to know about that. Or she'd seen Frank's shooting. Was she telling me Barker shot him? But if she had seen something, why the hell hadn't she told the detective? Unless she really was deaf and couldn't communicate? But that made no sense. She would have made an effort, written a note, or asked for an interpreter.

She continued gesturing, showing me repeatedly the action of the gun, followed by her manic dance, presumably to indicate violent death. At least I thought that's what it was. Charades was never one of my favorite games. The players are never precise enough with their gestures, and the guessing is all pretty much based on intuition, which was how I felt right then.

Finally, she wore herself out and stopped her pantomime.

My phone chimed that it was a few minutes to four. I waved and started toward the stairs. She didn't wave back.

65

Lorraine's apartment felt as spacious and clean as I remembered. It smelled of freshly baked brownies, but the odor wasn't oppressive and sickly sweet. It was warm and comforting, actually.

I put my purse on a table in the odd, rather pointless vestibule. When I stepped into the living room, Lorraine closed the second door behind me, which was strange. Why close a door to a tiny, unused space? I wasn't sure why there even was a door.

"I don't have the tea ready yet," she said.

"I can help you."

"It's not a two-person job. Have a seat and I'll be right back." She smiled. She turned and crossed the living room, disappearing into the kitchen, closing that door behind her as well.

I had the sense of being enclosed in the only space she wanted me to view. The dining room door and the hallway door leading to the bedrooms were also closed.

Instead of taking a seat, I stood in front of the shelf and looked at the photographs. If Lorraine had noticed Tess's was missing, she didn't seem to have guessed I'd taken it. There was a slight space where the frame had stood, so maybe she hadn't noticed. I went to the sofa and sat down, looking across the room at the illogical collection. Did she really view these women as candidates for daughters? I wanted to laugh at the thought. Who did such a thing? Maybe she was senile.

All my conversations with her had seemed fairly normal. She'd never forgotten what we'd talked about, or lost the thread of a conversation. When she didn't answer questions or changed the subject, it appeared deliberate.

The kitchen door opened and Lorraine pushed her cart into the living room. She walked around the armchair and stopped by the coffee table. She lifted a large silver tray holding a silver teapot, sugar, and creamer. It looked heavy. As her thin arms trembled under the weight, it appeared ready to crash to the floor. My instinct was to rush to take it out of her hands. I stood, but I didn't move quickly enough, and she managed to settle it on the table.

"I only use this for my most special guests." Her words had a crooning quality to them.

"I'm honored." I thought of Tess's warning about smothering.

The bottom rack of the cart held a plate with three kinds of cookies — Mexican wedding cakes, snickerdoodles, and some kind of crispy meringue thing.

"You can sit down."

"You're sure I can't help?"

"You're my guest. Someone I've waited for all my life."

I sat on the edge of the sofa and tried not to imagine her delivering that line in a 1940s film, overacted by today's standards. It was something you said to a lover, not a woman who was housesitting next door. But if she saw me as her daughter, what better way to ask for an invite to dinner with her son?

The teacups she placed on the table were so thin I could see the shadows of her fingers through the ivory china. She placed a spoon in the first cup. The tea flowed out of the perfectly shaped spout like a ribbon of amber.

"I know you liked the blackberry, but you should try different kinds. It's important to have a variety of tastes. Besides, the blackberry might stain this china."

"Why did you put the spoon in?" I said.

"It absorbs the heat and protects the china from cracking."

I'd never heard of such a thing. Weren't cups designed for hot liquid? Why on earth would it crack? I smiled and let her carry on with her ritual. We each took a sip of tea, which immediately seared my tongue. I ate a snickerdoodle to soothe it.

"We could have so much fun together," she said. "Shopping trips. Museums. Parks. The theatre."

I took another sip of too-hot tea.

"I should get your phone number, in case I hear of something that you might enjoy."

"The only phone I have is one that my company owns. I don't know if…"

"I won't bother you." She smiled. "Just if something comes up."

"I suppose. If you planned a dinner so I could meet your son, it would be good for you to be able to call me rather than hanging around outside until I came out for a walk. That's not sustainable, is it?"

"My son?"

"You mentioned you wanted me to meet him."

"Oh. Yes. I do. I did say that, but you seemed… disinterested."

I shook my head. "There it is again, a misinterpretation of what I meant. I guess I don't communicate very well."

"I guess not."

I searched my mind for something to say that would nudge her closer to a dinner invitation. Maybe it would be easier, and more effective, to find a way to meet up with Barker on my own, but since I'd only seen him the one time, that seemed like an exercise I didn't have time or patience for.

"You seem very proud of him," I said.

"Oh, yes. I couldn't have wished for a better son. He's so devoted. He's built such an amazing company."

"Does he have children?"

"His company is his baby."

"I know how that is."

"You do?"

"Not personally, but I've seen it."

"Yes. In some ways, I suppose that's more satisfying. You know it won't disappoint you."

I laughed. In the past, she'd assured me motherhood was the most satisfying life a woman could hope for. She clearly had mixed feelings on the subject. "Did he inherit your skill for gourmet cooking?"

She smiled and looked down at her tea. "I'm not a gourmet cook by any stretch of the imagination. And no, like a lot of businessmen, he eats out. More than he should."

"Then he must love the dinners you prepare."

Her smile widened.

"I'm looking forward to meeting him. And of course, I love your cooking. It's much better than anything I've had in a restaurant, if that isn't too over the top."

She looked at me, her eyes wide and her mouth partially open. "You really think so?" Her words came out in a slight gasp.

"I do."

"He's very busy. But I can ask when he might be free."

"Maybe tomorrow? Sometimes people are more likely to be available at the last minute than if you plan way ahead and risk something unavoidable coming up at work."

"I'll ask him. Will you give me your number?"

It was a big price to pay, but Tess's problem was that she'd answered the calls. Nothing says you have to. Nothing says you can't delete voicemail messages without listening. I picked up the teapot and held it over her cup.

"Wait. Put in the spoon."

"I think it's cooled."

"It hasn't. That pot keeps it extremely hot."

The tea was already running into her cup while she spoke. As if she'd willed it by her fear of something I still considered unlikely, the cup made a cracking sound. Liquid began to seep out along the thin line.

"Oh, dear. These cups were my great-grandmother's." Tears filled her eyes. "That's why they're so fragile. They're very old." Her tears dribbled over her lashes.

"I'm so sorry." I stood. "I'll clean it up."

"No. That's fine." She stood and reached across to grab the broken, leaky cup out of my hand.

"I'll get a towel." I hurried into the kitchen.

She came after me, walking quickly.

The kitchen had also been redone. The cabinets and drawers were white with small pewter handles. The countertops were pale gray granite. There was a small white table in a windowed alcove. A plate of brownies sat on the table.

Lorraine took the teacup from me and dropped it into

the trash. When she straightened the tears were gone from her eyes. She looked at me kindly. "Don't worry about it, things happen. Accidents. I know you didn't mean to do it."

Of course I hadn't meant to do it. What was she talking about?

She opened a drawer and took out a towel. She turned and opened a cabinet and I heard the rattle of china as she removed another cup. I went to the table and picked up a brownie. The cabinet closed and I heard a tiny shriek. I turned, still holding the brownie, my mouth watering at the thought of chocolate.

"Don't eat that!" She rushed toward me, moving faster than I would have thought possible. She grabbed the brownie out of my hand and set it back on the plate. After the panic that I might take a bite, it was surprising that she didn't mind a brownie with my fingers all over it being given to the intended lucky recipient.

"I suppose I should have asked. But I love brownies. Just one?"

"No. They're not for you." She smiled. "Let's go back and finish our tea."

We returned to the living room and she mopped up the spilled tea.

I was ready to leave, but I needed to make sure she'd recovered from the ruined teacup and the brownie. "I'll get you a business card with my phone number," I said.

"Oh. That would be nice." She settled into her chair and set the new cup on the abandoned saucer.

I went to the door leading to the vestibule and opened it. I stepped inside and picked up my purse. The table had a single drawer. It wasn't completely closed, which I hadn't noticed earlier. I rummaged in my purse with one hand and nudged the drawer out with the other, coughing several times to cover the sound of it opening.

Inside was a huge ring with six or seven keys on it. Each was labeled with a tiny paper tag — front door, vestibule, refrigerator, bedroom, bathroom, cabinet, cuffs. A lock for a refrigerator? Handcuffs? Without pausing, I slid the ring into my purse and pulled out my business card holder. I closed the drawer at the same moment as I set my purse on the table with a loud thud. I returned to the living room.

"Here you go." I placed the card on the coffee table.

She smiled. "Thank you, Alexandra. I'm already thinking about what I might make for dinner. You'll love my son."

"I'm sure I will."

I looked at the steaming cup of tea. "I need to get home. I'm expecting a call from my boss."

"What a shame she calls you in the evening."

"A small price to pay for the freedom to work from home."

"I suppose." She picked up her cup.

I swallowed steaming tea as quickly as I could, eating two snickerdoodles and three Mexican wedding cakes to diminish the burning.

Lorraine smiled with each bite, her eyes fixated on my face as if every movement of my jaw filled her with indescribable pleasure.

I swallowed the last of the cookie. "I've made a mess of this napkin. Do you mind if I have another?"

"Certainly." She stood and went to the kitchen. I pulled my phone out of my pocket and slipped it between the cushion and arm of the sofa. She returned and handed me a napkin. I wiped my fingers and patted my mouth.

We said good-bye and she promised to call with a date for our dinner.

I took the elevator to the second floor. The two labels — refrigerator and cuffs — screamed that Lorraine knew quite a lot about the woman locked up on the second floor.

I took the ring out of my purse, inserted the front door key in the lock and opened the door.

66

Jen waited just outside the lobby doors. She faced the street, forcing herself not to turn and look at the empty spot beside the entrance. The woman was never coming back. She knew that, but she hadn't been able to stop looking every time she left the building, as if something lingering in that space caught the corner of her eye, snagging it like silk catching on a hangnail.

In some ways, the woman's leaving was for the best. If she'd stayed, Scott would continue to abuse her, and security would continue to chase her away, and Jen would continue feeling awful.

Nothing ever changed. It was easy to think change was possible, but it was hard work, and the world fought against it.

She'd vowed she was going to find a way to a different kind of life, but she'd done nothing about it. She had no idea how to go about actually making that happen. It had felt so good when she'd stepped out of the car that night, confident in her vow. She'd felt certain it was her last time selling her body, or at least getting close to her last time.

She'd imagined that there would only be ten or fifteen more hookups, a manageable number she could count down, ticking them off like the days leading up to Christmas. But even as she'd stood in that hotel room, taking off her coat, letting her eyes glaze over so she didn't have to watch that guy eating up her body with his eyes, salvia pooling around his lips, she knew she was trapped.

How did you get out of something like making money from sex?

The whole reason she'd gotten *in*to it in the first place was a lack of options. She had no references for a real job. When Jake let out that string of profanity in front of her preschool students, her job options had been flushed down the toilet. The headmaster didn't care that it wasn't Jen's fault. She didn't care that Jen was unemployable. All she cared about was how she was going to answer the children's questions, and explain the whole ugly scene to the parents. All she cared about was the other teacher, filming it all on her cell phone. All she cared about was getting rid of Jen and punishing her by withholding a recommendation.

Jen shifted her position, moving her feet so her knees didn't lock up. Isaiah should have been here by now. She wished she'd told him to come to her apartment, or suggested meeting in the lounge before they walked to the Pho place. Standing out here made her feel like she'd descended further — a streetwalker after all. Lower even than what she did now, using technology to hook up with a higher class of men. At least that's what she told herself.

It was nice of Isaiah to get dinner with her. Asking him had been awkward, she'd worried she'd sound like she was asking him on a date, not a casual invite — neighbors grabbing a quick dinner. She'd worried for nothing, as smoothly as if she'd asked him to hold the elevator door, he'd said *sure, sounds good.*

Her phone buzzed. A chill ran down her neck. She'd looked forward to this all day. If he canceled…She pulled out her phone and looked at her text messages.

Isaiah Parker: *On the phone with my mom, be there in ten min.*

She texted back a thumbs up and took a deep breath as she slid the phone back into her purse. Her legs were killing her but there were no nearby benches. She could go into the lobby...

"Hey, hottie."

She turned so abruptly, her ankle twisted. She winced.

Scott walked toward her, grinning as if they were best friends. "What's up?"

She turned away. It was better to say nothing. She would never win a verbal battle with a man like him.

"Don't turn your nose up at me."

She felt the heat of his body behind her. Then, his hand was on her leg, sliding up her jeans. He grabbed her butt and squeezed, hard. It hurt.

She shrieked and wrenched away from him.

"Shut up." His voice was low, almost laughing. "Just checking out what you have to offer. Don't make a scene."

"Don't touch me."

"People want to know what they're paying for."

"You're an asshole."

"Aw. Come on."

"Go away."

He moved closer. "I know what you are."

"You don't know anything about me." She felt tears filling her head, as if her brain were turning to salty liquid, running down her throat, spilling into her nose and making it drip.

He grabbed her hair and pulled her head toward him.

"Hey! What are you doing?" Suddenly, Isaiah was standing to her right. He put his arm around her shoulders and pulled her away from Scott. "Leave the lady alone."

Scott laughed. "She's not a fucking lady, that's for sure."

"I don't know," Isaiah said, drawing his words out slowly. "Doesn't lady refer to a member of the noble class? Nobility cares about the unfortunate. She's certainly more of a lady than you're a gentleman."

Scott laughed. "I'm just having a bit of fun, don't get so worked up. Maybe the building management would like to know what she's up to, aside from being a lady and all that."

"You know," Isaiah said, "With a video camera in everyone's pocket, and public shaming on social media, I think I'd be more careful about where I piss. Your boss is always just a click or a tweet away."

He laughed and his tone was deep. Jen thought it sounded sinister, if that wasn't too much of a stretch, although it was probably her imagination, or wishful thinking. Maybe a sense of power.

"Are you threatening me?" Scott moved in a semi-circle around them until he was facing Isaiah.

"Take it however you want," Isaiah said.

"I don't believe you have a recording of me," Scott said. "I don't think my boss has ever looked at Twitter."

Isaiah smiled.

"There was no one out here but *her.*" He didn't bother to look at Jen when he said it.

Isaiah squeezed her shoulders and released her. "Should we get going? I'm hungry." He began walking.

Jen glanced at Scott. He looked more scared than angry. She hurried after Isaiah and they walked to the end of the block in silence. She paused at the corner.

"Wait. I have something to say."

He slipped his hands in his pockets and rocked slightly on his heels.

"First, thank you. I can't believe you did that for me."

"There are lots of nice guys in the world, Jen. They aren't all shits, and hating women. In fact, I bet nice guys are in the majority."

"Maybe."

"You've seen a distorted perspective."

"Well, anyway. Thank you."

"It's nothing."

"It's something. It's everything. No one ever stood up for me like that before."

"No one?"

"Not since I was a kid."

"I'm sorry."

"I hope you don't think I can't defend myself."

"I don't think that. Sometimes you just need a third voice to break the standoff."

She nodded. "You know, I'm not going to do this any more. The…you know." She waved her hand in a circular motion.

He smiled. "I know."

"But it's so hard, I don't…"

"You have friends, Jen." He moved to her side and put his arm around her. "You're not alone, and you're not ever going to be sleeping on the street."

She leaned into him. If only she could have him, or a guy like him. But he was right, she did have friends. She was going to figure out how to get a job. She'd move some place cheaper and maybe take some college classes so her absence of references could be explained. Or maybe Alex would help.

She could pretend Jen had worked for her. There had to be a way. The most important thing was, she had friends. She wasn't going to mess things up.

67

Inside the vestibule, I closed and locked the front door. I knocked on the interior door. I'm not sure why I hadn't knocked on the front door. I think I was so focused on proving the keys fit the second floor apartment, eager to find out who she was, and fairly certain that my knock wouldn't be answered anyway, I'd shoved in that first key before the elevator doors closed behind me.

After less than a minute without a response, I inserted the key in the vestibule door and turned the knob.

The apartment was filled with the silence of emptiness. The layout was the same as Lorraine's, but it hadn't been modernized. The thick carpet was dark blue with a pink floral pattern. The only furniture was an enormous sofa and two massive armchairs that looked as if they'd been in the room since the building was constructed in the early twentieth century. The twelve-foot sofa looked as if it weighed nearly five hundred pounds. A single recessed light glowed in the center of the room. The doors to the kitchen and dining room were closed.

The hallway leading to the bedrooms was also dark. I crossed the living room and flipped the light switch. It gave off barely enough light to see to the end of the hallway. I spoke in a loud, firm voice. "Hello?"

A gasp came from one of the bedrooms.

As I walked along the hallway, a woman stepped out of the farthest bedroom. She stared at me, then began moving toward me, her eyes wide, her pupils dilated, obscuring the color. Her hair hung over the front of her shoulders, so long and thick it appeared to be pulling her upper body into a slump.

"You." She put her hand on the wall and partially collapsed against it.

"What's your name?" I said.

"Jeanne. Who are you?"

"Does that matter?"

She put her hand over her mouth, squeezing her jaw.

"Do you want some water?"

She took her hand away and shook her head, moving it slowly as if her head weighed more than she could bear. Her skin was chalky, her lips without color, looking dry and difficult to move.

"Do you want to sit down?" I said.

She nodded. She walked toward me, keeping her hand pressed against the wall to guide her. As she drew closer the smell of unwashed hair came with her. A gray sweater and nondescript jeans hung on her thin frame. Her feet were bare.

We went into the living room. I sat in one of the armchairs. She sat on the sofa, curling her feet up to her hips.

"Is someone keeping you here?" I said.

She nodded.

"Tell me."

"My mother."

I waited.

In a whisper so soft, I almost didn't hear, except I half-guessed what she would say, and so the words were clear in my mind, she said, "Lorraine Clayton."

She began talking in a low, flat voice, a voice that

sounded as if the soul had been torn out of it. She took short, shallow breaths. "I..." she put her hand over her mouth again.

I thought of the letter *I* she'd drawn on the window with her blood.

She moved her hand. Her mouth was open, but she said nothing.

68

In a toneless voice, as if she were telling someone else's story, Jeanne began talking...

I think my mother was always, sort of...in love with my brother — Barker. Not incest, I don't mean to imply that. I hope you didn't think that's what I meant. But she was... flirty...with him. That's the best way to describe it. She giggled at herself, she talked in an embarrassing, high-pitched voice. Even when we were little kids it was like that. No one seemed to notice but me. At least no one said anything, or acted like she was strange. My father didn't, and Barker ate it up.

She adored Barker. She gushed over him for the most trivial things — if he hung up his towel after his shower or put the orange juice back in the refrigerator after he drank it. She asked his advice for everything, for stupid things. When he got older, she asked his advice about money, about decorating, about what shows and concerts she should attend, even her choice of clothes.

I don't mean to sound petty. Sibling rivalry and all that, but it was nauseating.

My mother was very proper, still is. Well, proper except for her shameful behavior around my brother. She's very dignified. I think she imagines herself as de facto American royalty, one of San Francisco's elite.

When I was about eight, I think, I started to realize I was different. Not just from my family. I think every child feels that a little bit. You're starting to be more aware of your separate identity and that makes you feel like you don't belong. But I thought I was different from other girls. I couldn't have explained it. They just seemed not like me, but at the same time, they were like each other. They connected with each other in a way that I didn't.

I'm not sure why, but I was almost eighteen before I realized I was gay. And it was another six or seven years before I found the courage to tell my family. All those years. It's shameful that I was so frightened, and that distanced from who I was. As if their reaction mattered. As if I had to explain myself or get their approval, as if I didn't exist without them.

The reaction was predictable. My father said nothing. Barker looked disgusted. And my mother shunned me. Literally. True shunning. Well, she allowed me into her home, still. In fact, she required it. But that was all. No phone calls. No chatty emails, not that she was ever particularly chatty with me. I received email when there was a family dinner, and I was expected to be at that dinner. I have no idea why I even went. Desperate for love, I guess. And approval. I had this ravenous need for the approval of everyone else, as if their good opinions formed my personality. Without them, I would disappear altogether.

When I showed up for these torturous dinners, my mother wouldn't look at me. She didn't speak to me. She talked to my father and Barker. She refused to even pass a bowl of vegetables to me. I really have no idea why I went. I guess I wanted to see my father. Barker was awful. He spoke in double entendres about gay people and then smirked at me. But at least he looked at me. At least he spoke to me.

I went, I think, because I kept hoping. Hope is a terrible, relentless, desperate thing. It makes you do stupid things.

I wondered if I might be a masochist because I couldn't stop picking at the wound. I had this sick need to keep re-experiencing the pain of my mother's rejection, brooding over it after, reliving every painful gesture. I couldn't stop.

I think maybe I was addicted to the rage I felt every time she treated me like that. That rage gave me an identity.

It was never clear where my father stood. He was kind enough to me, but he never spoke out against her or Barker. Around that time, my father moved out. My mother also owned the apartment on the fourth floor. It had been vacant for a year, so he moved into that. He couldn't live with her, but he couldn't separate from her either.

Almost as if I had a split personality, I became a bit of an activist. Well, a dignified activist, of course. No dressing up in crazy outfits, flaunting my sexuality. I didn't go to pride parades or any of that. But I started a blog, when blogging was a thing. I blogged about gay life in San Francisco, not just nightclubs and the bleeding edge, but normal life, normal couples. I had the tone and approach that being gay *was* normal and gay people were involved in normal living, not just in being gay. Along with it, I did some freelance writing for newspapers and a few online news outlets. I had this beautiful apartment, thanks to my parents. My mother, really. The money was, is, all hers. From her family. That's how she runs the show with my father. It's perverted, and I should have moved out. But I liked the blogging and the freelancing, and living simply. Without having to pay rent, I got by.

Of course, that gave Barker something else to sneer at.

During this time, Barker was building his company. He

was very impressed with his success. And so was my mother. You'd think he was the first man on earth to start his own company, to be in the right place at the right time, really. And he completely ignored the fact that quite a lot of his seed money was provided by my mother.

I guess he and I were both...dependent. No integrity in terms of taking her money.

A few years ago, Barker invited me to his company Christmas party. I really don't know why. Maybe he wanted to show me how extravagant it was, how he now had his own money, or maybe he felt sorry for me.

At that party, I met Miri. I don't care how silly it sounds — it was love at first sight. I feel like an idiot every time I say that, but it's true. I can hardly get the words out. I see people rolling their eyes at me. But I believe in connections that people can't see. It's that same invisible connection I have to my mother, so she's able to control what I think about myself even though I'm an adult woman. Her thoughts, her opinion of me, took root in my mind, as if they were my own thoughts. And so I let her abuse me.

Anyway...

Miri was a software developer. I didn't understand her work at all, but we had so many other areas where our minds connected. Everything. We liked the same food, the same music, the same movies, the same books. We both liked kayaking and hiking. Even our body clocks were the same — late risers. We loved to stay up until two in the morning watching horror movies. I didn't know my own life would become a horror movie.

We had ten glorious months together. We went everywhere and did everything. It was like one of those movies where you see a couple walking through a farmer's market to a peppy soundtrack, buying flowers, choosing fresh food for dinner, then you watch them laughing and cooking together, eating on a terrace and drinking wine. Dancing. That was our ten months.

One night in early December there was a terrible rainstorm, water lashing the windows, gusts of wind knocking everything around. It was so romantic, at first, but then we lost power. So we took a cab to Chinatown for dinner.

Barker moved in circles that didn't even brush up against the edges of mine. He liked the symphony and fine dining. Although it was naive on our part, we never thought we'd run into him. He had no idea about us. No one in my family did. Miri never came to my place, with all of them stacked on top of me, literally. We spent weekends together at her apartment. San Francisco is a big city, it's easy to run on parallel tracks and never see another person you know quite well. In all my adult years, I never ran into my mother in a store or restaurant. And I never dreamed Barker would eat in Chinatown.

Maybe the power outage changed his tastes, or he couldn't get into one of his usual places. I don't know.

Miri had her arm around me, holding the side of my head with her other hand. She was kissing me, wiping the rain water off my face while we waited for our wonton soup to arrive. Things got rather intense, maybe the sudden humid warmth in the restaurant, the smell of garlic and chili, the anticipated comfort of noodles and broth against the shivering rain.

When the soup arrived, we moved away from each other.

Barker was standing three feet behind the server. He stuck his finger in his mouth and made a gagging gesture. He pulled his finger out and gave Miri a look I can only describe as utter disgust.

I don't know why he hates gay people so much. I really don't. How can you live in San Francisco in the twenty-first century and think that way? He isn't religious. Part of it, I know, comes from adopting my parents' views, mostly my mother's. But also maybe because he had such a weird relationship with her? Maybe it gave him a distorted view of sex in general, made him put it in a box with clearly defined boundaries and rules? Maybe he's just insecure in his own sexuality. I don't know. Even now.

Miri's boss, one of the engineering vice presidents, reported directly to Barker. The company was private. It still is, as far as I know. They don't have the government breathing down their necks with the same intensity that a public company does, and they can find ways to skirt the laws. Even for a public company, there are ways to do things, to justify discrimination, covering it up with other manufactured judgments of a person's *weak contribution* to the team in a *very competitive environment.*

Within two months of Barker seeing us kissing, Miri was laid off. They never call it firing, of course: *her skills were no longer critical to the company's success.*

69

Jeanne went on with her story...

I wasn't going to take that. Miri loved her work, and she loved the company's vision. It was almost a part of her. Not to mention, it's illegal. And immoral. And all kinds of wrong.

Miri saw a labor attorney and they began discussing a lawsuit.

I felt personally responsible for what had happened, as if my brother's behavior was somehow my fault. The firing for not being at the top of her game made it difficult for her to get another job. Not impossible, she was enormously talented, but she had to explain. And no one wants to go into an interview explaining an HR issue. First, you have to get into a discussion about your sexuality. A job interview is the last place for that. It's invasive having to share information that no other person would ever bring up. It puts you on an unequal footing with other candidates.

No matter how much people say otherwise, it also makes you look like a problem employee. Companies don't want to deal with relationships or family matters of any kind, and if you're bringing it up in the first or second meeting, it sets the wrong tone. Suddenly, you're the gay chick instead of the one who graduated from Stanford or the one who has four industry awards.

I was so angry I couldn't sleep. I couldn't eat. My mind kept circling around how unjust it was, how unfair to Miri to sabotage her career like that, how frustrated she was. I couldn't do a single thing to help her, or change the situation. My mind kept gnawing on it, hating Barker, feeling like I wanted to kill him. Not that I would ever do something like that. Maybe I should have.

Finally, I thought about what I did have to offer — my blog. I had over seven thousand followers. It was a popular place to hang out online. The comment section was filled with side discussions, even conversations unrelated to whatever topic I'd posted about. It had turned into a virtual community.

I realized I had thousands of sympathetic listening ears.

I don't know what I thought I could achieve. It's not like it would get her job back, or even necessarily help her find a new one. Maybe I was just venting. Maybe it was all about me.

I wasn't entirely stupid. I let Miri preview the blog post. I asked her a hundred times if she was okay with what I'd written. She was thrilled. She didn't want it kept secret, she wanted to make news with it, really. If I could do that, she was behind me a hundred and twenty percent.

To be balanced, I decided to get a quote from Barker. Miri was okay with that, too.

He was furious, because of course I named his company.

For quite a few days, I didn't hear from him. I jumped every time my email pinged or my phone buzzed, expecting my mother's wrath or some threat from Barker. But there was nothing.

The silence should have made me take a step back.

Finally I got a very terse email from him that said — *no comment, dyke.*

The next day, Miri didn't come home after her appointment with her attorney. I called everyone we knew. I walked around for hours — her neighborhood, restaurants, some of the places we went to all the time. It got dark and dinner time came and went. I called the police and they said what everyone knows — call back in twenty-four hours. When the officer I spoke to found out she was gay, I could hear something come through in her voice and I knew she was judging us — gay girl fight, and all that crap.

I slept on Miri's side of the bed, too scared to even cry.

The next day, right after lunch, the police came to the door. They'd found Miri's body in the bay near Sausalito. She didn't have any stab or bullet wounds, but they did think she was dead before she drowned. It turned out she'd suffocated, most likely with a plastic bag.

Of course I told the detective what happened. Barker became a suspect for a few days, but he had a very complex alibi provided by my mother. Miri's boss had been home with his wife the entire evening. There was nothing. It was reported in the paper and they mentioned the suit, but of course not the company, so no mud splashed on Barker.

When I got hold of myself enough to return to my apartment, my computer was missing. I wanted to edit my blog, express my feelings about her death, my grief, the technology world's loss, but still post what I'd written about discrimination and her job loss. I tried to access it on my phone but my entire blog was missing — *404 page not found.* Just like Miri.

I got into bed and didn't get up for three days. I lost a lot of weight and got dehydrated. I was a mess.

Then, my mother showed up. She had a key, of course.

She was frantic to make sure I didn't destroy Barker's stunning creation. She took over the kitchen, made me beef broth and brought it to me on a tray. She still wouldn't look at me, didn't speak to me beyond telling me how I'd almost destroyed his life. She made clucking noises to show her disgust, but that was it. No actual words. There was Seconal in the broth and I fell asleep.

When I woke, I had no idea what time it was, or even what day. The mug was gone. I tried to move and found I was handcuffed to the bed.

Every day she came into the apartment. She offered food, sometimes laced with pot, other times with Seconal. The meals were small, enough to keep me alive.

When she knew I was defeated and too weak to fight, the routine changed. Once I dozed off, she unlocked the handcuffs so I could move around when she wasn't there. Since the refrigerator was padlocked and there was no food in the cabinets, I couldn't eat except when she arrived. I usually got half an apple for breakfast, a slice of turkey and some grapes for lunch, and a bowl of soup for dinner. But sometimes there was no lunch. And sometimes the soup was simply broth. Now that she had me, she'd enter the vestibule and shove the handcuffs under the door. I was told to lock myself to the headboard before she came in. After she fed me, once the drugs kicked in, I fell asleep and she unlocked them and left. Not that I could overpower her anyway. I could barely get out of bed sometimes.

I didn't even try. Who can fight a will like hers? I'd tried all my life. She won. She always, always won. Even before the all-out war that we have now, she won with her passive-aggressive games — freezing me out, whispering cruel comments to make me feel useless or guilty or ashamed. She had me locked up long before she put handcuffs on me.

70

After Jeanne finished talking, I didn't say anything for several long minutes. There's no way to respond to a story like that. I still wondered why she didn't fight back, but I guess everyone isn't like me — born to fight.

She looked at me, waiting. Her breathing was ragged, exhausted from all the effort.

"What changed? When you saw me?" I said.

"You weren't the first. When I saw people, I tried to get their attention, but they ignored me. I don't have soap. My mother bathes me and takes the supplies with her. Or pens. I don't have much of anything." She extended her hands to show me the ripped skin and the exposed bloody remains. "I wrote with my blood. It scared people, so they stopped looking up at my window the minute they realized what it was. They wrote me off as disturbed. No one wanted to interfere. You were the first person who didn't just walk by and turn your head."

"I interfere all the time."

She smiled, but her mouth seemed to grow tired quickly and the smile slipped away. "So what are you going to do?"

"Interfere."

"How?"

I held up the key ring. "I need to get these back to Lorraine before she notices they're gone."

Jeanne nodded.

"But I'll be back. It might be a few days, but I promise.

I've never had a problem with interfering."

She smiled again, although she didn't look like she believed me.

I left her apartment, locking the two doors behind me, and took the elevator to the fourth floor.

When I knocked, Lorraine spoke to me through the closed door. "Who is it?"

"It's Alexandra. I think I left my phone here."

"Oh. Where is it? I'll get it."

"I'm not sure. Can I come in for just a minute?"

Thankfully, she opened the door. I went to the sofa and dug between the cushions. I held it up. "Found it."

"Oh, that's good."

I grinned. "I was wondering...do you mind if I take a few of those cookies with me? They're so good!"

"Of course." She smiled and hurried into the kitchen. I stepped into the vestibule, put the keys in the drawer, and closed it. It was another minute or two before she returned, holding a small tin. She handed it to me.

When I left the building, I looked up at the window on the second floor. Jeanne wasn't there. Maybe she didn't need to be anymore.

71

Locking Jeanne back in her apartment wasn't fair to her, but if I was going to deal with Lorraine, it was the best plan. The only plan.

It felt as if I'd stumbled into a gothic novel. The whole family lived in a single, stoic but ornate building, each isolated in his or her own apartment. The mother was one step away from taking her son as her husband — no wonder Frank had moved into the empty apartment. She controlled the whole bunch of them with money that had come down through decades into her hands. You don't have to let someone's money turn you into their bitch, but once you start down that path, it's hard to get off, I suppose.

And there was more.

Jeanne was sure Frank was the one who had murdered Miri. Under pressure from Lorraine to protect her son's company — his baby, as she'd put it. She probably didn't have to apply all that much pressure. Frank, who wanted women to be little ladies, ashamed of his daughter flaunting her sexuality. Blogging about the gay lifestyle. I could picture him tugging his hat lower on his brow, briefly closing his eyes as the pain shot across his face. And Barker with his tidy alibi from mommy, while daddy was out making sure she and her son retained their perverted, over-sized dignity.

Jeanne had been standing at the window, long after midnight, staring down at the empty street. Frank had come home, staggering a bit, his hat missing, his head looking frail and old. The gray of his hair shimmered white under a bright moon. Lorraine had appeared on the front steps. She walked down slowly and stood facing him.

They spoke for a few minutes, then Frank spit on Lorraine's shoe. He turned and stumbled up the stairs.

Before Jeanne could even raise her weakened arm to pound on the glass, Lorraine took out a gun and shot him in the back. Jeanne couldn't see the stoop from her window, but she'd heard the shot. And she'd seen the aim of the gun.

The next day, Jeanne had begged her mother to explain, but all she got was the usual silence. Nothing would break her. Lorraine went about preparing her minimalist meal, waiting for the Seconal to take effect. Jeanne found herself wishing her mother would do the same for her.

I knew why Lorraine had killed him. She was worried Frank's guilt was getting the better of him. She didn't like him smoking and chatting with the young woman next door. No telling when he might spill his guts.

I didn't have a lot of time to get ready, Lorraine had arranged our dinner with Barker for the following day.

When I moved into Tess's place, I hadn't anticipated killing anyone, so my roofie supply was at my apartment. I went to the apartment while Isaiah was at school, to avoid answering any overly curious questions. It was also pretty much impossible to get something out of a hiding place in a studio apartment when there's another person inside. The roofies were deep inside a throw pillow on my sofa. It was a dark purple pillow with white embroidery, not as cheap looking as it sounds. The embroidery said — *Lie down at your own risk*. It seemed appropriate.

I unzipped the pillow, shoved my hand into the hole I'd

cut in the foam and pulled out the cotton-stuffed bottle. I zipped up the pillow and put it back on the couch. I got a hooded all-weather coat out of the closet, a black scarf, and a pair of black leather gloves. I shoved everything in a Bloomingdale's shopping bag and left. I took an Uber to South San Francisco where I bought two pairs of steel handcuffs, duct tape, a new pair of scissors since I'd forgotten those at my apartment, and some rope. Just to be safe.

This was going to be a risky event, aside from what Jeanne might figure out. The hooded coat and scarf would keep identifying features from showing, but if someone saw me, the detective might recall an overly curious young woman living next door. Unless the brain-fog created by his cold medicine had blurred his memory.

I was on edge. I would be walking over there in plain sight. It would be after dark, but it's a well-lit street and I was sure my shape and movements would identify me as a young female. Most times, I work completely unseen.

Despite all the risks, I had to do what was necessary. Even though Lorraine didn't have that many years left on the earth, she didn't deserve a single day for what she'd done to her daughter. She didn't deserve another hour. Neither did her son.

Once Lorraine and Barker turned up dead, Jeanne would know it was me. Who else? I'd never had to trust another soul with my secrets. I'd known the woman for all of thirty minutes, unless you counted our silent dramas over the past few weeks. She wouldn't know for sure, and I wouldn't tell her, but she would have a pretty good idea.

Still, in a few days, I'd be gone, disappearing into the

twisting, hilly, foggy streets of San Francisco. There wasn't really any way for Jeanne to locate me, nothing I could think of that she might identify about my life. She knew I lived nearby, but she didn't know I was a temporary resident. She couldn't connect me to Tess. She didn't really know anything, except that she'd seen me with Steve. I hoped she hadn't seen enough of his face to truly remember him.

I was relying a little too much on luck for my taste, but it seemed relatively safe. And there was no choice.

72

I brought a very expensive bottle of wine to Lorraine's for my dinner with her and Barker. I arrived ten minutes before the time she'd suggested, but she opened the door wider for me to enter. Without any change in expression she surveyed my dress and shoes. "That's quite an outfit."

"I realize I'm early." I lifted the wine bottle slightly. "I'll open this so it can breathe while you finish up."

"I already have wine," she said. "And champagne."

I allowed a wounded expression to cross my face. "I chose this especially for you. And Barker. I have to contribute something. You've already prepared two fantastic meals for me."

She walked toward the kitchen and I followed. "I suppose we can serve your wine, if it's that important to you." She gestured toward a narrow drawer. "The opener is in there."

"It is." I went to the kitchen table and set the wine down. I turned so my back faced the area where Lorraine was working. As she began tossing the salad, I removed the cork and slipped the powder of two finely crushed roofies into the bottle. I'd thought about using three, to be on the safe side, since I couldn't predict how much wine either of them would drink, but I didn't need them falling asleep at the table, forcing me to do the extra work of moving them to the sofa.

I asked for her decanter and slowly poured wine into the wide mouth, swirling the crystal container, not to help the wine breathe, but the roofies to dissolve completely.

Avoiding a glass of my own wine would be a little difficult. Champagne glasses sat beside each place setting, but the last time, we'd only had one glass each. I would insist on finishing the bottle while she and Barker enjoyed the Cab. The other difficulty would be watching that lovely wine go to waste.

I placed the decanter on the dining room table and returned to the kitchen.

"Can I help you with anything?"

"Of course not, you're my guest."

I went to the alcove and stood looking out the window. "I think I forgot to mention, I met Barker a few days ago."

I could no longer sense her moving around behind me, touching the various serving dishes. "How is that possible?" she said.

"I ran into a man I know. Barker came out of the building while we were talking, and it turned out those two knew each other. Isn't that strange?" I turned.

"Why didn't you tell me?" She glared at me. "What's the point of hiding something like that?" She looked annoyed, as if I'd ruined her dinner party.

"I don't know. Honestly, I really don't." It's amazing how often that kind of answer is sufficient. People don't know what to say. They can accuse you of being insincere, but you're sort of admitting that you were, so the accusation dies. They find themselves pitying you for not being in control of your own actions and they ease off on the attack.

There was a knock on the door.

"Should I answer it?" I said.

Lorraine scowled. "Since there's no need for an introduction, I don't see why not."

When I opened the door, Barker looked startled, but recovered smoothly, as most CEOs do, after years of encountering all kinds of unpredictable situations. He extended his hand and gave mine a quick shake. "Good to see you, Alexandra, right?"

"Yes."

He stepped around me and went into the living room where Lorraine had come out to greet him. He kissed her cheek. She grabbed at his shoulders, her fingers reminding me of Damien's claws. He grasped her hands and lifted them off his shoulders, taking a few steps away from her before she finally allowed him to break away.

He eyed my four-inch heels and my black dress with the scooped neckline that went out to the edges of my shoulders. It was cut low enough in the front that delicate supporting cups were sewn into the dress. There was no bra in San Francisco that would remain hidden below that neckline. He had the same poker face as his mother, and his facial muscles remained unchanged as his eyes moved up and down, taking it in.

"I'll get the champagne," Lorraine said.

Barker and I seated ourselves — him on the sofa, me on the armchair facing him.

"So you work for Steve Montgomery?" he said.

It didn't seem necessary to correct the false way Steve had described our working relationship. I smiled at the dull, obvious opening line. "Who wants to talk about work?"

He smiled. "What would you like to talk about?"

Lorraine returned with the opened bottle of champagne. She placed it on the table and went to the dining room table for the glasses. Barker filled them, pouring so rather large heads of foam remained for nearly half a minute.

We lifted our glasses. "Cheers," I said.

Lorraine looked disappointed, as if she'd planned a more elaborate toast, but she said nothing and took a small sip. She left her glass on the table and returned to the kitchen.

"So you're my mother's latest...companion?" he said.

I smiled and sipped my champagne. "She's a very dignified woman. And she thinks the world of you."

He laughed.

"Your achievements are impressive." My voice sounded false in my ears, but he didn't seem bothered. Maybe he was used to the phony formality, given his continued proximity to his parents.

"I thought you didn't want to talk about work?" he said.

I lifted my glass, smiled, and took a sip. I leaned forward and set my glass on the coffee table. He studied the top of my dress in that barely noticeable way that many savvy businessmen have developed. They're keen to keep their hands clean from a harassment accusation, and the habits from work bleed into the rest of their lives. Although his care for not being obvious hadn't extended to Miri Toffler. He thought he'd gotten away with letting her go, then hiding behind his parents as they planned her murder.

I asked him whether he'd seen any good movies lately, and before he could figure out when he'd last seen a movie, Lorraine called us to the dinner table.

Lorraine outdid herself on the meal. Instead of soup for the first course, she served Gyoza she'd made herself, followed by a traditional Caesar salad, sans anchovies, with homemade croutons. Dinner was stuffed sole, wild rice, and peas. Thinly sliced pumpernickel bread circled a plate, with a ceramic dish of unsalted butter in the center.

Once Barker tasted the wine and Lorraine explained that I'd insisted on serving it, his attitude toward me shifted ever so slightly. Lorraine took it in stride that I was happy finishing the champagne, while Barker took control of the decanter and kept their glasses filled with red wine. He out-sipped her by about two to one, obviously enjoying the Cabernet. It couldn't have been more perfect if I'd planned it that way.

Both of them made it all the way through the stuffed sole before their eyelids began to droop. They fought hard to keep their speech clear and their eyes open. Barker was less successful, his head nodding forward then jerking upright.

"You look tired." I stood. "Why don't we have dessert and coffee in the living room? You can relax and I'll serve it."

"I am very tire' but I'm your hostess," said Lorraine.

"You've done so much for me. You should sit down."

"I am sitting down." She giggled softly and yawned.

"Just tell me where it is. I'll take care of everything."

She yawned again. I walked to her side and helped edge her chair away from the table. I took her arm, guided her to her feet, and walked with her to the living room. I returned to the table. "Barker. Why don't you keep your mother company while I make the coffee. It looks like you could use some."

He tried to smile but his face sagged. "I could. I feel a little...strange. Almost..."

"Maybe a bit too much wine." I laughed softly.

"Maybe. It doesn't usually affect me this way."

"Go on. I'll be right there."

He stood and stumbled away from the table. I went into the kitchen and rattled around as if I was setting up the coffee maker. After a few minutes I went into the living room. They were seated beside each other, leaning close. Barker's eyes were closed but he was mumbling something to his mother. Lorraine nodded.

I smiled, pleased that she was still awake. I faced Lorraine and her son, hands on my hips, like an angry mother myself. "What you did to your daughter is despicable. That you did it to protect your son is worse. I've known women like you since I was a child," I said.

Lorraine's eyes opened wide. She sat up, glaring at me.

"Even if you have daughters, you think your son is something special. A man. A different species. A male to treat you like his queen for the rest of his life. It's Oedipus in reverse," I said.

"It starts at infancy, calling him your little man and telling him how tough and strong he is. You laugh about his ability to spray pee and compare his prowess to his older sister. And do you think that infant boy isn't receiving messages right then and there — that he's better, more entertaining, more interesting, more able to get a reaction out of mommy because he has a little nub of flesh between his legs?

You let him climb higher in the tree than his sister, telling her to be careful. What he hears is that his sister is weak and not very capable. You let him ride his bike farther from home and stay out later, and he learns his sister can't quite take care of herself out in the world. She's made to feel like half a person.

Mothers like you dote on their sons and turn away from their daughters the minute the boy opens his mouth to speak. They bury their own needs for their sons, and put their daughters in second place. Their sons can do nothing wrong, and their daughters are wrong by their very nature.

You allow them to think they're superior, because you make them better than yourself. You make excuses and you fawn over them and sometimes come dangerously close to flirting with them.

Women like you treat their sons like substitute husbands. When their husband is emotionally distant or works too much and travels too frequently. Instead of trying for a more satisfactory relationship, they turn to their boys. They tell their sons secrets they shouldn't, and rely on their boys to make them feel beautiful, preening in front of them, always aware of where their son's attention is. Always keeping him at the center of everything.

And all these tiny messages build up in the dinosaur regions of their brains and they grow up with a latent disdain for women.

Now that the remainder of your sick, disturbed family is about to be removed from the earth, maybe Jeanne can finally have a life."

Lorraine's eyes narrowed. "Jeanne?" She squinted, as if she wasn't sure who I was. "So disappointing." Her head wobbled slightly. Barker was letting out soft snores. After a few minutes, her head joined his, lolling against the back of the sofa.

I cuffed them and tied their lower legs. I covered their mouths with duct tape. I smothered him first, just in case she had a pinprick of awareness, deep in her mind. It took all my strength to keep the pillow over his face, and quite a long time for him to stop thrashing. Lorraine was easier.

I nestled the pillow back in the corner of the sofa.

I went into the kitchen and sat at the table. I opened one

of Lorraine's bottles of wine and drank a glass while I waited for my heart to slow to its normal pace. Finally, I stood and tied one of Lorraine's aprons over my dress. I kicked off my heels and got to work.

It took an hour or so to wash and dry all the dishes and wipe the tables and chairs and counters that I'd touched, including the picture frames and the table in the vestibule. I tied up the garbage bag, filled with paper towels, and poured bleach down the garbage disposal to make sure the smell and any trace of the leftovers was eradicated.

I returned to the living room and removed the rope, duct tape, and cuffs. I left them settled close to each other on the sofa, Lorraine's head resting on his shoulder, which seemed fitting.

73

When all of my things were packed up, I took the keys to the various locks in the second floor apartment and went out. First, I returned to Tess's place and went down to the parking garage. I put the trash bag in my trunk for disposal later that day, then went up to her condo and changed into jeans and a sweater.

It was three o'clock in the morning when I returned to the building next door. I wanted everything done and wrapped up before dawn. I knocked on the outer door to let Jeanne know I was there, then unlocked the door and went in. Jeanne was seated on the sofa staring at the vestibule as if she hadn't slept, had been waiting for me the entire time. I handed her one of the individual chocolate cream pies Lorraine had made for her son and me, her pseudo-daughter.

She smiled. "A dessert without dope. No more falling into a stupor and dealing with the freaky dreams." She took a bite.

"There's a bit of a mess you'll have to untangle," I said.

"What's that?"

"I can't say." I held out the key ring. It would allow her the freedom of her own apartment, but I'd left the door locked on the floor above. It would be a few days before anyone got inside.

She ate the rest of the tiny pie. "What are you talking about?"

"I need to leave, but just know that you're free to come

and go now." I opened my purse and took out two hundred dollars in cash and placed it on her leg.

"Why are you giving me money?"

"To tide you over."

I turned and started toward the door.

"Wait."

"I can't. You'll be fine."

I left the vestibule door open as I let myself out of her apartment.

I would have to tamp down my raging curiosity, because I'd likely never know what happened, beyond what got reported in the news regarding the murder of a San Francisco matriarch and a bio-tech success story. I worried a little that Jeanne would face a lot of scrutiny for murdering her mother, who had *too much* money. She had no alibi. It would be horribly ironic injustice if she ended up locked in a prison cell. But she was obviously in a very weak condition. One look at her slender arms and malnourished shoulders would tell any physician she couldn't possibly smother a healthy adult male.

During my remaining days at Tess's apartment, I would only come and go in my car, ensuring Jeanne would never get a glimpse of me. She was on her own, and I trusted she would find her way through the mess of her mother's and brother's estates and enjoy a life of freedom and good food.

It wasn't a very tidy solution, but it was the best I could do.

74

It was my last night in Tess's condo. Her flight from Sydney would land in the early morning the next day and she'd be back to her place before lunch. The timing was perfect. As far as I knew, the bodies next door had not been discovered yet. I had no idea whether Jeanne was still hanging out in her apartment or had found friends to meet up with and explain where she'd been for the past few years. Maybe she'd gone straight to an internet cafe and re-launched her blog. Or to a hair salon, or out for lunch.

Locking the door to Lorraine's apartment made things more complicated for Jeanne, but better for me. I needed to do my best to make sure I was gone from Tess's place before the bodies were discovered. The other thing niggling at the back of my mind was Steve. I trusted that he fully believed the story he'd told himself about me, that he wouldn't come looking for me in Tess's neighborhood — full on stalking. If Tess saw him anywhere near her condo, I was dead, and most likely out of a job.

But one problem at a time. If a situation arose, I'd deal with it then.

Mostly I hoped, believed, that leaving Tess's was like every place you leave — the water closing over the spot you'd occupied, wiping you away without a trace. In the same way, Jeanne's memories of Lorraine and Frank and Barker would become faint outlines on the horizon, then disappear altogether.

I mixed a martini and sat in the sunroom, watching the sky turn inky blue and then black. When my drink was half gone, I ate one of the olives.

Chardonnay time!

I stood and went into Damien's room. I settled in the armchair across from him. I took a sip of my drink.

Dangerous woman!

I looked at the bird. He cocked his head to the side. For the first time, he lowered his crown feathers in a friendly acknowledgment that he didn't view me as a threat. *Dangerous woman.*

"Yes, I suppose I am." I lifted my glass. "Cheers, Damien. It's been a pleasure getting to know you."

Likewise, he said.

A Note to Readers

Thanks for reading. I hope you liked reading about Alexandra as much as I enjoy writing her stories.

I'm passionate about fiction that explores the shadows of suburban life and the dark corners of the human mind. To me, the human psyche is, as they say in Star Trek — the final frontier — a place we'll never fully understand. I'm fascinated by characters who are damaged, neurotic, and obsessed.

I love to stay in touch with readers. Visit me at my website: CathrynGrant.com
To find out when the next Alexandra Mallory novel is available you can sign up for my new book mailing list here: CathrynGrant.com/contact/
As a thank you for signing up, you'll receive a free Alexandra short story — *Death Valley*.

CPSIA information can be obtained
at www.ICGtesting.com
Printed in the USA
LVHW051059250520
656497LV00003BA/447